Praise for *Beneath the Blonde*

"Saz Martin is . . . an ebullient heroine of courage and wry wit . . . Duffy's third novel removes her from the category of 'promising' and confirms without doubt that she's very near the top of the new generation of modern crime writers" Marcel Berlins, *The Times*

"Stella Duffy's writing gets better with each book" Val McDermid, *Manchester Evening News*

"Always a pleasure to find a new Stella Duffy novel . . . a good read and highly recommended" *Diva*

BENEATH THE BLONDE

Stella Duffy

Library of Congress Catalog Card Number: 99–63597

A full catalogue record for this book can be obtained from
the British Library on request

First published in 1997 by Serpent's Tail
4 Blackstock Mews, London N4 2BT
Website: www.serpentstail.com

First published in this 5-star edition in 2000

Printed in Great Britain by Mackays of Chatham, plc

10 9 8 7 6 5 4 3 2

For my sister Veronica,
with love and thanks for all the Marvellous Bumps.

Thanks to Bev Fox and Ian McLaughlin for practical inspiration, location scout Mandy Wheeler, sanity specialists Shelley and Yvonne, and the legal team: Graeme Austin, Claire Bonnet and Steve Harris. Special kihinui to Sandra Morris, kuia-in-waiting and Dave Perese, writer-in-residence.

ONE

I would sit in your mother's kitchen and watch the sun come up. The kitchen is blue. I remember when your dad painted it. He is dead now. They both are. You killed them. Like you killed me. Like you killed everyone in your past. You do not know your mother and you do not know your father and you do not know me. Because that would mean them all knowing who you were. But I remember.

I know enough to conjugate the tense into who you are.

I remember when this was fun, easy. When the long summer holidays were six weeks that seemed like years, punctuated by the melting chocolate peanut slabs at the school pool and the warm Fanta and trips to the beach and the sweltering turkey of a midsummer Christmas afternoon. And it always rained on Christmas afternoon.

And then not many years after that the changes began. The small town grew constricting, the black and white two-channel TV became a symbol of how much you needed to run away, how far we both needed to go. You went further than most.

At eleven you wanted to leave. Told me where you'd go— and why. I didn't believe it, I called you a liar. We fought, didn't talk for half a year. By which time our seven-year friendship had faded. You had been leaving me for a long time. You had been leaving everyone. But I never left you.

I helped your dad paint this room. We were almost friends, he and I. Some work together, a beer in the garage. By then it was just postcards from you. They shared them with me. The scribbled writings from New York, London, Amsterdam, Rio. Your parents shared you with me. Their generosity knows no bounds. That was their choice. I have never chosen to share you with anyone.

Then you killed yourself and the postcards stopped.

And now you say crisps instead of chips and off-licence instead of bottle store and sweets when you really mean lollies. But I know what they're really called. And I know your name.

You say it was a phoenix reinvention. Say you created yourself new. Recreation. And was it fun? I know all about it. You told your mum and she told me. Neither of us believed it. And anyway, who gave you permission to be reborn? Not me. You're the Catholic. Resurrection and transubstantiation are foreign words to me. They stick on my tongue like the wafers of dry Jesus you smuggled me one day after Mass. It tasted of nothing.

I'm doing this in memory of you.

TWO

A pigeon shat on Saz as she left St Pancras Station. She climbed from the train tired, still slightly hungover from the excesses of the day and within four paces, one of London's lesser creatures deposited its multi-textured blessing on her front. Her whole front. The tip of her chin, the flare of bare flesh just below her collarbone and the top of her black wool Bloomingdales cardigan. The dark yellow and white crap ran down her left breast and into the top of her bra, leaving an egg yolk stain across her skin. She shifted her old suitcase into the other hand and hurried even faster out to the street, slimy pigeon droppings sliding from her underwired breasts down the ridges of her scarred stomach. Molly hooted from behind a taxi rank and Saz opened the car door, flung the case in the back, herself into the front seat and burst into tears.

Molly said nothing until the sobbing had subsided, just passing Saz a box of tissues and stroking her right leg whenever gear changes allowed. At Camden Lock, a dated black-clad youth holding hands with two baby goth girls skinned his shins on Molly's new Renault and a drunken old man grinned into the passenger window. Saz finally held back the tears and snot long enough to wind down the window and shout at the pedestrians, "Fuck off, you bunch of complete wankers, this is a road not a fucking shopping mall, use the fucking pedestrian crossing." The drunk man jumped back in surprise and narrowly missed being run over by a black cab.

When the congestion cleared a little Molly took her eyes off the traffic long enough to look clearly at Saz. She took in the almost dried bird shit in all its glory. "It's supposed to be lucky, you know."

Saz snarled, "Being obliged to attend the wedding of your brother-in-law's homophobic sister and her fascist army husband where the only conversation possible is one in which you tell all present that they're nasty Tory bigots for whom shooting is too good and then get kicked out of the reception and unceremoniously dumped on the next train home?"

"No. Bird shit is supposed to be lucky."

"Must be great being a lion in Trafalgar Square."

"Are you going to tell me what happened or don't you remember?"

"I remember, I just don't think I want to. Anyway, it's your fault, if you'd have been there I wouldn't have drunk so much."

"If I'd have been there we'd probably both have been dumped on the next train home and then we'd both be covered in bird shit."

"It's still your fault."

"You knew all along I couldn't come."

"Wouldn't come."

"I'm not going to argue with you, Saz. I was already committed to working this shift months ago, I'd promised Jim I'd cover for him—for his own wedding I might add— and much as I love your family, there's no way that my respect for the extended family concept extends all the way out to your brother-in-law's sister."

Saz grunted and blew her nose, Molly slowly joined the uphill out-for-dinner traffic in Hampstead High Street.

"And you still haven't told me what happened."

"The best man, Jonathan the soldier, is a racist, sexist pig who didn't realize I was gay when he started slagging off queers."

"I guess he didn't know it was a reclaimed word then either?"

"It's not reclaimed the way he uses it. Nor are nigger, paki or not—in his mouth—girl."

"So you had a go at him?"

"No, I should have but I didn't. I was being 'good'. I was being the quiet sister."

"Must have been hard."

Saz ignored Molly and continued with her description of the day's events. "I sat quietly listening to his bigoted ranting until Tony had a go at him and then Cassie joined in. I just sat there like an idiot, thinking it was only my family by marital extension and Emily Anne couldn't help being so stupid and I really shouldn't interfere and I'd had too much to drink anyway and I was so angry that I'd only talk rubbish—"

"Or burst into tears."

"Exactly. So I sat there and listened to my brother-in-law and my sister try to reason with him, telling all those pathetic placatory stories, you know—'Molly's Asian and she's wonderful . . .' "

"All absolutely true."

"That's not the point, Moll, and you know it. Anyway, he's probably the kind of bloke who has one friend in every shade just so he can prove he's not racist. So finally he turns his attention to me, telling Tony and Cassie, 'Your sister's no better, even if she is a dyke she should still have the decency to wear a dress to a formal occasion.' Tony was about to hit him and so I just stood up, climbed on to the table—by this time we were all sitting at the bridal table itself—and I took off the trousers and the jacket of my beautifully cut and incredibly expensive deep-red raw silk suit to show him and the rest of the assembled guests just exactly why I wasn't wearing dinky little mini skirts so often this season."

Molly pulled the car up outside their flat. "Oh, I see."

"They certainly did."

"And then?"

"Then, while no doubt one or two people were enjoying the sight of my Janet Reger underwear, everyone else was gasping in shock at my horrifically scarred legs and stomach."

"They're not that bad."

"Not to you, darling. You love me, you're used to them. Anyway, you're a doctor."

"So what happened next?"

"Well, it got even juicier after that. Tony swiftly hit the bastard best man—causing his nose to bleed copiously all over the chief bridesmaid's lemon taffeta dress and Cassie retrieved the kids and bundled us all back to the bed and breakfast before the remaining guardsmen took it into their tiny heads to see to Tony. They stayed the night and I got the first train home to you."

"So you didn't exactly get kicked out?"

"Not as such. But I'm tired, hungry, hungover, furious with myself for letting him get to me and ... oh God, you know. This."

She hit her right thigh in frustration and Molly took Saz's scarred hand to stop her hitting herself again.

"Yeah, babe, I know."

That night Molly lay in bed beside her girlfriend, stroking the heavy lines the burn scars had left on Saz's stomach and legs. The scars from a job that had gone badly wrong. Scars that, although they were slowly fading, could never be removed completely, either from Saz's body or her mind. Molly let her hand travel up the thick ridge of burned skin along Saz's thigh, gently easing pressure where scar tissue turned to sex tissue. After more than a year of various treatments and painfully slow healing, Saz was almost used to what she referred to as her "branding", but there were still many times when she reached her hands down her own body and felt disgust, when she looked at her newly mottled body and longed for the smooth single-coloured skin she'd grown up with and had loved to both feel herself and have others discover. Saz's physical strength and a large dose of body image politics had steered her through much of the pain of healing, but Molly knew that her lover's defiant, drunken gesture at the wedding would no doubt leave its own scabby residue to pick over in the coming weeks.

Molly started to kiss Saz, slowly drawing her back from sleep. Her hand followed the map lines of burn scars back to breasts and stomach. Saz roused herself enough to hold Molly's hand fast and draw it to her face. She kissed the hand and then turned away, her back to Molly, whispering, "I'm sorry, I can't babe, I'm all raw."

Molly cradled her lover and listened to their twin-rhythmed breathing as Saz fell asleep beside her. After nearly eighteen months of patience, Molly was starting to wonder when the rawness would end and Saz would finally be cooked enough to eat again.

Six hours after they'd fallen asleep together Saz came in from her usual run across the Heath, headed straight for the shower and stood for a good ten minutes under the fast running cold water. The shower sluiced away the sweat and aches in her muscles and the chill raised her heartbeat another notch or two. Her body cold and dripping, she climbed back into bed beside Molly.

"Hold me?"

Molly turned over, still dreaming and took Saz in her

arms, acknowledging the cold wet skin with a grunt and a lick like a kiss to the forehead and then they slid together back into sleep.

An hour later they were wakened by sun twisting in around the wooden slatted blinds and Molly groaned as a bright beam hit her, a shot in the right eye.

"Saz, I hate this. I told you these blinds weren't dark enough. We should have kept the curtains."

Saz shuffled closer and laughed as Molly pulled a pillow over her face, barely stifling her own complaint, "And I despise your early morning cheeriness."

Saz hushed Molly's objections with a long soft kiss, nibbling at her lower lip and then smoothed her girlfriend's sleep ruffled hair.

"My darling Moll, it's a beautiful crisp day, the Heath is covered in trees doing their red and gold thing, I have no work and you have a day off. Let us greet the sunshine and play in the world with joy and gratitude that we are happy, healthy, alive and, best of all, together."

"God, I hate it when you wake up all Pollyanna."

"Even when Pollyanna's feeling sexy?"

"Hayley Mills feels sexy?"

"I do."

Molly opened her eyes wide. Saz laughed, "You're so predictable Molly Steel!"

"Yeah, and you so rarely feel sexy these days, let's get on with it!"

Molly pulled off her own T-shirt and rolled over on to Saz's naked body, nibbling at her shoulders, arms, breasts. She closed her eyes and ran her fingers lightly over the four heavy ridges of scarring that counted her down from just below Saz's breasts to her groin, her hand hovered, dived and then stroked up, over the more heavily burnt right thigh then over the lightly scarred left. Saz's legs and stomach were once again strongly muscled, and Molly could feel the long thigh muscles tense under her touch. Her exploration of Saz's torso nearly over, Molly bent her head to kiss the breasts that had, to her unspoken relief, escaped permanent injury. Her mouth to Saz's nipple, her hand reaching for her groin, Molly was lost in the pleasure and enjoyment of her lover. It took two or three rings and Saz's decidedly unsexual stirring underneath her before she heard the phone. Molly barely paused, just moving her mouth from the skin long enough to say, "Leave it, I like this."

Saz shook her head and pulled herself up on the bed, away from Molly's kiss, "I can't, babe, it might be my sister."

"She'll leave a message."

"No she won't. Not if she's pissed off with me. Please?"

Molly threw back the bedclothes and stormed into the lounge, picking up the phone just as the answer machine cut in. Saz heard her irritated greeting and then a few short sentences were exchanged and the receiver was replaced with an echoing click from the phone in the kitchen. Molly walked back into the bedroom, a piece of paper in her hand.

Saz looked up sheepishly, "Not Cassie? I'm sorry. I'll call her later." Saz was looking at Molly's confused grin as she held out the piece of paper.

"What? Why the look? Who was it?"

"Siobhan Forrester would like you to call her—when you have a moment. If you're not too busy."

"Who?"

"Siobhan Forrester. The singer, I suppose. Wonder what she wants with you?"

"*The* Siobhan Forrester?"

"Well, yeah. She had a Scouse-ish accent and she said this was her private number and would I please be very careful about who I gave it to. I suppose she thought I was your secretary which is why she talked to me like an idiot."

"I'd better call her."

Saz started to get out of bed and Molly lunged at

her, pulling her back. "Oh no you don't. We were busy, remember? And anyway, like the good secretary I am, I told her you wouldn't be back for another hour. So you can just lie back and think of me for a change."

"Is that the same as lying back and thinking of England?"

"Only if an Asian Scot counts as English. Now, Ms Martin, what do we think about sexual activity in the workplace? Or is having an affair with your bimbo secretary just too much of a cliché to contemplate?"

Saz didn't bother to answer and Molly regained her rightful position at Saz's breast while Saz did her best to ignore thoughts of why the lead singer of Beneath The Blonde should be calling her at eleven o'clock on a Sunday morning. A few moments later Molly was nearing her target and Saz had no trouble forgetting Siobhan Forrester. She sailed with Molly's experienced hands and mouth into a body and mind mix where her burn scars were as irrelevant as the tiny tattoo on Molly's left thigh. And twice as sexy.

THREE

At barely twenty-three, Siobhan Forrester didn't really appreciate what the man from NME meant when he had called the promising newcomer: "the dream reincarnation—Deborah Harry face with Patty Smith vocals and lungs like Janis Joplin never left town".

Five years later, after she'd invested in the works of her musical godmothers to wile away months of negotiating the M1 at five in the morning, she knew when she was being praised by a master, even if only as a newcomer. She also knew that their second album would confirm the band's status and keep them forever out of the flash in the pan bracket. Getting ready to gear herself up for the next press launch, she reminded herself that as long as she kept her lips apart just a little for the photo calls and wore a short enough skirt, all the baby boy journos (and at least a third of the girls) would fall over themselves, and each other, to be nice to her, taking great care with their sharp muso prose to note her looks first and her music second. It was tedious and predictable and if it annoyed Siobhan, it probably annoyed the boys in the band even more, but all five of them knew that the perfect packaging they'd chanced on by accident—blonde girl singer, four boys backing—was the glitter that sold their music. While the press was slowly starting to acknowledge that the music could stand by itself, no one yet felt brave enough to test the waters and allow Siobhan more than a moment or two out of the spotlight. So the four men of the band prepared for the press part of the launch by buying matching charcoal grey Paul Smith suits, with a different coloured linen shirt for each and Siobhan prepared herself by buying most of South Molton Street with half of Top Shop thrown in for glitter trash value. Their manager, their tour promoter, the record company and the band itself knew that Beneath The Blonde was made up of five people, only one of whom happened to be Siobhan. The buying public knew that too, but only as much as it knew winter follows summer and first love always dies. Truth, but not the kind of truth you think about too much. For the world outside the band, Beneath The Blonde was the Blonde.

In the past five years Siobhan and the guys had learnt more about the business than they'd ever hoped to know. They'd had a fairly slow start. The first single, a minor triumph, had been followed by another year of student gigs and record company stonewalling. Then they'd eventually managed to record a very well received first album with a willing if disorganized indie label. That album had been a huge and very surprising success. However, the subsequent tour had been followed not by the weeks of glory they'd expected but by another agonizing year in which they eventually sorted out all the business details. And rather messily extricated themselves from a tricky relationship with the guy who had been acting as their manager until a real one happened along. An old friend of the bass player Steve, Alan had known far more about managing stand-up comedians than bands and had only been looking after them as a favour. Manager-free (after a great deal of negotiating and a greater deal of cash), they accepted an offer from Cal Harding, a Texan businessman their record company had introduced them to. He'd commuted between LA and New York for thirty years and, in his early fifties, he knew the business inside out. Or certainly seemed to. With one success under their belt and badly needing to realize the promise of so much more, the band couldn't afford not to make a leap of faith on the manager front. They signed away the next five years to him and then, for the first time in their career as musicians, they were able to leave business to someone else and get on with being creative. Greg and drummer Alex churned out over forty songs, Siobhan and Dan edited, pruned, arranged and then rearranged. After five major arguments between Alex and Dan, yet another monumental fight between Siobhan and Greg, and a single moment in which even Steve was ruffled, they finally had the sixteen tracks they felt ready to let Cal offer their record company. The album was whittled down to thirteen songs, at least one of which everyone hated, and another which needed virtual blackmail to get the record company to agree to. (Cal had proved himself a man of great artistic integrity by simply sending a fax to the most difficult company executive: "No 'Pink Pleasure Please?' No Blondes.") Luckily for all of them, his bravura show of force was successful.

And now, with the second album due out soon, Cal had set them up with a new tour manager, dates were being booked and time on the road was coming up in the new year. Only three months to start with, but that was three months too long for Alex and Steve who both hated to go away—and nine months too short for Dan who, having just broken up with his boyfriend, would have been happy to go on the road forever and never come back. Siobhan knew that they stood a chance of becoming something with this album, of building on their first success and actually making all the work really matter, not just the years she'd been with the band but everything else too: the hundreds of nights in grotty clubs and pubs since she was sixteen, the effort she'd put into trying to make homes out of sad bedsits and worse shared squats with Greg. She knew that Beneath The Blonde On Tour had to be something incredible.

She also knew that the silent phone calls she was receiving at three in the morning were starting to annoy her. The nasty anonymous letters weren't very pleasant and when the first bunch of yellow roses arrived, she realized she was frightened and maybe it wasn't just a joke after all.

FOUR

The band had been Alex's idea. Stoned again in the muggy summer of 1988, sitting on the roof of his squat in Vauxhall, gas tanks and the Oval hazy in the near distance, he was burning his back and rewriting his fourth poem of the day. Stuck on line three, he was relieved to hear Greg shout up from the street. He stood on the warm pavement with a twelve pack of beers and the bongos he'd borrowed for a party the night before. Alex threw the keys from the roof and watched after them as they floated down to the street on their pink silk handkerchief parachute. Five minutes later Greg dropped a cold beer two inches in front of his new friend's face. "I bought them this morning and left a couple out so they'd warm up for your crap taste buds."

"Very considerate. Unusual for a colonial. Smoke?"

To Greg's nodded agreement, Alex rolled his fourth joint of the day—it was one-thirty in the afternoon, he'd been up since ten and he was cutting down.

The two young men smoked and drank through the heat of the afternoon, enjoying the solid wall of breeze-free London heat and the freedom of summer. Greg was an engineer for a recording company and loathed every minute of his weekday job. He'd taken the job hoping it would help him with his own music, but found that the best of his work involved recording cheap radio ads with bad voice-over actors, while in the worst moments he was just a glorified (and slightly better paid) runner. Alex was signing on every second Tuesday morning and putting in twelve-hour days at a pine furniture factory in West London for twenty quid a day cash in hand. He'd just arrived back from two weeks with his family in Cork and was gearing himself up to the regime of fortnightly lying to the government and daily lies to the tube inspectors and then wasting himself at the weekend as a relief from hating his weekdays.

As they sat and smoked and drank, Alex occasionally made forays all the way down to the cellar kitchen to bring up another slice of bread and jam for himself or bread and Vegemite for Greg, who complained that the Vegemite in Alex's kitchen was Australian, not New Zealand, and therefore not the real thing. And then ate it anyway. After two warmish beers and a half-hearted attempt at conversation about cricket, Greg, who had cleared his own flat of party goers at six that morning, fell asleep and Alex finished his poem. Then Alex fell asleep, Greg woke up, rolled another joint, read Alex's poem, edited Alex's poem and wandered downstairs to chat in the kitchen to Alex's Spanish girlfriend. Mariella had spent the day at Kennington Lido and after too long asleep by the reflected water, was applying after-sun to the backs of her arms and legs. He stayed long enough to make coffee until three of her dyke friends arrived with two dogs and a puppy on a string and he felt the warmth of Mariella's welcome quickly turn to a more politically correct animosity. Waking Alex with the coffee, Greg told him that Mariella was back.

"Are those 'wimmin' with her?"

"Yep."

Alex grabbed his coffee and growled. "Fuck it."

Greg shook his head, "Nah, they're all right. They're just not very . . ."

"Nice?"

"Chatty."

"Yeah, well it's my fucking kitchen, man, and they're always bloody here."

"Is Mariella . . .?"

"I dunno. Not yet anyway. Oh fuck it, why me?"

"Why you what?"

"Why do all my fucking girlfriends become lesbians?"

Greg laughed, "Only one of your girlfriends has become gay, and you knew Hannah was more or less a dyke when you started going out with her."

"So why'd she go out with me then?"

"Last fling? Sad and desperate? Just to persuade herself of what she wouldn't be missing?"

"Bitch."

"Nah. Just confused. It's the *zeitgeist*."

"The what?"

Greg picked up the bongos and started drumming while Alex rolled another joint. He explained, "Sign of the times. It's trendy for girls. The girls we know anyway. Look at Mariella, I mean she's probably more or less straight."

"Oh, she's more, believe me."

"Ok, but if most of her women friends are gay, and it's not as if she really knows that many other people in London anyway, she's bound to get a bit curious. And you know . . . they're women. They're girls. They're nicer, softer, cleaner— all that shit. I'd be a lesbian if I was a girl."

Alex snarled, "Not if the lesbians you knew were those lesbians."

"Yeah, well, maybe I could do without the barbed-wire tattoo on the face . . ."

"And the fucking dogs everywhere."

Greg drummed faster, Alex holding the joint for him so he didn't have to move his hands from the rhythm. "That's not the point. These specific lesbians aren't the point. I know some lesbians who don't have tattoos or dogs."

"You do?"

"Yeah. There's a girl in my photography class. And she doesn't live in Brixton either."

"Well, she must have got lost."

Greg stopped drumming. "You're deliberately being a wanker now. My point is that when you say all dykes are ugly or nasty or whatever . . ."

"I didn't."

"No, but you implied it. And that's just the same as when they say all men are crap or all men are slobs—which, come to think of it, is probably true . . ."

"Fuck off, you might be, but I did my washing this morning. And I'll be ironing tonight."

"Or all men are liars . . ."

"Or all men are rapists?"

"Maybe that's stretching the analogy a little too far, but you know what I mean. You know, all Irish are thick?"

Alex stood up and started pacing the small roof area, looking down at the square he'd lived in for the past four years, once a haven for squatters of all kinds, now slowly reverting to "society" as the housing associations and co-ops bought up the properties and normalized them. He sat on the edge of the roof and looked back at Greg. "Yeah, all right. Of course I know what you mean. And I also know that this is my house. I found it. I opened it, I got the electricity and water put on, I cleared the garden, I fixed the roof, I put in the windows and when Mariella brings that bloody Autumn round here . . ."

"Autumn?"

"Yeah. Her girlfriend's called Evechild."

"Oh."

"See? Anyway, the problem is, I don't exactly end up feeling that this Englishman's home is his castle."

"Fair point. Even for an Irishman. Pub?"

"In a minute. I just want to finish this." Alex looked around for his notepad, Greg pointed it out under the several empty cans of beer.

"I did it for you. Edited the poem. It's finished."

"You bastard. That's private."

"People who get stoned as much as you do should never attempt to keep things private, they fall asleep too fucking much. It's good though."

"Thanks, you'd know."

"But I've made it better."

Alex grabbed the notepad and stared at it for a couple of minutes, frowning hard. "Fuck me, but you have. Hah!" He tossed the notepad down and opened the last can of very warm beer.

The young men shared the last beer and watched the sun set on the other side of the river and talked of Greg's photography course and the relative merits of Split Enz and Crowded House, football and rugby, until Mariella joined them with three glasses, two bottles of Spanish wine and two mammoth portions of chips swimming in salty vinegar. When she went inside to get her after-sun cream for Alex, having kissed him for a full five and half minutes, Greg looked across at his friend and smiled. "Yeah, she certainly looks like a dyke to me."

Alex threw a handful of cold chips at him. "Fuck off. Let's start a band."

Alex always maintained that he'd been thinking about suggesting a band to Greg for months, but it was Greg's editing of his poem that decided him. Greg believed Alex was too unnerved by the honesty of their earlier conversation about sex and sexuality and wanted to get back to any safe topic. Football, music, anything as long as it didn't involve sexual truth. Whatever the reason, Greg agreed and the idea became real. Alex brought in his old friend Dan as keyboards player and singer, gleefully pointing out that Dan was gay and wasn't it strange that Greg didn't seem to have any gay men friends, and Mariella pointed them in the direction of Steve, bass player, sometime playwright and Autumn's brother. The band rehearsed on the roof for the rest of the summer and moved down to Alex's bedroom when the days turned colder. For a while, Mariella sang with them but when she left in October, with Autumn and the two puppies, Alex wrote their first real song "Welcome Winter" and Greg brought in his new flatmate, Siobhan, to sing. Greg and Siobhan weren't yet lovers. That grew over the following months, but by late November of 1988, the line up of Beneath The Blonde was firmly established.

FIVE

Since 1988, Siobhan Forrester had created one hell of a reputation for herself. When the band was performing she strode the stage like a manic sex goddess. Alternating between her whispered intros and proclaiming the songs with cut-glass attitude, she held court between chord changes—rude, crude, loud and powerful. The music press, at a loss to describe her adequately, took the easy route, comparing her to other women performers. Gig reviews were crammed with quotes like "A cross between Sinead O'Connor and Jenny Eclair with the voice of Annie Lennox". And always, no matter how erudite the publication, the reviewer would find some way of getting in a description of the physical Siobhan—long lean limbs, impressive height, amazing mouth, tits that shouldn't be allowed near hips so sheer and, inevitably, all that hair. The celebrated blonde locks. Blonde that changed from week to week, gig to gig— elemental silver and platinum, alchemical peroxide, edible strawberry and honey, and occasionally just pure out-and-out white. Whatever they thought of the music, and most were agreed the band was close as fuck to perfect, every reviewer, male or female, gay, straight or raving queer was in agreement on one thing—Siobhan Forrester's looks were phenomenal.

So, turning up at the Chalk Farm address on Sunday after-noon, Saz had expected a collection of security guards and

a video entryphone at the very least. What she didn't expect
was to stroll up the overgrown path, climb the three steps
to the purple front door of the baby pink house, ring the
bell and, after a fish eye had glared at her through the peep
hole, to be greeted by Siobhan herself. At least she thought it
was Siobhan. The mouth looked like it belonged on Siobhan
Forrester, but very little else did. Saz was just starting to
wonder if every beautiful woman had a dowdy little sister
hidden away somewhere when the tall, thin woman with
short brown hair held out her hand. "Saz Martin? Thanks
for coming so quickly. I'm Siobhan. Come in."

Saz followed her into an open entrance hall, decorated
in a mini rain forest of tropical houseplants and pots of
yellow and orange flowers against a backdrop of draped
purple muslins.

The newest icon of female pop sexuality shuffled away
on holey socks and called over her hunched shoulders, "I've
just put the kettle on, would you like some tea?"

"Yeah, thanks."

In the first floor kitchen Saz sat on an extremely modern
and very uncomfortable stool, four inches too tall for her
legs to reach the floor. She watched while the darling girl
of Britpop poured boiling water on round Tetley teabags in
chipped yellow china mugs and then fished out the soggy
bags with a bone caviar spoon. She knew it was a caviar
spoon because Siobhan told her so. "It's since we've had
some money. Greg's got this thing about caviar. I don't get
it myself. The only time I like seafood is when it's a tiny
piece of anchovy with a thin crust pizza base on one side
and a lot of melted mozzarella on the other."

Saz could see that the woman before her was the Siobhan
Forrester she thought she knew, but only just. She had the
distinct feeling she was looking at the "before" photo from
a trashy magazine makeover. This woman was tall enough,
but hardly the giant she seemed on stage, closer to Molly's

height, maybe five foot nine or ten. Saz knew most of the
hair must be a wig though she wasn't prepared for the ordin-
ariness of the mousey brown bob. But what really got her
was the body. It just didn't seem to be there. She looked up
from Siobhan's T-shirt covered chest to see the younger
woman smiling at her.

"I know. It's a shock. Or so the men tell me. And of
course I don't answer the door like this to the press—our
manager would never allow it. It is me though. It's easy.
Really. Same old girl shit just taken to extremes."

"Girl shit?"

"Yeah, you know. Hair, height and hips. Hair's obvious—
just wigs. Height's shoes. And hips—well, there's never really
any hips anyway. I'm lucky I suppose. Prancing around the
stage for two hours a night does wonders for the bottom
line—that's why I like doing the big dates last, so I'm even
thinner than usual by the time we get to them. Makes the
waist go in and so the hips go out—with the right clothes
they do, anyway. The rest of it's just makeup."

Saz nodded. "All of it?"

Siobhan grabbed a breast in each hand, pulling the T-shirt
material tight across her front. "Almost. These bits are all
mine—with a little help from Mr Gossard of course."

Saz had the grace to blush. "Yeah. Right. I'm sorry. It's
none of my business. I just . . ."

"Expected Bette Lynch?"

"Maybe. Or Bette Midler."

Siobhan laughed and put a cup down in front of Saz.
"Christ, even drag queens get to take their heels off at
home!"

Twenty minutes later Saz was listening to Siobhan's stories
of Beneath The Blonde—the early years. She'd just heard a
catalogue of particularly disastrous motorway journeys and

hideous B&B's when Greg Marsden walked into the kitchen. He appeared not to have seen Saz as he grabbed Siobhan by the throat, turned her to face him with a growl and then pulled her off her chair. Saz was about to stand up to protest, but stopped in her tracks as Siobhan burst out laughing and then swung both of her legs around Greg's waist, attaching herself to his body with her own and her face to his mouth with her big famous lips. What seemed like an embarrassed eternity later to Saz, Greg put Siobhan down, ruffled her flat bob and, putting the kettle on for the third time that afternoon, said, "Hi honey, I'm home. Going to introduce me to your new friend?"

He flicked the switch on the wall and held out a hand for Saz to shake, adding, "New Zealand, not Australian, so don't even ask."

"Wouldn't dream of it."

Siobhan threw a cushion at Greg, narrowly missing the top of his almost six-foot frame. "Don't mind Greg, he has a massive antipodean chip on his shoulder."

"I do not," he countered, returning the cushion with rather more accuracy. "I have a massive Aotearoan chip on my shoulder—and I'm not a bloody Australian."

"That's nice, darling, but I don't think our guest cares much. Saz Martin, this is Greg Marsden. My lover of ten years, the writing force behind the band, though don't tell Alex I said that, and a New Zealander who has lived in England for . . . ooh, I don't know . . . six weeks from your accent isn't it, hon?"

"Sixteen years. Almost half my life. But don't let that stop you getting it wrong in your article, Saz—who do you write for?"

By the time she left for home, Greg knew that Saz was about as interested in writing music articles as she was in having her tongue pierced and Saz had two new jobs. One as assistant to their PA and the other, rather more importantly, as unofficial investigator/bodyguard for Siobhan Forrester.

SIX

"No, fine, darling. You go on tour, all that extra work, all those late nights, wonderful idea, it'll do you the world of good."

"I hate it when you use that tone, Moll."

"I hate it when you do stupid things, Saz. Doesn't stop you doing them though, does it? And really, it's not as if we need the money."

Saz ran her fist up and down her left thigh, a new gesture of irritation she'd developed in the past eighteen months—although her hands had healed fastest, they'd also been covered in burn gloves for long enough for her to learn to do without her fingernails. She got up from the old wooden farmhouse table and took their dishes to the sink.

"Jesus, Moll, this is the first real job I've been offered in ages. I'd have thought you'd be pleased."

"Right. Sure. Of course I should be pleased. A pop band wants you to go on tour with them for months, just at the point where you're almost healthy . . ."

"They're hardly a 'pop' band and I am healthy."

"I'm the doctor. 'Almost healthy' and just when I could actually start having you to myself again."

"You've had me all to yourself for the past eighteen months!"

"Except for all the other people I've shared you with— the physiotherapists, occupational therapists . . ."

"Psychotherapists. Don't forget them."

"Yeah, well they obviously didn't bloody well work. Not

to mention your mother, your sister, her husband, her kids and every ex-lover you've ever had."

Saz ran water over the plates, keeping her voice low and trying not to get caught up in Molly's rising anger. "A slight exaggeration, babe, it was only Carrie really, I don't see any other ex-lovers. And being with her has usually been more work than socializing."

"Well, Carrie doesn't seem to be able to tell the difference between work and fun and she takes up enough space and energy to feel like half a dozen old friends."

"I think she is. Anyway, she cares about me."

"I care about you."

"I know. So admit that having a real job, one I can concentrate on . . ."

"One you need to go away for."

"Yeah, that too. A job where I need to go away and look after myself will be good for me. You've been looking after me for ages. Earning all the money—"

"You had sickness benefit for a while."

"Yes. That went a long way, didn't it? Come on, Moll. You know I'm right. I'm not sick any more. Maybe I'm always going to be a bit tender, but I can't hide behind you forever. It's not good for us, for our relationship. And anyway, I don't want to."

Molly picked up her glass of wine and poured the rest of it down the sink. She kissed Saz's shoulder and picked up a tea towel.

"I know it would be good for you to have a job you can get involved in. I know you need a job. I know I can't keep you wrapped in cotton wool forever."

"Not even silk suits."

"Not when you rip them off at weddings, no. But this is different, Saz. You don't know anything about music, about bands."

"I can learn."

"I thought you were there to detect, not to gain new career insights?"

"I'm being an assistant. I'm just helping. Being the runner, whatever. So I can find out what's going on. Find out about them. If I see what there is to know, then I'll know what there is to find out. Anyway, I won't be doing the business thing much. They've got a band manager and a tour manager and they've got a PA working for them at the house. Alex's little sister. She'll do most of the work."

"Right. And she'll never ask you to do anything."

"I'm quite good at office work actually."

"And body guarding? You're not exactly Kevin Costner."

"Dances With Dykes?"

"I'm serious. All your work until now has been investigative stuff."

"So's this. It's just in more glamorous parts of the world than South London."

Saz rinsed the last of the glasses and continued with her attempt to persuade Molly of the value of getting back to work full-time.

"Look, it's really not going to be that complicated, surely. I've just got to find out who's been delivering the flowers to her. I can get Carrie to help out. She could do with the cash. Once we grab the flower sender, I'll persuade Siobhan to make a complaint and then hand it all over to the men in blue. Here's your stalker, deal with it."

"So why doesn't Siobhan just go to the police herself?"

"I don't know. Shy. Private. She probably feels stupid to be worried. It's not as if she's actually being threatened as such, more like irritated, annoyed. Letters, flowers, that sort of thing."

"Doesn't sound very annoying to me."

Saz turned her head to look at Molly, her yellow-gloved hands still in the washing-up water. "That, my darling, is because you expect all flowers and surprises to come from me. What if you didn't know who they came from?"

Molly kissed Saz's upturned forehead. "I might find it a turn on. I might find it exciting. Like I'm finding you exciting."

Saz turned to kiss Molly back. "Yeah, I know, there's just something so goddamn sexy about a girl, a washing-up bowl and a pile of dirty dishes, isn't there?

Saz extricated her hands from the sticky yellow gloves and Molly slid her own hand down Saz's bare arm. Saz hooked her leg back between Molly's and pulled her even closer. Beneath the knee, beneath the line of burn, Saz's legs were smooth like Molly's touch, Molly's mouth. Lips to legs, to stomach, to breasts, to back, sweet pointed eye teeth clawing their way through scarred skin. Saz was body-pinned to the kitchen floor, newly laid slate tiles cold on her back. Molly found her experienced way through the clothes straight to the skin, the soft flesh, taunting Saz's body with her fingers, her hands, whipping at Saz's centre with her rope of long hair, the two of them as the same shudder. Saz's body joined Molly's, centring herself on her lover and into the slate and into the cold of the kitchen night and, after the sweat and the holding and the last turn away from the hot two-body cave, eventually into sleep.

Hours later Saz and Molly pulled themselves from the cold kitchen floor, Saz complaining that their new tiles should have an anti-sex warning, and stumbled through the dark flat into their bed. As Molly stroked Saz to sleep, Saz mumbled, "You won't miss this when I'm away, will you? At least you won't have to look after me all the time. That'll be a relief, won't it?"

Molly smiled into Saz's hair, "I love looking after you,

babe. I've always loved it. It's my favourite thing. Which is why I know it's a great idea that you should go."

But Saz was asleep before she heard the permission granted.

SEVEN

Saz was sitting on the attic floor of Siobhan's house, looking out as the heavy rain lashed across her view of the city. In just one night the weather had made its usual London leap from late summer sun to early autumn damp and she was delighted that at least this part of her job was to involve being indoors for much of the time.

Siobhan and Greg had each claimed a room of their own when they moved in. His was the basement; dark and padded, it was half studio, half playroom, the walls lined with recording gear and corners stacked three deep in guitars. On one wall was a red formica and chrome bar, on another a fifties' juke box and a pool table stood in the centre of it all. Siobhan's room was the converted attic. It was a stunning space, stretching the width of the house with windows all along one wall looking south down to the city. Siobhan lay on a double chaise longue—custom-made by an old friend of Alex's and upholstered in padded gold and purple. The walls were pale lilac, and the room was carpeted in dark green for half its length, while at the other end, in front of a wide-screen TV with huge speakers, was a small wooden dance floor. Siobhan pointed to a shelf beside the TV on which were more than twenty exercise videos, "That's how Siobhan Forrester gets 'the body of an Amazon princess'. But with two tits, you understand. Every bloody morning I'm up here and getting on down with Cindy and

Claudia and Elle and all the other barbie dolls who wish their sculpted limbs were made from plastic and not sweat."

"You don't like gyms?" Saz asked.

"I like privacy. I like to be alone." Siobhan whispered in a very bad Garbo as she rolled herself off the chaise, managing to crumple the sheet music she was studying as well as several copies of an incongruously paired *Smash Hits* and *GQ*. She opened a cupboard built into the sloping back wall, which turned out to be a small fridge and took out two short frosted glasses and then reached into the tiny freezer compartment and took out a selection of frozen vodka miniatures. She offered them to Saz. "Not that I'd do this if I was really seriously in training, but what do you say? Since it's such a lovely Monday?"

Saz looked out at the rain weeping horizontally against the windows, at the gold-painted clock which read almost noon, laughed and chose the cherry vodka.

Saz had asked Siobhan if she could come over before she started her official job the next day so that she could get clear on exactly what she was supposed to know and, more to the point, just what it was she should be looking out for. Saz started by asking Greg about himself. He answered hesitantly, "Well, I don't know that there's that much of interest. My parents died ages ago. I was brought up by my aunt and uncle, got on with them well enough, but I just always knew I wanted to leave New Zealand. See the world."

"To do the back-packing thing?"

"Not really. I pretty much came to London and stayed. I've been to Amsterdam a fair few times, bits of Europe, the States. But I was just interested in the music really. Alex and I started the band in '88 and since then, that's been my main focus. Well, the band and Siobhan." He added the latter with a kiss to his girlfriend's forehead and then got up to leave the room.

Saz looked at Siobhan, "Sorry, touchy subject?"

Siobhan shook her head. "No, you're all right. He's just not very good at talking about himself, that's all. Basically, his family were really pissed off with him when he left New Zealand so young. He was only sixteen, after all. He didn't really have anything when he came here. Did loads of crap jobs, lived in squats and put all his efforts into getting into music—not really the ideal career path for a number one son. Or nephew for that matter. He doesn't like to talk about it much."

Saz turned from the floor-to-ceiling windows, grabbing another handful of toasted cashews from the bowl at her feet as she did so. "OK. Fair enough. It's unlikely that your stalker is a long lost cousin anyway. And your family?"

"Yeah, well my lot are cool. Really, they're great. I love my family."

"Do you see them often?"

"Twice a year, Easter and Christmas. That's probably why they're so easy to love."

Saz nodded, "Absence certainly seems to make the heart grow fonder as far as families are concerned. What are yours like?"

"Very TV typical. One of those classic Liverpool Irish Catholic families they make all the documentaries about. And the soap operas. All the clichés, all the shouting, all the affection. And all the problems. Which is why all this is still so much like playing to me. Having this house, these things—it's like having someone else's life. And we got a really good deal with it too, because we so often rehearse in the basement, a whole chunk of the mortgage is paid for by the band itself. One of the good things Cal managed to sort for us."

"There must be a payoff though?"

"Yeah," Siobhan shrugged, "my life." Then she smiled, "No, it's not too bad really. The record company get to keep an eye on us and there's no way we could have afforded all this before them." She interrupted herself and smiled gleefully at Saz, "Actually, things are going pretty well right now, we could have paid for the lot ourselves ... but why should we if they wanted to help? And with all these rooms, we realized we could have what we'd always wanted. A music room for Greg, the acoustics are good enough for rehearsals and because it's the basement we don't really disturb the neighbours. Then there's the three spare rooms, our bedroom, the living rooms, kitchen, office and this"—she waved her arm around the room—"my boudoir. It's important for the promotions people too—everyone knows Greg and I are together but we have to play it down a bit for the fans. We're supposed to look as if we're both eligible, apparently one Ben Watt and Tracey Thorn is enough in British music. So I get to have this all to myself. As different from the basement as possible and as far away from Greg as possible too—just in case we should happen to have a tiny tiff, you understand." Siobhan laughed, throwing her head back on her long, arched neck and Saz nodded, thinking that if the huge screaming fight Siobhan and Greg had been having when she arrived twenty minutes earlier was a tiny tiff, then she didn't plan on being around when they were having proper rows.

Over another vodka, Siobhan showed the letters to Saz. There were only three, each neatly printed up in a different font, but all on the same expensive creamy white paper. The first just asked how she'd liked the flowers and the second, while longer, was fairly innocuous, though Saz understood that it was enough to be concerned about. She herself would have been very perturbed to receive a letter that said, "I know what you feel like".

She pointed this out to Siobhan who laughed and asked, "You don't know much of our back catalogue, do you?"

Saz winced a little and answered, "Sorry. I don't have a lot to do with 'young people's music' these days. I was a Radio One girl once, but I always knew when the time came that I no longer cared about Top of The Pops, I'd be a grown-up."

"And that's now?"

"Now I listen to Farming Today and the start of the Today Programme while I run, then I usually go back to sleep for the rest of the morning."

"So do I when I'm awake."

"Go back to sleep?"

"Listen to the Today Programme."

Saz sipped at her drink, the alcohol warming her more than was warranted on an early autumn morning, "I'd have thought you'd be a morning TV girl."

Siobhan shook her head, "Too much bloody shouting far too bloody early for me. I do all my shouting on stage. Real-life I like to be as calm and quiet as possible. Mind you, they were very nice to us when we went on the Big Breakfast. I suppose you missed that too?"

"You suppose right. And so, in order to remedy this appalling lack of knowledge, I went out first thing this morning and harassed the assistant at Virgin . . ."

"Oxford Street?"

Saz nodded.

"God, that's what I call dedicated."

"No, that's what you call desperate. I harassed this poor spotty girl until she found me not only the album—which, you'll be glad to know, she was visibly shocked to learn I didn't already possess—but also the two single CDs. I haven't had a chance to listen to any of it yet. Sorry."

Siobhan stood up and reached for an apple from the fruit

bowl on top of the television. "You didn't need to buy them. I would have made you copies."

"Isn't that a breach of copyright?"

"Not as much as these letters are."

She proceeded to explain to Saz how both letters quoted from Beneath The Blonde songs. The first letter was very short, the second was a virtual paraphrase of their first hit—a "my lover done me wrong" song, written by Alex and more than a little angry. Siobhan read the letter out loud, grimacing as she did so.

"Dear Siobhan, I know what you look like beneath the blonde. Beneath the dress. Beneath the knickers. I know what you look like. I know what you feel like. I know you, Siobhan Forrester. I won't forget you. Don't forget me."

She then quoted the lines from "I Know You". "See, the real words are 'I know what you look like, beneath the dress, I know how you feel, dressing to empress'—with an 'e'—that's a very Alex line, you don't know what he's fucking talking about unless you read the lyrics. Then there's some other stuff, blah, blah, blah . . . 'bitch'. That's it."

Siobhan threw away her apple core and grimaced, "Bitch of course rhymes with witch; the boys weren't quite as eloquent in the early days as they are now. Then it stops rhyming altogether and becomes this really fast, furious rant which I sing, if I do say so myself, fucking brilliantly."

Then she sang it and, sitting at her feet on the attic floor, Saz understood why that voice had made so many people tout Beneath The Blonde as the future. Siobhan's fierce, atonal scream made the hairs on the back of her neck stand on end as she launched into the last few lines—"I know you, I know what you feel like, I know you. Beneath the blonde. I know you. Beneath the hair. Under the dress. I know you. Under the underneath. Under the skin. Under you. I know you."

When she'd finished, she sank beside Saz onto the floor and swallowed a long draught of her vodka. "Then there's this really long pause with just a drum beat and it ends with me whispering, 'Don't forget it, bitch'. Which is, of course, where the early dyke rumours came from."

Saz grinned, "So they are just rumours?"

"Primarily. Certainly there's been no chance, or desire for that matter, since I've been with Greg. Sorry."

"Don't be, I'm practically married too. It'll disappoint my ex-girlfriend though."

"It's not that I wouldn't, or that I haven't. Dabbled, you understand. But I'm with Greg. I love him."

Siobhan reached into the fridge and took out another vodka for them both.

Saz accepted hers readily and asked, "So why is it 'bitch'? Why didn't they choose a boy word?"

"Alex had written it about a girl he'd been going out with, and he originally meant for it to be sung by both me and Dan. Like a duet for two people breaking up—all that bitterness and nastiness. I thought it was a great idea, even if it did come from Alex." Siobhan shrugged her shoulders and pulled herself back up on the chaise, "You know, a duet version of what you walked into this morning. Only Greg and I aren't breaking up, we just always fight over trivia."

"We don't call six hundred pound phone bills trivia in our house."

"Neither does Greg. So anyway, me and Dan dueting was a good idea, but when it came to the recording, I got on much better with the arrangement than Dan and the last bit, all that ranting and then the drum and the whisper just sounded so much stronger with only my voice."

"Didn't Dan mind?"

"Yeah, sure. But nobody would actually go out of their

way to pick a fight with Alex if they could help it, so the rant was mine and we left it as 'bitch' because it was better that way. The record company wanted me to whisper 'bastard' but that was pathetic. Bastard sounds too nice. Bitch sounds mean."

"Going by the words of the song, Alex sounds mean too. Or was he just horribly hurt?"

"Oh no, Alex is, well, nasty—in a funny sort of way, you understand. But in this case he was horribly hurt as well. Alex has this unfortunate habit of falling in love with women who turn out to be gay. Not when he meets them—just when they leave him."

"Ouch."

"He thinks so."

"Has it happened much?"

"Only twice to my knowledge."

"But twice too many?"

"Yeah, maybe. I don't know. Alex is just an angry shit anyway. You know, he's Greg's mate and I do like him and everything—I mean, it feels like I've known him for forever. We've worked together for long enough now and he does write fantastic stuff for me, but, well, it's like he's only really happy if he's got something unhappy to obsess about. He's a really good writer but he's even better at being a moody git. Which, to be honest, is fine with the rest of us really, 'cos on the rare occasions he's in a good mood he writes fuck all."

By the time Siobhan had explained all the references in the letters, listed the several three am telephone calls where the caller just hung up, and showed her the three bunches of now dried yellow roses, their cards simply reading "I Know You", they had finished another two vodka miniatures each and Saz was feeling like she'd better get out of that warm room soon or the concept of coming to work the next day would be more painful than morning usually necessitated. Molly, who was at home preparing dinner for the select gathering they were expecting that night, wouldn't be too impressed either. But to clarify her thoughts and what Siobhan expected of her, she went over it once again, retying the laces on her boots with clumsy fingers.

"You've had two letters in the past month?"

Siobhan nodded.

"And they're both postmarked WC1?"

"Which is where our record company's offices are."

"True. But it's also where very many other London offices are. And while they read like letters from a man, we mustn't discount the possibility they may be from a woman. They're definitely from someone who knows your work well."

Siobhan giggled, her dimples flashing in the perfectly smooth makeup free skin, "Someone who knows it better than you do, yes."

"And no one knows about the letters except Greg?"

Siobhan stopped laughing at this and sat herself up on wobbly arms.

"Yeah, and I meant what I said about not mentioning them either. I told Peta, our PA, that you're not very experienced as a production person. I said you were a friend of a friend who needed work and we'd offered to give you some office stuff to do. I just want you to suss it all out. If you need time to go off and check up on things, or do any of that detective following stuff—"

Saz shook her head, thinking of the rain falling outside, "I tend not to do a lot of 'following stuff' if I can possibly help it, but I know what you mean."

"Right, so just let me know and we'll say you're doing something for me or Greg. But I don't want any of the others to know why you're really here. I think it would be . . . I don't know, bad for group morale or something. These letters are crap but that's all they are. Just letters. So far anyway. Hopefully it'll stay that way and we'll have bothered you for nothing."

"Do you really think it's nothing?"

"I'm not as worried as Greg. He kept pushing me to tell the police about it, but I just can't stand the thought of that lot prying into our lives, so I settled for the next best thing. Chick detective, just like in the movies."

Saz stood up, "I hope not. The ones in the movies tend to get beaten up with alarming regularity."

"Yeah, but they always bounce back, don't they?"

"That's why they're in the movies. So you really don't care about any of it? Not even the phone calls?"

"I do care. I don't like it, but then again one part of me actually thinks it's quite cool."

"Cool?"

"Yeah, you know. Makes us real. Like a proper band. With a stalker and everything. But I . . . well, Greg and I, we value our privacy. In a way, it's exciting and on the other hand, it's just another bloody intrusion. I expect the press to want to know about us—I think I'm almost prepared for how it's going to be if the next album does even better—but the guys can be such arseholes sometimes."

"How do you mean?"

"Nothing really, I do love them, the men, but I really don't need them to start getting on my case about . . . well, about anything. Alex is always such a grumpy shit and just at the moment he's being particularly bad. Steve's a honey but even he's a worrier at the best of times and Dan's just broken up with Jeremy. I'm well aware that promoting the new album and getting the tour together is going to be more than enough work, a lot more fuss. I just don't want to bother them any more than I need to."

Saz nodded. "Ok, if that's how you want it, it'll be our

little secret. Just don't expect me to win PA of the month, that's all."

Siobhan showed Saz out and gave her a quick hug at the door, then Saz ran out into the rain and Siobhan wandered into the kitchen to rummage through the cupboards and find something sweet and tasty with which to placate Greg.

Saz decided to walk the fifteen or so minutes home, the sharp wind and slowing rain would sober her up and give her a chance to buy Molly some flowers to make up for being no help with the dinner. It would also give her a chance to work out why she didn't quite believe Siobhan's protestations about wanting to keep Saz's real job secret from the boys. Or rather, she certainly believed the protestations, what she didn't believe were Siobhan's reasons. Either Siobhan was a control freak who needed to keep all information to herself or there was something she wanted to hide from the others. Saz was looking forward to finding out—tactfully, of course. She was also looking forward to Molly's broccoli and stilton soup with Delia's sage and onion bread and quickened her pace up the hill.

EIGHT

In the early seventies Gaelene and Shona used to spend most of the summer holidays down at the beach with Shona's cousin John and the rest of the family who gathered around Aunty Ruby's place for the summer. The two little girls had already been best friends for nearly three years. Kindergarten and Primers, now waiting through the summer to go on up to the Standards. Big kids nearly. Their birthdays were two days apart and on the day that Gaelene's mum had brought her to kindy for the first time Shona, with a whole two days' more experience in the ways of the sandpit and the Library Corner, was given the important job of "being Gaelene's friend". A job she'd taken seriously for almost half her tiny life. Summer holidays, before the advent of skin cancer and burn times and sun block, meant long days swimming and running from the sea to the estuary and back again, panting out their feverish six-year-old energy with only huge sandwiches of homemade bread and big blocks of dairy factory cheese to sustain them until the tide went out. From the flattened, damp shore they would dig for pipis that Ruby and Wai cooked into fritters, the kids eating handfuls of them in the back garden. Ruby always refused to let them take the fritters back to the sea, saying it wasn't fair to show the baby pipis sleeping in their closed shells under the sand what had happened to their mums and dads.

Gaelene and Shona had far more in common with John and the other Maori kids, whose dads worked in the forest and whose mums worked on factory floors all over town, than with most of the other kids at Sea View Primary with their Choppers and their skateboards and their patent leather shoes. Gaelene and Shona didn't think they were any different to all the other kids at Ruby's. Shona and John were first cousins because John's mum and Shona's dad were brother and sister and when John's uncle on the other side had married Selma—Scottish, Arawa and Tuhoe—with family stretched down the East Coast all the way to Te Kaha, Shona and John's family had just been glad of the extension of their own—for a start, it helped with the babysitting.

Anyway, summer holidays lasted a long hot six weeks, the ocean gave up pipis and mussels and paua for free and if none of the kids was quite sure if she was their aunty or their great-aunty or their great-great-aunty, Ruby didn't seem to care. She was happy to welcome whoever John brought home with him; her daughter's nephew was a sweet boy and she knew there were no mums at the other kids' houses to make them lunch and check that the sun didn't burn too hard into their little freckled white shoulders. Anyone was welcome at her place, just as long as John reminded those Pakeha kids to take off their shoes before they came in the house.

At six, Gaelene and Shona were as interested in John's Maori ancestry as they were in the Irish heritage that gave Shona her green eyes and black hair or the older Danish generations that bred Gaelene's white blonde locks and darkly tanning skin. By the time the girls were sixteen though, New Zealand had just about stopped kidding itself that it was the godzone melting pot and prejudice was only to do with who you supported to win the Ranfurly Shield. And by the time he was eighteen, John had been Hone for three years and New Zealand was starting to name itself as Aotearoa. In the blinding summer of '71 though, the name changes to come didn't mean a whole lot to a bunch of little kids who swam together in waves higher than their heads.

But they would.

NINE

Siobhan greeted Saz at the front door on Tuesday morning, flushed and sweaty from an hour spent with Elle Macpherson, and directed her through to Peta's office. Saz walked into the room, her mind concerned with the usual debate of whether or not Siobhan had already come out for her and if not, when would be the best time to do it for herself. She'd tried to get an answer to the coming-out question by bringing it up at dinner the night before, but the resulting conversation had been no help at all. Molly maintained that immediate and frank assertion of one's sexuality was vital, while their friends Helen and Judith held to a mainstream line of telling people only as much as they had to know. As Molly said later, perhaps Helen and Jude's long years in the police force had made them a little more circumspect than was absolutely necessary. Carrie and her new lover Blair seemed surprised that anyone thought a world might exist where people didn't automatically know the two of them were dykes. That Blair was wearing a too tight T-shirt, perfectly outlining her surgically perfect breasts and reading "cute baby dyke" and that Carrie had not managed to move her lips from Blair's body for the entire month of their relationship, meant that neither of them could quite envisage a world where people might not be able to tell their sexuality at a fifty-pace glance. As the only straight couple at the table, Molly's ex-girlfriend Elaine and her new Brazilian husband added their belief that all people should be out all the time, drawing accusations of "You can't know how hard that is" from Carrie. Equally forthright, and to Molly's smirking joy, Albert then took the opportunity to enlighten Carrie that not only had the forty-two-year-old Elaine been gay—and out—for most of her adult life, until she'd surprised herself by falling in love with him, but that he'd actually had a boy lover of his own at high school. The conversation then degenerated into an alcohol-fuelled debate about just where was the dividing line between straight and gay, finishing up with confirmed dykes Judith and Helen looking on in amazement as Carrie finally admitted to having enjoyed more than a few men in her time and Blair telling Carrie that she was glad to hear it, because she had an ex-husband of her own hiding in her Cardiff closet. None of which gave Saz any insight on how to deal with her own introduction to Peta, but did give her and Molly a chance to congratulate themselves on having fed and watered such an interesting array of sexualities, congratulating themselves even more when they finally managed to get rid of them, sometime close to three in the morning.

Saz, then, had approached the office with little sleep and mounting interest only to find that her fears were groundless when the tiny white-skinned, red-headed woman stood up from behind her desk, greeting her with a smile, an out-stretched hand and the first surprise of the day. "Hi. I'm Peta. I'm twenty-three, I'm single and I'm gay. Have you had breakfast?"

Saz's second surprise in her new "office" job came when Peta asked her how she liked her coffee. Saz had suffered more than the usual variety of temping jobs before setting up her own business. She managed most for no longer than a month or so, but even in her best temp job where she'd actually been given real work and trusted to get on with it unsupervised, she'd also been expected to make the coffee, to run out and fill meters with twenty pence coins and to open the post as if that task was actually valuable and couldn't be performed by anyone with half a brain. She wasn't used to the person who was ostensibly her boss offering coffee and she certainly wasn't used to that offer being followed up with morning snack sandwiches of wafer-thin, honey-smoked turkey slices on fresh ciabatta and just a touch of Peta's homemade cranberry and orange relish to liven them up.

Saz enjoyed working with Peta. She enjoyed it so much that, after the first hour, she almost forgot why she was supposed to be there as she scoffed at Peta's long-winded stories of her sexual exploits, tales delivered in a shouted Cork brogue over the booming Aretha Franklin and Gladys Knight Peta had chosen to accompany their work. Peta showed Saz around the basic filing system and a rather less basic computer.

"I adore technology, Saz. I forced Siobhan and Greg to go on the net when they moved into this house and set up this office—everything to my specification. You can't imagine how much simpler it's made things like liaising about tour dates."

Saz, who could only just cope with receiving her itemized phone bill, let alone deal with being e-mailed, certainly couldn't imagine how it could make anything simpler to throw more technology at it, merely nodded an appearance of enthusiasm while making a mental note to go through all the old-fashioned files, the 'paper junk' as Peta disparagingly called it, to check any fan letters against the letters Siobhan had received. She also checked her enthusiasm for Peta long enough to ask her a few pertinent questions about her relationship with Siobhan, but the fulsome answers and Peta's obvious devotion to the band in general and Siobhan in particular meant she placed Peta very low on her early suspect list. As did the fact that while Peta was single, she was certainly not celibate and her frank description of her varied sexual exploits over the past couple of months meant that Saz couldn't imagine Peta having time to go out shopping for yellow roses, let alone finding the energy to have them secretly delivered.

The morning passed in dealing with fan letters, several calls to the tour manager's office to check dates and times for press interviews and, for Saz, the slightly more onerous task of working out who was who. Between the tour manager, the tour promoter and the several other people ringing every five minutes claiming to be something to do with the management of the band, she was finding it all rather confusing. Peta called a lunch break at two in the afternoon and went down to the kitchen to reheat the carrot and lentil soup Greg had made that morning. She came back with the news that Alex and Dan had arrived and were just waiting for Steve to join them and if Saz wanted to meet the lads before they retired to the basement until the early hours of tomorrow, she'd better grab them in a hurry.

Saz followed Peta back downstairs and put on a brave face as she entered the kitchen. The heads of three men turned as she walked into the room. As she told Molly that night, "A straight girl would be in heaven. They really are beautiful guys."

Dan stood up first, wiping his right hand on his jeans before he held it out to her. Saz figured he was about six three, his black skin a burnt caramel brown, jet black eyes, long curly hair caught back in a pony tail and an incredibly well worked out body which he made no attempt to hide under a very thin, just buttoned shirt. Steve introduced himself next, an inch or two shorter than Dan but his wider girth actually made him seem bigger. His close cropped hair revealed a dragon tattoo across the back half of his head when he bent over to kiss Saz's hand. Peta pushed him away playfully with a shake of her head and a stage whispered, "No chance, darling, she's one of us."

At which point Dan burst out laughing and shot his left hand in the air with an exultant "Yes!" and Alex fell back in his seat, groaned and pulled a ten pound note from his pocket which he then passed to Dan. Peta glared at Alex and turned to Saz, "I'll have to apologize for my brother, he's not normally such a rude bastard."

"Fuck off, Petey," Alex interrupted her, "I'm a rude bastard most of the time actually. I pride myself on it. And I don't need my baby sister apologizing for me either."

He pulled himself up off his chair and walked over to where Saz still stood in the doorway. He looked down at her, the shortest of the three men but still a good few inches taller than Saz. He had the same bright blue eyes as his sister, but his accent was muted from many more years living in England. He smiled at her encouragingly as he held out his hand, "Saz, is it? And you're sure that you're gay, are you?"

Saz smiled back equally encouragingly as she shook his hand and to the delight of the other two men answered, "Well, I was last time I checked. And are you sure you're straight?"

Dan's whoops of laughter were silenced when Alex dragged him to the ground, the two men mock fighting for a few minutes while Steve provided a commentary which dealt rather more with the finer points of Alex's sexuality than his battle technique. Which is where Siobhan found them when she poked her newly highlighted and perfectly made-up head around the door to call them to their rehearsal.

"I see you've met my men, Saz. Leave Alex alone, guys, he's valuable. And get a move on, Greg's waiting downstairs."

And all three of them meekly rose as one and followed Siobhan down to the basement. Saz watched after them as Peta grabbed a bar of chocolate from the fridge. "Does that sort of thing happen a lot?"

Peta ripped open the giant-sized bar of fruit and nut and crammed six squares in her mouth, nodding her head. "Depends. They're good crack when they're happy."

"That's happy?"

"Sure. Have you no brothers, Saz?"

Saz shook her head, "Just a sister. But I'm quite close to my brother-in-law. We have an understanding. Doesn't involve a lot of physical interaction though."

Peta nodded. "Right. Well, I'm the youngest of five. Four big boys and then me. Alex is the oldest and I love each and every one of them to pieces. And he is a bastard too, Alex. An angry young man, even at his age. This, the being with them, playing about with them, I love it. It's like being at home again."

Peta smiled as she walked out of the room, "I make every man my big brother, Saz, that way I'm not tempted to fuck any of them."

That evening Saz described her day in minute detail for Molly. As they sat down to eat Molly poured Saz a generous glass of Chilean Pinot Noir and asked her if she thought she was likely to be affected by big brother syndrome.

"I don't know, Moll. I mean, I can see that Siobhan is stunning, it's common knowledge and confirmed in real life, and I suppose I'd noticed that the boys were good looking too. But I can't say watching them on telly prepared me for meeting them in the flesh. Their size, their energy. And they're funny too. To tell the truth, I was impressed. Dan in particular is very beautiful."

Molly left her Spanish omelette to go cold while she

bodily reminded Saz that testosterone or oestrogen, which-
ever hormone is only as impressive as its results, and Saz
went to sleep that night smugly thinking it might not be a
bad thing if she could manage to make Molly a little more
jealous just a little more often.

TEN

Having spent her first day helping in the office, thereby setting herself up in Peta's and the boys' minds as the general help, Saz was itching to get on with her real work. But when she met Siobhan the following morning and asked for access to her and Greg's old correspondence and some time to talk about any other leads either of them might have—not so friendly old friends, for example—she was met with Siobhan's claim that they were far too busy to go through all that "old stuff". When she volunteered to go through their things herself, the response was icy. The shutters came down on Siobhan's usually smiling huge grey eyes and the dimples fled her chiselled cheeks.

"Saz, I'm perfectly happy to have you rummaging through my past, if you must, but there's nothing about me and Greg—as a couple—that could possibly have any relevance to the case."

Saz tried to disagree, "Surely if someone is out to have a go at you, then all your relationships are relevant . . ."

She was cut off by Siobhan with a wave of the hand, "Greg is not the one being hounded here. I am. This is about me and I'd like to keep him out of it as much as possible. Greg and I are very private people. I don't like being asked about him, I don't like being asked about my past. What I do now is public, that's fine. What I've done, what I've been, that's old news."

She carried on talking, not giving Saz a moment to interrupt, "Believe me, no one I grew up with has ended up wealthy enough to send huge great bunches of yellow roses. And as far as Greg goes, I can't imagine it's anyone in New Zealand. Do you have any idea how much it costs to order yellow roses on Interflora these days?"

With that she twinkled a "See you later, must work" while slamming the basement door on Saz, ending the conversation with a bang. Saz stormed back to Peta's office more certain than ever that Siobhan was hiding something and determined to look into Siobhan's history at the earliest possible moment.

Alex walked into the office half an hour later looking for his little sister. He looked tired and dishevelled and didn't bother wishing Saz a good morning, simply growling, "Where's Peta?"

"She's gone to the Post Office. Anything I can do to help?"

"Got any drugs?"

Not especially prudish, but all the same surprised at his audacity, Saz didn't quite know how to reply and Alex sneered at the confusion on her face, "Pain killers I mean. Christ, it's only eleven in the morning, what kind of an arsehole rock and roll band do you think we are?"

Figuring that honesty was likely to get her more information than anything else, Saz replied, "I don't know. I'm not that much into music and I don't know a lot about you guys."

"Yeah, well, that's obvious."

"You've got a headache?"

"Hangover. Brain fucking shafting bitch of a hangover, aching stomach and a mouth that tastes like . . . oh fuck it, I don't know, not enough sanity for clever similes. Now where does the silly tart keep her drugs?"

He then rifled through the drawers of Peta's desk until he found a box of Nurofen, swallowed the last four dry and left the office, slamming the door behind him. Saz watched after him, delighted to have been of use.

Later that morning Saz asked Peta about Alex's drinking habits and she was treated to a lecture on the drugs of choice of the whole band.

"No, it won't be just a hangover on Alex. Too much bloody coke, that one. He wants to watch it, last time we were all home for Christmas my mother nearly caught him at it and there'd be hell to pay if she did."

"They use a lot of drugs?"

"The band?" Peta shrugged her shoulders, "Depends what you call a lot. They're hardly the Velvet Underground. The boys smoke dope. Every day, I guess. Well, not Steve, he hardly ever touches anything other than lager—his body is a temple, if you see what I mean."

Saz did. "The others?"

"Alex and Greg and Siobhan like a line or two of coke. Several lines in Alex's case. Addictive personalities run in my family . . ."

Saz could see that Peta was about to launch into a tale of alcoholic aunties and uncles and drew her back to the band, "Dan?"

"A little of whatever's going, I suppose. When you've got the money and you need to keep working and half the time the work looks like partying, well it does the trick, doesn't it? Dan's more into your young person's drugs though. Clubbing and all that. He likes E. I don't touch any of that stuff myself, I can't stand the music that goes with it and I prefer my chemical release in liquid form."

"What about Siobhan?"

"She doesn't smoke, but she'll do the rest now and then."

"She doesn't like dope?"

"Bad for the voice, you know. Actually, it's bad for the band really. The five of them, they're ready for an argument

almost any time these days, but with the drink and drugs—
it just makes them even nastier to each other."

"When they're off their faces?"

Peta laughed, "Oh no, that's the only time they seem to
like each other anymore. They're all the best of friends when
they're pissed. Even Alex. Mostly. It's when they have to be
sober and get on with the work while they've still got the
hangovers from the night before that the shit really starts
to fly."

"Like Alex this morning?"

"Exactly. Mr Happy coming down. It can get very nasty.
Alex picks on Siobhan. That's normal enough, he's always
picking on Siobhan. But then maybe he goes just a little too
far, Greg sticks up for her and Alex turns on Greg. Then
Siobhan screams at Alex, Dan has a go at Alex, blah blah
blah. Eventually even Steve gets pissed off and then they're
all at it. It's why Kevin left in the end. He couldn't stand it."

Saz sat up at the mention of a new name, "Who's Kevin?"

"Ex-tour manager. He was an old mate of Siobhan's. He
was with the band from the beginning—at least, from the
beginning of doing gigs anyway. Started off as just a mate
humping the gear, then as they did better and better he went
from roadie to crew to tour manager."

"But not any more?"

"They had a big bust-up last summer. Alex was screaming
at Siobhan—"

"It sounds to me like he's always having a go at Siobhan
about something."

"He is. She and Greg might be the centre of the band but
Alex thinks he's her svengali—she couldn't do it without
him, wouldn't have the right words to sing without him—all
that bollocks."

"Not true?"

"He's probably right. She's pretty—well, let's say flighty.
Alex is the only one who can get her to really concentrate.

And he does write really good stuff for her. Everyone knows that, he's just dead arrogant with it. Anyway, last summer, they've just got off stage, everyone's really hyper, it had been a brilliant gig but Alex doesn't see that. Alex is off his face and screaming at Siobhan about fucking up some line or other, on and on about how she's ruined the whole gig with that one mistake and eventually she starts crying. Greg's not there, he's gone off to talk to some journalist and Kev just comes up and smacks Alex in the face."

"You saw it?"

"I mopped up the blood gushing out of his nose. Now, the guy's my own brother and I'd be the first to admit he deserved it, but Siobhan sacked Kevin anyway."

Saz shook her head, "I'm sorry? Siobhan sacked the man standing up for her?"

"I know it doesn't make any sense. He was one of her oldest friends too. But you see, I don't think Kevin ever really understood—I think they need it, the five of them."

"Need what?"

"All the shouting and carry on. It's just part of the game."

"Of the band?"

"That's right. The dynamic is just that—Alex is hateful and everyone puts up with it. They just shut up and are relieved to listen to him being nasty to someone else. Anyone else, as long as it's not themselves. You know, when someone else is getting it in the back of the neck, it's actually almost funny. Alex's sarcasm is brutal but it's definitely witty."

"I've noticed."

"And the more hungover he is, the nastier he'll be. Siobhan always gets the worst of it but it just seems to suit her. I think she actually likes him screaming at her. She gets off on the drama of it all."

"So what happened to Kevin?"

"Slunk back off to Liverpool, I suppose. I've no idea actually."

Then Peta looked at the pile of unopened letters that had come in the second post, "Look, I'm quite happy to tell you all the juicy gossip if you're really interested, but d'you think we could get on with some of this work at the same time?"

Peta kept Saz fully occupied for the rest of the day opening letters, checking tour itineraries with the band in an attempt to accommodate all their individual requirements. While Alex had been single for some time and Dan was newly alone, quite a few important details had to be co-ordinated with Steve's model girlfriend Tiana and the seven stone Canadian princess was not easily satisfied. Saz had to content herself with brain-filing her own little pile of information. She planned to check out the peremptorily sacked Kevin as soon as she was free and she'd also make a few more enquiries about Alex. If he and Siobhan really did have such a vicious relationship, then it wasn't inconceivable that he might choose to upset her just that little bit more. With a bunch or two of roses perhaps.

Saz went home to complain to Molly about how on earth she was supposed to proceed while not letting Peta know why she was really there. As she explained over their takeaway pizza—American hot with extra pepperoni and chilli sauce, "I mean, I like the woman, Moll, I'm sure she'd be cool if I told her the truth, but I'm not allowed to and so she's really just . . ."

"In the way?"

"Exactly. I did what I could with her around. This afternoon I went through all the fan letters the band had ever received. Thousands of them, all neatly filed in cardboard boxes."

"Thousands? Really?"

"I exaggerate. It just felt like thousands. I wanted to give up after ten of the bloody things. How many different ways can you say 'Siobhan Forrester, I fancy you?' "

"Didn't Peta think it was weird you were rifling their archives?"

"Official business. My task was to alphabetize the letters, thereby helping her compile a fan database."

"And did you?"

Saz swallowed a fingerful of stretchy mozzarella and sneered, "Ms Steele, that's a very stupid question. To do that, I'd have had to actually use the bloody computer. However, one of the more useful things was finding correspondence about this Kevin bloke in with all the fan stuff. The latest address was about a year ago so I'll follow that up tomorrow. I also made a note of the twenty-two letters with the same sort of expensive writing paper as the letters sent to Siobhan—only eight of which were printed, the others were written by hand. Once I've sussed out Kev, I'll get on to checking out the addresses. Then I relocated to Siobhan's room for a couple of hours and called practically every florist in North London."

"Exaggerating again?"

"All right, I didn't bother with too many in the outer reaches of Colindale. Anyway, it's not as if any of them can remember someone coming in and asking for more than the usual number of yellow roses."

Molly laughed, "And what's the usual number?"

"It's an engrossing statistical study actually, you might be very interested."

Saz sat up from where she was lying on the floor at Molly's feet and pushed the finished pizza carton away. She had been absent-mindedly forwarding through the pile of old video tapes, one of which she knew held the Orson Welles version of *Jane Eyre*, which she and Molly planned to settle in and watch that night. If she could ever find it. She pulled three sheets of close printed figures from her file and looked down the numbers. "According to my research, most people buy red roses, then white, followed by tacky red carnations, then even tackier pink carnations . . ."

"What's wrong with carnations?"

"They're nasty, cheap and I hate them."

"Carrie?"

"Who else? Sent me three bunches in one week."

"To say sorry?"

"No. She sent them the week before she left me, buttering me up."

"I'll remember that."

"Please do. I'd prefer lilies. And finally, a surprising fifth in our top ten poll of flower buyers' favourites, yellow roses."

"All of which means?"

"Absolutely nothing as far as I'm concerned. No one's jumped up and said, oh yeah, sure, bloke comes in once a week for an armload of yellow roses, then takes them off to his pop star love. None of the letters match directly, and even if I found one that did, I couldn't do any more without fingerprinting and all that analysis nonsense."

"I wouldn't let Helen hear you say it's nonsense."

"It's only nonsense when I don't have access to it."

"Ask her to help."

Saz shook her head. "Can't. Siobhan won't let me contact the police at all and the other reason is . . ."

"You know that Helen and Jude don't approve of you working alone after the last disaster."

"Thanks for the memory. The fact that since my recovery I've had two cases of missing fathers, addresses and phone numbers passed on to the mothers—"

"So they could make their own decisions about the Child Support Agency?"

"I'm nothing if not politically correct. Further, I've proved one cheating wife and disproved one cheating husband."

"None of which involved a mystery caller who may or may not be dangerous."

"May or may not be a member of the same band. Very juicy."

"Very risky."

Saz sighed, "Moll, I like my job. I know you're worried for me, but this feels good. I'm enjoying it."

"You just said it was frustrating."

"Don't be such a pedant, it's meant to be frustrating. It's work. And yes, I am still a bit scared. But it's bad enough living every day with the scars, I'm not going to let what happened in the fire make me give up. You fell in love with a woman who had a life; you've just accustomed yourself to living with an invalid. You have to learn to trust the old Saz, not the needy burnt one."

Saz knelt up and pulled Molly down to her, kissing her hard. Then she drew away and turned to look at the television. Elizabeth Taylor was simpering sweetly on her death bed.

Saz laughed, "See, Molly. Now that's what I call a burns victim. This one however," she added, pointing to herself, "this one, is risen again and in control. Now pass me those tissues and get ready to sob."

She rewound the tape and they watched the movie in silence, Molly's hand occasionally and gently stroking the scars on Saz's bare leg.

ELEVEN

Making the bouquet happen can be quite an art. I liked choosing the flowers. It gave me satisfaction. I would go to a flower shop or stall, far from her, and choose them one by one. Pick each perfect yellow rose, one by one. It can be hard to find twenty-one flawless yellow roses. Sometimes I would have to go to three, even four shops in one morning. It was like work. Like having a job. It was my mission. I wore gloves. For my safety, you understand. Thorns. Fingerprints. The fingerprints of bloody, pricked fingers are a double giveaway, double bind. When the Prince finally hacked his way through to Sleeping Beauty he must have been scratched to ribbons. Maybe he liked it. Maybe it was a Jesus thing. Perhaps he'd left his own crown behind. Anyway, I wear gloves. I'm careful with my hands. I'm an artist.

Having gathered my rosebuds, cut their stems, water sprinkled the petals, I would take them to another shop, the gift wrapping shop where the nice lady with the sweet soft smile and the sweet soft hands would take such care to get the paper just right. Painstaking. She was taking pains. She liked me, she said I was a sweetheart. Perhaps I am. I am charming. Lots of people have said so. And then back to my car and laying them down so softly on the back seat. Laying down on the back seat. The delivery of course was my *coup de grâce*.

I would take them into the city and find myself a vagrant. Not hard to find, it's true. A homeless person, a dirty, city-encrusted baby. I'd give them cash to get the flowers to her. I know she received some of them. Some of the flowers, some of the time. Maybe not all. I don't mind, the money went to a good cause. It was ideal really, touching her and doing a little charity work into the bargain. I'm very philanthropic at heart. Underneath this tough exterior lies a heart of pure mush. Honest.

But then, aren't we all something else really? Underneath?

TWELVE

Saz took the morning off from work at the office, lying to Siobhan about following up a lead with the flowers so that Siobhan could lie to Peta about why Saz wasn't coming in, so that Saz could go to visit Kevin the ex-tour manager. The series of untruths were rather more convoluted than the directions to Kevin's home. Kevin hadn't gone back to Liverpool. In fact, Kevin was living just a mile or so from Siobhan in a tired first floor bedsit in Camden, not yet elevated to the lofty heights of "studio flat" by the simple landlord strategy of stripping the floorboards and putting up blinds instead of faded red curtains.

Kevin Hogan, tall, stooped and unshaven, was not exactly Beneath The Blonde's Number One Fan. He and Siobhan had known each other at school—the kind of knowing that Saz suspected involved at least a fumble of early sex. He'd moved to London around the same time as she had, they'd shared friends, shared a squat for a few months one summer and then when she'd joined the band, he had too. He'd gone along to rehearsals first just as Siobhan's mate and, once they'd managed to finally get a few gigs, he went along as driver. The fact that Kevin's big brother loaned them his old PA and Kevin himself had access to a van that could fit the dodgy gear and the rest of the band—at an extremely tight squeeze—meant that he was very valuable to them. Over the years his value increased in direct proportion to his growing knowledge of the music scene. Eventually, however, with the band's greater success, the status of their relationship changed until rather than the band needing him, Kevin was the one who needed the band. Not that he expressed the situation in quite those terms. Drawing heavily on his third cigarette since letting her in, he exhaled his bitterness at Saz, "Fucking cunts used me for years. Took advantage of my generosity and all my hard bloody work and then the minute things started to go really well for them, it was over. Goodbye, matey, thanks but we don't need you anymore."

Saz had introduced herself as a journalist doing a background story on the band and had no problem getting Kevin to talk. For a start, he was drinking cheap whisky in his instant morning coffee and secondly, he was hugely bitter about being left out of Beneath The Blonde's success and perfectly happy to tell Saz anything she wanted to know—as long as it was likely to make the band look bad. And it did. Kevin detailed the early years of rehearsing in Alex's squat, the dreary South London pub gigs, the signing on and working at rubbish jobs to get the money to pour back into the band. He told it all in glorious shades of drab squalor. "I don't suppose you know about Dan's early career either?"

Saz shook her head.

"Yeah well, Mr Petty Poof hasn't always been so bloody clean. Spent most of his teens in and out of care getting done for petty theft and burglary. You know, videos, TVs and the like. They've managed to keep that out of the press so far. That one's too fucking groovy by half if you ask me—doesn't care if the whole world knows he's queer but got to keep the criminal record hushed up at all costs."

Saz bit her tongue and offered a non-committal shrug, "What about Steve?"

"Nah, Steve's all right. Bit of an odd job boy until the band started to make money. He's big, strong. I offered him work as a bouncer once—I used to do a bit of work at a mate's club—but he'd rather hump sideboards up staircases for three quid an hour for his dad than run the risk of getting himself messed up. Steve would always shag anything in a skirt and he didn't want to ruin his future chances with a bent nose. Spends hours down the gym, that one. Very proud of his body—all his own work, apparently."

"Apparently?"

"Nah, you'll not get me having a go at Steve, luv. He's the only one I'd trust out of the whole lot of them. Let's just whisper steroids and leave it at that, yeah?"

Kevin looked at the dirty clock on the kitchen wall and then at Saz's jacket hanging on the back of her chair. "You got any cash in those fancy leather pockets of yours?"

"Some."

"Good. Because the pub's about to open and I haven't hardly started on what I've got to tell you."

Saz spent the next three hours with Kevin in a smoky pub off Camden High Street. Kevin bitterly attacked Siobhan for deserting him, sacking the only old friend she had. According to Kevin, she didn't see any of their Liverpool friends these days—"Not since she's become the poncey blonde one. Course, we all remember when she had puppy fat and brown hair and bad skin." He raved for about half an hour about Greg, not that there was anything particularly bad to say about Greg, in fact that was Kevin's main problem with him—"The guy's a bore. All he cares about is music and the band and Siobhan. In that order. Now if Siobhan was mine, I'd put her right at the top of the list."

"Even now?"

Kevin grinned a lopsided, half drunk smile, "Yeah, even now. I've always fancied her. More than fancied her. Ever since we first met when we were fourteen. I've always fancied girls with guts and Siobhan's got that—in truckloads."

"So you think Greg's not good enough for her?"

"Oh no, he's good enough. I know he loves her. And she loves him, it's just she had more balls when she was single."

"She seems pretty strong to me."

"She is. But she used to be more. Stronger, faster." He shook his head, "There just used to be more to Siobhan before it all became about making her look as if she was tough, instead of just letting her be her own staunch self."

"It could just be age, couldn't it? It is fairly normal to tone it down a bit as you get older."

Kevin almost conceded with a slight incline of his head, "Maybe, it hasn't slowed Alex down any."

"Do you blame him?"

"For getting me sacked? Yeah, I do. It's all down to him. Even in the beginning he didn't really want me around."

"Is it to do with Siobhan?"

Kevin frowned, "Why? What?"

"Maybe he fancies Siobhan too. If he knew you did . . ."

"Nah. He doesn't fancy Siobhan. He fancies himself. He fancies themselves. The famous fucking five." Kevin finished his pint, "Get me another one, love, and a whisky chaser."

Saz obediently went to the bar where she also ordered a fourth diet Coke for herself and a couple of bags of crisps in an attempt to keep Kevin on the coherent side of sobriety.

He downed his whisky in one and launched back into his tale, "Alex is only interested in the band. Always has been. Can't keep a girlfriend, doesn't have any friends outside the band . . ."

"It doesn't look as though they're exactly best of mates inside the band either."

"Don't let the act fool you. They love it. All of them, but Alex most of all. They like being the chosen ones, the élite little crew. They'll fight and argue and scream at each other, but let some poor bugger from outside try and come in to sort things out and they're all over him."

"Like you?"

"Exactly like me. I was with them for seven years, then just when things are getting really good, I'm out on my ear. I got too close, see? And Alex didn't like it and Siobhan didn't like it either—not that she'd ever say as much—and so I was gone. Why do you think they went with a manager that doesn't even live in the fucking country?"

"I assumed it was because Cal's good."

"Yeah, well, he is. But they could have found someone good in England too. It's easier for them that way, they stick together and get to keep all the outsiders out. I worked for them—with them—for all that time and I still never got to be an insider. There's just Beneath The Blonde and the rest of us. I mean, they're doing bloody well and the only real staff they have is Alex's sister—how's that for keeping it in the family? Everyone else is just hired in for the current gig or tour or whatever or comes from the record company. They wouldn't give you the time of day if the management didn't force them to talk to outsiders occasionally for the publicity and all. It's sick, I reckon. Five grown people all living in each other's pockets like that. What they need is someone to get in there and shake things up a bit".

Kevin was just getting into the stride of his rant when Beneath The Blonde's first major hit came on the juke box. "Oh, fuck this. I'm out of here. I can't listen to this shit."

He downed the rest of his pint and struggled up from the low table, looking down at Saz, eyes bleary with alcohol and reminiscence, "Ok sweetheart, I'm off. Now how much are you getting paid for this article?"

Saz, lost in thought about Kevin's fury at the band, didn't quite understand his question, "I'm sorry?"

"My fee, love. What am I getting? There's no pension scheme for sacked roadies, you know."

"Oh yeah, sure." Saz reached for her coat and fumbled in her pockets, "Um, fifty quid do you? I'm freelance. I haven't exactly been commissioned for the piece yet."

Kevin took the proffered cash and stuffed it in his back pocket. "That's cool. We're all doing what we can."

He turned to leave the pub, calling over his shoulder as he went, "Give my love to Siobhan if you see her."

Saz thought she probably wouldn't bother. But she would keep an eye on Kev.

THIRTEEN

Saz returned to the office late that afternoon determined to make some headway with the band. An hour after dropping her bag by the desk and doing her best to look efficient for Peta's benefit, she went downstairs to make their coffee and managed to corner Greg in the kitchen, where she forced a conversation from him while he chopped onions, garlic and shallots for the sinus clearing soup they would eat before rehearsing that afternoon. He answered all her questions about how they had formed the band, his friendship with Alex whom he'd met one night in a pub and how Siobhan had been first his flatmate, then the band's singer and then his lover. He told her a little about their several false starts, the time when he and Siobhan had already booked a trip to New York when the offer for their first real gig came up and about the huge fight between Alex and Siobhan when Siobhan insisted she and Greg go to New York anyway. He further explained that Siobhan's temperament—"hot and cold running egocentricity", as he described it—meant that even now their schedules were subject to change at a moment's notice.

He explained, as he added the chopped vegetables to the bubbling butter in a pan, onion tears running down his cheeks, "You see, Siobhan's just so bloody contrary. The boys couldn't stand it at first, didn't know how to be with it. She takes some getting used to. But as we've become more successful—well, I guess we've all just resigned our-selves to the fact that you can't ever completely plan anything with her around. Even our manager accepts it as artistic licence. Mind you, I reckon he's probably more used to performers acting up than we are. Certainly Alex had never come across it until Siobhan. Alex prefers to be the only one to make a fuss, if you get what I mean."

"What does he do?"

"Tells her off in no uncertain terms." Greg shrugged, "Alex and Siobhan have a love-hate relationship. More hate than love at the moment."

"They're not getting on right now?"

"It's always a bit fraught when we're rehearsing—and Alex does bring out the best in her. She'll fuck around for hours and then be brilliant just to spite him."

"And he knows that?"

"We all know it. Even Siobhan." Greg stirred vegetable stock into the pan, "Knowing what's going on doesn't stop us getting back into our roles though. It's the family thing."

"Band as family's a bit of a cliché, isn't it?"

"Maybe, but true. Siobhan knows that whenever she stays with her parents they'll want her to go to church with them. She refuses. There's a big fuss. Every time, regular as clockwork. It's the same with Alex. We rehearse, she fucks around, Alex gets pissed off, they have a slanging match, she sings like an angel."

"Couldn't she just sing like an angel anyway?"

Greg laughed, "I don't think it would be as much fun that way. It's not just Alex. Siobhan gets off on her tantrums too. And we all get annoyed with her, she just gets to him the most. He also can't stand it if she acts up outside the band, at gigs or whatever. He likes us to keep our little traumas to ourselves."

"You make it sound like Alex is Dad."

Greg shook his head, "No one's in charge. Officially. Or maybe everyone is. I don't doubt that Alex thinks he's the boss though."

"Doesn't that annoy you?"

Greg grinned at Saz, "Well, I don't want to sound too sexist here, but I just don't think guys care about that stuff as much as girls. Like, Alex is my mate, you know, he's a really good friend."

"But he's horrible to your girlfriend."

"Yeah, I know. But um . . . well, it doesn't really affect me. I just try not to get involved. As long as it doesn't do the music any harm, Alex can think what he likes. If thinking he's in charge makes him happy, I'm not going to tell him otherwise. I like an easy life wherever possible."

Greg's reference to Alex was further underlined when the man himself arrived in the kitchen, grabbed Greg by the arm, allowing him time only to place a lid over the pan, and led him to the basement door. Alex called over his shoulder to Saz, "Whatever he's been telling you, it's all bullshit, darling. We're just a pitiful foursome of satellites floating around the queen bee. She's the one who's really in charge of it all. Only, you see, Greg is a man blinded by lust."

At which Greg tried to protest his innocence but Alex shouted over him, "He always has been. Ever since he first laid eyes on her. Siobhan Forrester's just a fancy pants who likes to do what she wants whenever she wants it. A right little bism, as my granny would say. If Granny hadn't been rotting in her grave these past twenty years."

Alex stopped, as if knowing what Greg would say next, gave him just a moment to open his mouth and then added, "And no, Gregory, that's not what I call artistic temperament, that's just showing off."

He then pushed Greg out the door ahead of him and smiled sweetly at Saz, "And I do hope you don't mind my saying, but are we really paying you to stand there and ask questions all day, or are you actually going to do some work?

'Cos if it's just a star-struck fan is all you are, then we can get half a dozen of them any time we like. For free. Or for fucks. Or better still, both. Off you go now. Petey's waiting for you."

He then flicked his hand, shooing her out of the room and Saz heard him laughing as he went down the stairs to the basement, announcing to the rest of the band, "I just saved him, lads, the lovely lezzie had him in her clutches!"

Dan and Siobhan's loud condemnation didn't stop the bile rising in Saz's throat but it did prompt her to whip through her business in Peta's office in record time and then out of the house as fast as she could.

With Peta mostly out of the office at meetings with the tour booker and PR company, Saz was able to spend all of the following day on the phone. She contacted over two hundred florists to no avail. She made contact with sixteen of the twenty-two letter writers, all sounding very sane on the phone, mostly female and mostly in the thirteen to sixteen age range. She also managed brief chats with Dan and Steve over morning coffee in the kitchen. Both were helpful and rather more friendly than Alex, but both were also a little too concerned with their own roles in the band to be paying much attention to Siobhan's problems. Saz left them with the feeling that success had not necessarily cemented their friendship ties, particularly not now that Alex and Greg were starting to earn royalties from their songs. And while Dan and Steve acknowledged that this was fair and right and just, they couldn't help comparing their rather smaller bank accounts with those of their co-workers in what had started out as a collective endeavour and was now becoming much more of a financial oligarchy.

After a couple of hours of phone calling for Peta so she could look like she wasn't entirely avoiding all office work, Saz enjoyed a more successful post-lunch conversation with Dan, getting what else she could on the genesis of Beneath The Blonde, although she felt no closer to finding anyone who might be considered a threat. So far her only suspects were Alex, for no good reason other than that, from what everyone said about him, he might enjoy upsetting Siobhan even more than usual, or the disgruntled Kevin, who didn't look like he could get the cash together for a bunch of daisies, let alone huge bunches of yellow roses. From Dan she learned that the New York trip wasn't the only time Siobhan had disturbed the schedule for the rest of the band. He told her about the several other occasions on which Siobhan had changed their plans at a moment's notice. "There were the two surprise trips she arranged for Greg. Once to Casablanca after we'd all been watching the bloody movie on late TV and she just got it into her head that Greg would simply love it and the other time to Rio."

"Why Rio?"

"She was doing another of her 'I'm more Catholic than Madonna' trips and was suddenly seized with a passionate desire to go and see that big Jesus on the hill."

"Must have pissed you all off?"

"To say the least. It's not only the dropping everything just because Siobhan wants us too—sure, that's annoying, but a few days off every now and then isn't that much of a hardship. It's that it never really is only a few days, there's all the aftermath too. Every time they go anywhere we usually lose at least a week because one of them comes back with a stomach upset or a cold or some new and exciting viral infection. And then Greg and Siobhan can't just be sick by themselves, one of them always has to take time off to look after the other. That's love, I guess."

"They're prone to illness?"

"Not Siobhan especially. But Greg's a bit pathetic, he'll catch any cold going."

These incidents of Siobhan's unreliability, while doing little to flesh out Saz's suspect list, actually made for good stories, particularly as Dan tended to act them out, impersonating Greg hobbling through arrivals at Heathrow and Siobhan dramatically throwing herself into the backs of cabs, demanding he be taken home via their specialist homeopath.

Before she left the office that evening, Saz cornered Siobhan, fresh from her second workout of the day and tried again to get a little information on her past. This time Siobhan was more amenable, cheerfully recounting every difficult friend she'd had as an adult—although Saz noted she didn't mention Kevin once and certainly didn't seem to view any of her band relationships as difficult. But she professed to remember virtually nothing about her schooldays. As she told Saz over her second lemon vodka, "I loved my childhood. Well, I loved my family but I hated every bloody minute of my school life. Nuns." She said it as if the one syllable explained everything. "I forgot it all as soon as I could, and what I didn't forget I wiped out in a coming-to-London haze of alcohol and cheap speed." She grinned, "And a few more exciting drugs as soon as we could afford them."

Remembering her earlier discussion about royalties accounts, Saz figured that had to be fairly often these days. Siobhan went on, "I tell you, Saz, my real life only started ten years ago. It's why I only go to mum and dad's once or twice a year if I can help it. I'm happy for them to come down here, I love it when they do. I get on really well with them, but oh God, I hate to go home. Doesn't everybody?"

Saz, who fully understood about the deadly dull Sunday afternoons of teenage suburbia, nodded and left it at that.

Having called Molly to suggest they meet for Mexican in Camden, Saz got her things together, still puzzling over the quick change in Siobhan's attitude from one day to the next. To be fair, while she had been very little help about possible stalkers, to the extent of not even mentioning Kevin when Saz directly asked her about ex-workers, Siobhan had endeavoured to give Saz a belt-by-button account of every item of clothing she'd ever worn on stage and her preferred makeup to go with each outfit. Their little chat ended with Saz convinced that Siobhan was either a genius or a complete idiot because no normal person could possibly care so much about what didn't matter and so little about what really did. Or tell the stories with so much charm and seemingly little conceit. When she crept into the rehearsal to say goodbye that night and heard the band playing at just five feet distance, she knew that no matter what stupid things Siobhan said or how very much she pissed her off or how maddeningly naïve she was being about the stalker, the woman standing in the semi-darkness, looking like a tainted goddess and making her voice climb scales and dance jigs right at the top of her range, had to be a genius. Though not everyone agreed. When the song finished she heard Alex bark out his judgement that the rendition had been, "Barely adequate. You're just not fucking working hard enough. Take your time, listen to the bloody music and fucking well get it right!"

Hearing Siobhan's tired acknowledgement and immediate acquiesence, she was left to think that perhaps Kevin was right, maybe Siobhan really did enjoy Alex's nastiness. They'd started the first bars again before she left the house.

Just as she was lying in bed, explaining to Molly that she thought Siobhan was probably ok after all, the phone rang.

It was Siobhan, "Hi, babe. Listen, I forgot to tell you,

we're going to Sweden on Sunday, you need to come—ok?
Bye."

After spending time pretending to be an office junior, Saz
figured a relaxing couple of days in the land of sauna might
be just what the doctor ordered. The doctor beside her,
however, was rather more keen on the concept of bed rest.

FOURTEEN

They were playing at home. The kind of playing that their East Coast pretty sunshine homes weren't really designed for. Childish playing that only solid northern hemisphere brick homes can properly enjoy, making little children feel warm and safe in their smug cosiness, an architect's dream of Enid Blyton winters. Not the sort of playing made for these thin weatherboard houses set in sectioned-off quarter acres of the New Zealand myth, cabbage trees framing the backyard, now toe-deep in a baby lake of cold tropical rain. Winter rain lasting three days and nights of fast, fat drops kamikaze killing themselves on the corrugated iron roof. Drops that kept the kids awake even longer than John's scary stories about the tapu on his grandfather's old house, a beating tattoo of rain that left them tired and grumpy when they woke in the morning, all three of them crammed into Shona's faded pink bedroom with the lavender ballerina curtains her aunt had sent up all the way from Wellington. But this was the May holidays and with eight-year-old intensity they ignored the wet outside and the damp inside, engrossed in the life of their combined Lego sets, the girls' long bronze-legged Barbies discarded in an ungainly heap for the greater joy of creation in red and white plastic brick. Two or three hundred of the bricks of varying ages and various teeth marks had been shaped into farmyards and car yards and building sites, punctuated by Corgi trucks and tiny earth movers that covered a kitchen floor landscape of old lino and Shona's mother's hand-made rug, the thin pieces of red and orange wool knotted into a dishwater-stained base extending out to the very edge of the draughty door-frame where they'd placed a saucer of water for the pond.

They'd been playing for an hour, a game they played day after day, John staying with Shona, while Ruby took a brief respite from her home-based extended family and went to the relaxing embrace of her own cousins further south. Shona's mum had gone to work at eight, leaving their usual lunch on the table—a half loaf of buttered white bread, a family-sized jar of Vegemite, an even larger jar of sticky smooth peanut butter and, stacked in the fridge, ten slices of thick cut luncheon, wrapped in greaseproof paper. The kids would smother the rounds of fatty sausage meat with peanut butter then roll them up into fat cigar shapes, munching through them as the day progressed. Gaelene had made up the Tang, a bitter-sweet powdered fruit drink, full of colour and flavouring—though no one really cared about that in 1973. She had her back to Shona and turned, peanut butter and luncheon roll in one hand, overfull glass of drink in the other, to see Shona, three quarters of the way through creating a building.

"Shops?" she enquired spitting a lump of half-chewed, thick white bread from her mouth as she did so.

Shona mumbled an unheard reply.

"Is it shops? For the car yard? Or a garage for the trucks? 'Cos we need one of them."

"Nah," Shona mumbled, not looking up, "it's a house."

Gaelene nearly spat out her lunch with her sneer, "What the fuck for?"

"For the people to live in. They need a house. And it's a really big house, a flash people's house. Look, there's heaps of bedrooms and a rumpus room for a ping-pong table and a garage for three cars and a really big kitchen and a lounge with a verandah with ranch sliders and everything . . ."

Shona, in her excitement with the plans, didn't see

Gaelene and John coming closer, engrossed in the room-by-room description of the beautiful edifice, she didn't notice the look of disgust as it filtered across Gaelene's face, a look which flashed from face to fist and into her naked left foot which came crashing down onto the creation.

"Crap. Fucking stink fucking doll's house!"

Gaelene smashed the house and then mashed her peanut butter and luncheon roll into it. Shona, knocked off balance, reeled back for a second before jumping up and knocking the glass from Gaelene's hand, the juice spattering over John and the kitchen wall as she splattered her hand across Gaelene's mouth. The three kids caught each others' hair and clothes, throwing themselves into the fight as easily as they had earlier thrown themselves into tearing up the pieces of luncheon, rolling on the house, the tiny cars, the plastic cows, liberated just that morning from their cornflake packet and now grazing in a green plastic field. For five minutes they rolled in a frenzied eight-year-old tumble of kicking and spitting and hitting and biting, then, exhausted, they withdrew for a moment.

Shona's eyes flashing, she glared at Gaelene and John, "What the fuck did you do that for? It's not fair. This is my house, I can do what I want."

"We don't play fucking dolls' houses, we play building! It's what we always play. You can't change the game."

"Yeah," John chimed in, "You can't change the game, Shona."

Shona and John had cleaned up the kitchen by the time Shona's mum came in from work, cleaned up the kitchen and wiped down their faces, the only trace of their fight a small bruise on the side of Shona's left eye. Her mum was used to it, though, used to the kids fighting, used to their pretending they hadn't, used to ignoring the signs of frustrated rage in her tiny girl. Most of all, she was just tired of trying to explain that it was ok for John to fight, but not Shona or Gaelene. Tired of explaining and not certain it was true anymore anyway. And the next day the kids were playing together again, as if nothing had happened.

To Gaelene, violent in temper and quick to forget, nothing had happened, it had gone, she was already in the next thought, the next thing, the next action. For her it was all forward movement, hurrying on. John didn't care, he was already starting to think that maybe his place wasn't at Shona's house anymore and a year or so later he would stop playing so much with the girls, he would stop being a child and become a boy and then a man and therefore other. Shona, however, would hang on to the pain for years, taking it out late in the dark to tremble in silent night rage and frustration at the unfairness—she'd only wanted a nice house.

And anyway, who said she couldn't change the game?

FIFTEEN

With only a day to check up on Alex, Saz took a short cut. First thing on Saturday morning she rang Helen and Judith. Old friends, they were both cops and, while not approving of her choice of career any more than she condoned theirs, they had proved helpful in the past. Knowing that Judith would be in touch as soon as she turned up anything on Alex, Saz then initiated the other branch of her attack. If Alex had two ex-lovers who were dykes, and now that he was more than just a little famous, then someone she knew ought to know something about him. And her gossip-fuelled ex-lover would be the one to find out. Although getting Carrie's help could be costly—in this case a fifty pound reduction in her next month's rent—Saz's investment was quickly returned. Carrie called back three hours later to say that she'd contacted three ex-lovers of her own and that one of them knew a girl who knew a girl who knew a woman who was definitely not a girl. Who was willing to talk to her this afternoon.

Expecting an extreme politico-dyke from the description, Saz was galled to find that the woman Carrie had described as someone who "sounds like the kind of chick who wouldn't exactly approve of me calling her a babe," was sitting in the Islington café with two babies on her knee and a husband beside her. It seemed that while Alex's ex-girlfriend had become a dyke after going out with him, she had also returned to her true inclination in the end. The American earth-mother who cradled her twin babies on her lap didn't seem much like Alex's sort. Saz had rather more expected his ex-lovers to look like lesbian Bond girls. When Hannah showed Saz old photos of herself and Alex, Saz noted that indeed she used to give a good Bond girl impression—tall, strong coffee black and razor-cut sharp. She was still tall, but the cooing and sweet mama baby talk, passing from her to the babies and back via their father, was anything but sharp.

Hannah wiped milky baby vomit from the front of her dress and smiled, "I wasn't really cut out to be a rock chick."

"From your past, it wouldn't seem that you were cut out to be a wife and mother either?"

"I never knew what I wanted. Not for years. So I tried it all. I came to London, I worked in alternative theatre, I dabbled in music—that's how Alex Cramer and I met— I lived with him, I left him, I lived in a lesbian co-op, I left that, I lived in a black lesbian co-op, I left that. Eventually I went back to New York and met Will."

"And found true happiness for the first time ever," Will added, returning with coffees for Hannah and Saz and reaching for one of the twins. "I'll take them out for a bit, give you women some peace—half an hour do?" Hannah handed her babies over with obvious reluctance, "If you have to. I don't mind keeping them."

"No. But I mind hearing all about your ex-squeeze. This way I can at least get the good father kudos on the street."

He walked to the pushchair parked against the door, a baby in each arm, and already two young women on their way to a table were falling over themselves to help him load them in.

Hannah shook her head, "And that just never happens to me."

Saz was always amazed at how the journalist myth could encourage almost anyone to unburden the secrets of their lives in return for a little fame. She'd told Hannah that she was writing a *Guardian* article about the changing nature of women's sexuality. Or, in this case, for what Hannah redefined as "the hope that my story might encourage other women to search for their own truths". Trying not to feel too guilty—and succeeding—Saz launched into her list of questions. To make the ruse look real she did pursue something of the hasbian line, but primarily centred her interview technique on the part of Hannah's life that involved Alex. After half an hour of following Hannah through her stories of incarnation workshops and sexuality training and therapeutic dolphin sessions, Saz was in quiet despair. The woman before her was a fount of knowledge about the "alternative world", what she wasn't doing was dishing any dirt on Alex. Eventually, though, it came out, hidden in a spiel about her years in the world of London squats, Hannah unwittingly gave away a gem about Alex.

"Of course, once that band started rehearsing no one ever saw Alex anymore. He and I had already broken up but I still saw him every now and then. He'd even manage to be quite civil to me if I didn't mention my girlfriend."

"So you didn't see him because of the band?"

"Kind of. The band and Siobhan. What with his working on the music and then seeing her, he never had time for any of his old friends. We all just sort of drifted away."

Saz was jolted from praying for Will to return. "Seeing Siobhan?"

Hannah stretched her long mouth into a skewed apology, "Whoops. That's still a secret, I guess. They had an affair. Just when the band started."

"I thought Siobhan Forrester was with Greg? The guitarist?"

"She was. Still is, apparently—I don't know, I don't exactly get invited over to Alex's for afternoon tea, not that I'd know what to say to him. I don't imagine he likes kids any more now than he did then. What did he used to call them? 'Midget parasites', something like that . . ."

Saz interrupted her, "Alex and Siobhan had an affair when the band started?"

Hannah looked at Saz, licked the cold milk foam edge of her coffee cup, "You won't use this information?"

Saz shook her head, "No. Sorry. I'm just interested in the gossip. Forget it. It's got nothing to do with this story, of course."

Hannah put down her cup, "Well, in that case, I don't suppose it matters if you know. They were only together for a month or so. Not long enough for it to be common knowledge anyway. Alex only told me about it because I was still his sort of confidante. Greg took Siobhan along to some rehearsals and they all liked her voice, so she stayed with the band when the first singer left, then Alex and Siobhan got together, then Greg came on to Siobhan and she dumped Alex for Greg. It was all kept very quiet."

"Why?"

"Alex is extremely proud. He'd just been dumped by his last girlfriend. Before that he'd been rejected by me—I guess he just didn't want Greg to know she'd chosen him over Alex. Male pride, that sort of thing. But I expect he still holds a bit of feeling for her somewhere—Siobhan was quite exceptional, even then."

Will's return and Hannah's joy at seeing her babies after a sixty-minute separation meant that Saz could easily depart without having to discuss Hannah's private life any further. She left promising to send Hannah a copy of the article and rushed home to check on Judith's news. The information awaiting her was neither surprising nor particularly enlightening—Alex had encountered the Metropolitan Police Force on a number of minor occasions. He'd been done for breaking and entering when trying to open a squat, he had one youthful caution for disorderly behaviour and another for a little dope possession. Judith did point out that somewhere along the line the band's manager must have done some good work in getting him an American visa. But Saz merely answered that that showed how Judith foolishly trusted that everyone declared everything as honestly as she did. Except, of course, her sexuality. The conversation ended on a somewhat frosty note.

Alex's "criminal record" was no worse than several of Saz's friends and rather tamer than she'd been expecting. But while the police details told her nothing new, she was rather more excited about the knowledge that Siobhan and Alex had once been an item, however briefly. Her next plan of action was to try and puzzle out whether she should tell Siobhan that she knew or confront Alex himself. Saz decided it could wait a day or so, reasoning that she might as well try to elicit confidences from Siobhan in a relaxing Scandinavian sauna as in a hurry at the airport. That would also give her time to apply the new information to her earlier perceptions of the band dynamic. Besides, as long as she was waiting for inspiration to strike, she still had her packing to do—and long goodbyes to linger over.

SIXTEEN

Saz had read that Beneath The Blonde were "big in Europe", but she hadn't quite expected them to be so very big in Scandinavia. Or Scandinavia and what she now knew to be the Nordic Countries. Or Scandinavia, the Nordic Countries and the Baltics. Just as she now knew the correct forms of address for those lands, she'd also been well and truly assured that the fame of Beneath The Blonde stretched north well beyond Scotch Corner. Saz hadn't known Beneath The Blonde were big in Estonia. But then, she hadn't known where Estonia was either.

When Siobhan rang to say Saz was going away on tour with them, she omitted to add, until they were safely on the plane to Copenhagen, that part of the reason she wanted Saz with them was the arrival of yet another bunch of yellow roses. The flowers had been hand-delivered to the doorstep and this time the card read "Getting closer", also a line from a Beneath The Blonde song—Siobhan explained that the rest of the line was "Getting closer to finding the end of you". The difference was that this bunch of yellow roses also included a single red one. Siobhan didn't know what that meant, but she also knew she didn't really want to find out.

Peta had readily agreed to stay behind in London, saying that Saz would learn more about the workings of the band through actually touring with them. Neither Siobhan nor Saz had let on to Peta that there was more to Saz's job than just helping out with the band, and neither Peta nor Saz bothered to tell Siobhan that Peta had recently embarked on an affair with a wealthy German woman who would be in London all of that week, so Peta was delighted to have a good reason to stay at home. It fleetingly crossed Saz's mind that maybe Siobhan and Peta also had a secret they weren't telling her, but she dismissed the thought as she squeezed herself into the packed Piccadilly Line train for the journey to Heathrow.

Saz, then, was accepted as part of the entourage. As a combined prelude to a few days in LA meeting people from the record company and, as an added softener to Cal (who would only allow Siobhan and Greg their long-anticipated New Zealand break if they worked their butts off, up to and immediately after the seven days allocated to the Antipodes), they were now on what Peta called a "baby tour", designed to give them a little taste of what they could expect on the real thing to come early in the new year.

They started in Denmark, followed by a ferry crossing to Göteborg in Sweden for one night, a drive to Oslo for the next night's gig, then a quick flight back to Stockholm for their main Swedish date. They then flew into Helsinki on Friday where they performed that evening, had one day off and on Sunday caught a horribly early morning ferry to Tallinn, capital of Estonia, medieval city, ex-USSR since 1991. This Saz wrote on a series of postcards, one to Molly, one to Carrie and another to Judith and Helen, noting that if she was to be fully informed of the modern ways of the ex-eastern bloc, then they might as well get educated too. They stayed in Tallinn for a day and a half, using it as a base from which to make their other Baltic gig in Riga, flying back to London via Helsinki, and loaded down with far too many bags of duty-free vodka, smoked salmon, Russian caviar and, in Alex's case, bear paté and reindeer steaks—which he threw out as soon as they arrived at Heathrow, admitting he'd only bought them because he wanted to see the look on Siobhan's face.

Saz was very fond of travelling, but to her that concept was best embodied by two weeks on a quiet Greek island with Molly. In this instance it meant a week which stretched to nine days, exhausting her in the process, and spending just long enough in each city to form a lasting and probably completely inaccurate picture. Stockholm, for example, had been such a rushed trip with only an hour and a half to wander through the circular island labyrinth of the old city that, despite the great harbour view from her hotel window and the wonderful sound of big boats mooring and moving in the night, was now simply confirmed in her mind as Ye Olde Ikea—with trees. Even worse, what she was really likely to remember of their day and a half in Copenhagen—mostly taken up with Alex and Greg both having tantrums at the sound check—was Siobhan's intense and childlike disappointment at just how small that bloody mermaid turned out to be. In Helsinki they had a little longer to make their whirlwind judgements and made the most of their first whole day off, sleeping late and breakfasting far too well. Saz contented herself with fresh cranberries and rather too many cups of dark fresh coffee, while the boys overdosed on a rich delicatessen variety of meats and cheeses and Siobhan made it to the breakfast room just in time to make a grand and gorgeous entrance, demanding French toast with a fresh pot of Irish Breakfast tea. The kitchen had closed but she was Siobhan Forrester and she got what she wanted. After stuffing themselves with food, the boys went down to the harbour to check out the ferries for the next day's sailing and Saz and Siobhan took a vigorous walk to the famous (famous to Siobhan, Saz had never heard of it) Church in the Rock, looking from the outside alarmingly like a sixties' underground carpark, the circular inside hewn from rock with a roof of glass that looked right up to the blue sky above. Not often moved to religiosity, Saz found herself buoyed up by the sheer audacity of the architecture that allowed something so simple to be so beautiful. Despite her heavy pink and purple makeup, glitter-blue false eyelashes and bum-scraping black mini skirt surmounting thick pink tights, all topped with a fake fur pink jacket, Siobhan knelt beside her in rather more traditional pose, saying the rosary she had fished from the depths of her bra with all the fervour of a virgin acolyte.

As they left the church Saz took the opportunity of Siobhan's moment of peace to question her about Alex. "Um, can I ask you something personal?"

Siobhan, replacing her rosary in the elaborate engineering of her wonderbra, didn't bother to look up, "Go ahead."

Saz took a deep breath, "Your relationship with Alex. Will you tell me about it?"

"What's to tell? You've seen it. He yells, I jump. Four or five times higher than I thought I could. Then he yells one time too many and I tell him to go fuck himself. It's push me, pull you and no Doctor Dolittle to translate. I hate him, I love him, he's a cunt, we work well together." Siobhan straightened her top, "That what you wanted to hear?"

Saz exhaled, her breath frosty in the thin morning sunlight, "Ah no. Not exactly. I was thinking more of your sexual relationship with him."

Siobhan slowed her fast, long-legged pace, "Oh. Ouch. Well . . ." She turned to look at Saz, "Who told you?"

"One of Alex's ex-girlfriends."

"I suppose I should congratulate you on doing your job so well. I had no idea that anyone else knew."

"Sorry."

They picked up their pace and continued the walk back to the hotel. Saz tried again, "So, the two of you?"

"We had a fling. A month at most."

"And no one else knows?"

"Nah. They were mates. Alex didn't want Greg to know I'd dumped him for Greg."

"Is that why Alex gives you such a hard time?"

"What? With the work? Hell, no. Alex is just being himself, and good at his job, of course. The band was his idea in the first place, me and Greg—well, me really—I've sort of become the figurehead, but Alex is the real thing. The mastermind. He and Greg do all the really creative stuff. I guess it makes sense that Alex only wants me to do the best I can for his songs. It's his material, after all, his and Greg's."

"But he isn't only nasty during rehearsals or gigs though, is he? He's pretty rough the rest of the time too."

"Yeah, so Alex is a bastard all the time, what's new about—," Siobhan stopped again. "Oh, my God, you don't think he's got something to do with the flowers and all that?" She looked hard at Saz, "You do, don't you?"

"It's not impossible, is it? Certainly he has access to all your dates, knows how to get hold of you. What's more important, he also knows you well enough to be fairly sure what will upset you."

Siobhan shook her head. "I don't think so. I mean, Alex isn't exactly Mr Polite, but he's always very open about being a bastard. He prides himself on it. You've noticed that, haven't you?"

Saz had to admit, having been on the receiving end herself, that she certainly had.

Siobhan continued, "I just don't think so, Saz. I can't know for certain, things are really fraught at the moment, there's been loads of hassle with the next album and the boys are starting to fret over the disparity with things like royalties going only to Greg and Alex . . . but trying to spook me? I just can't see it. He's too concerned about the product. I really don't think Alex would do anything that might fuck me up too much. He always knows when to call a truce."

"Which is when?"

"Around about the time my voice starts to crack from the strain. Or the tears. Right up until then he's perfectly happy to push me as far as possible—once it threatens the 'art' though, the guy's a pussycat."

They made it back to the hotel just in time to see the pussycat shouting at the desk clerk who'd made a minor mistake with a message from their record company.

Siobhan noted this with just a little pleasure, whispering to Saz, "See? A big old softy."

The conversation was left open-ended, Siobhan denying the possibility of Alex's involvement but Saz still uncertain. A record company official arrived to take them all out to lunch, but unfortunately the elaborately coiffured executive had not been warned about Siobhan's passionate vegetarianism. She had booked a table at one of Helsinki's prime spots for showing off to tourists—a Russian restaurant specializing in bear and reindeer. Winnie The Pooh and Rudolph, as advertised on the shiny menu outside the door, weren't exactly Siobhan's idea of a great day out and Greg had some difficulty persuading her to actually go in and enjoy the vegetable skewers, thereby calming the look of rapidly growing discomfort on the record exec's face. The trauma was somewhat relieved when they finally got the reluctant Siobhan through the door and found that they were booked not into the main restaurant, but a private dining-room, with gold cloth-covered walls, a silk padded chaise longue, a table large enough to hold all seven of them very comfortably and a shiny samovar in the corner by the roaring fire. And

Siobhan eventually pronounced that the vegetable skewers were very good too. Saz also noticed her directing a couple of questioning looks at Alex during the meal.

That evening, after even more food, they were taken to a local and fiercely fought ice hockey match where Siobhan, in direct contrast to her loudly professed vegetarian beliefs six hours earlier, screamed in delight every time a member of "their" team (that is, the one supported by most of the record company staff) smashed a resounding body blow into a member of the opposing team. She yelled even louder when their team—the reds—beat the blues, provoking Alex to tell her to shut up and save her voice and Saz to ask how she would have felt if the blues had won. Siobhan, living as always in the present tense, with no awareness of either the past or the future conditional, just looked at Saz in utter incomprehension. "But they didn't, did they?"

In fact, the entire evening was a huge success as far as Siobhan was concerned, eighteen requests for signatures, her very own Helsinki Stars baseball cap, another night of late drinking great vodka and loud laughing with the few fans they'd picked up along the way and even Alex had the good grace to simply get very drunk and keep his anger to himself. The record company exec's day had been fairly good too, following what she'd thought might be a near disaster at lunch, the evening had ended almost perfectly. Though, as her husband explained to Saz, it was not quite as ideal as what he described as the "most best ending"—when all the forty or so players erupted into a frenzied fist fight and the red stuff on the ice was not from the tassels of the chilly cheerleaders' pompoms but the blood of the captain's nose. "Still," he reasoned, "you can't have every-thing, could you?" Adding "can you" as an afterthought in

case imperfect grammar might take the gloss from an otherwise perfect night.

Saz saw Siobhan and Greg to their connecting rooms, glad
to see that Siobhan's near insobriety was likely to give her
a good night's sleep. While the boys regularly went to bed
and fell into the drunken sleep that affected them after
eight or nine pints—thirteen pints if it was what Alex called
"pissing Euro-lager"—for Siobhan, carrying her secret
worries, sleep had recently been proving as elusive as
success was now becoming effortless. While she ordinarily
used a little drugs or alcohol to smooth her life in London,
she did so, despite appearances, with a great deal of care
and only when her schedule promised her at least a day to
recover. Nordic vodka, however, was taken to be the kind
of exception you made when it just wouldn't do to offend
your hosts. So for once she crashed into a dreamless sleep,
with the kind of inebriation that made Alex's nights so worry
free. Then again, she never had to deal with his daily whisky,
wine and bitter hangovers either.

The break in Helsinki and Siobhan's apparent lack of nerves
had done the band a great deal of good. Other than a scary
moment when Siobhan saw a flower seller coming at her in
the market loaded down with yellow chrysanthemums—a
flash of panic swiftly noted and calmed by Saz and Greg—
nothing untoward had happened. Whether it was just the
difficult telephone system at the hotel or the fact that Interflora can't always deliver the same day, there hadn't been
any calls or yellow roses to disturb the star's sleep. And in
seeing Siobhan less tense, having had a real "girl" conversation about her relationship with Alex and in getting a
chance to laugh with her, Saz found she was starting to

quite like Siobhan. Like her and looking forward to spending the next day with her.

As she explained to Molly in the nightly phone call that connected her to their world—what Saz increasingly saw as the real world—"It's not that I've stopped thinking she's the most irritatingly contradictory person I've ever met, it's just that sometimes those contradictions are quite charming."

"Such as?"

"Such as expressing horror and disgust at eating Santa's little helpers and then whooping like a banshee every time one heavily padded male body slammed another into the ice."

"So it's not only hippy dykes who have coin tossing views on eating meat and blood on the street?"

"Hell no. Siobhan's more fiercely anti-meat than the hippiest Hackney dyke you know."

"Hate to tell you this, Saz, but I don't think I know any Hackney dykes. Judith and Helen eat meat—well, Hells eats fish and Judith doesn't eat pork, but kosher's not quite the same as vegetarian, and Carrie sometimes is veggie but then she lives in Camberwell, not Hackney . . ."

"You know what I mean."

"Yeah, I do. And I know I don't want to waste our phone calls talking about Siobhan bloody Forrester. I know she's your job but I have to admit that I'm getting a bit . . ." Molly's voice faded on the other end of the line.

"A bit what?"

Molly sighed and said quietly, "I'm jealous."

"What of?"

"You keep talking about her."

"Siobhan's straight as."

"So's Madonna. Doesn't stop her using girls like us when she thinks it'll do her good."

"Come on, babe, I have to spend time with her. That's what they're paying me for. And at least liking her a bit makes it more enjoyable than hating her a lot. Would you really rather I was having a crap time?"

Molly laughed. "Yeah. Actually I would. Sorry, but I'd love you to be having such a crap time that you'd get on the next plane and fly home to me. I miss you and I want you and if you're nibbling on Rudolph burgers you should be doing it with me, not them, and I just want you here. I want to be us."

Brought back to the reality of her relationship, Saz chatted a little longer to Molly about nothing and everything. The upholstery material they wanted to recover the sofabed and what movie they might see when she got back and the fact that Molly wanted to spend every minute of the rest of her life with Saz, ideally in person and not on the phone.

Five minutes later Saz put down the receiver and looked out of her tiny hotel window at the harbour. Despite having calmed Molly's fears, she could find no comfort herself in the wind-battered water as she climbed into the sterile, narrow single bed. She turned the television on for a semblance of company and glared at CNN for a while and then turned out the light. She lay alone in the light of flickering American blue and tried to sense Molly beside her. They'd lain so long in the same embrace that sleeping alone now felt like amputation.

Later, fitfully asleep, Saz stretched out in the night to scratch the ghost itch of Molly's hand on her arm, thigh, face, but there was no hand and no touch, just the aching left unscratched, turning slowly from itch to ulcer.

SEVENTEEN

The gig in Estonia was a spirited affair in a huge marquee in the old town square of Tallinn. Sponsored by two different breweries, the main aim of the young, mostly male, punters seemed to be to imbibe as much of the proffered liquid as possible and then use the alcohol-fuelled energy to propel themselves towards the stage. The numbers of young men flinging themselves against the flimsy plywood dais increased in direct proportion to the amount of flesh Siobhan revealed as she disrobed through each number until, at the end of the gig, she stood on the stage in just a pair of gold platforms, tangerine hot pants and a see-through silver shirt, while the swaying structure beneath her looked in imminent danger of collapse.

Flushed and breathless from the gig, Siobhan was given just five minutes to swallow a quick glass of vodka and then Greg whisked her back to the hotel where a selection of local journalists were waiting to dissect her precious thoughts. The boys were going on to a restaurant—Alex to drink, Dan to eat and Steve to ply with wine the Estonian beauty who was taking seriously her role of "hospitality hostess". Tiana had turned down the chance of coming to Estonia at the last moment to go to a photo shoot in Milan and Steve was making the most of his free time. Not wanting to cramp Steve's style, and not interested in yet another night fending off Alex's drunken aggression, Saz went back to the hotel alone to spend an hour or so on the fifteenth floor where the plate-glassed sauna looked out over the dark Baltic and the scarcely lit city.

Fifty minutes later she was loosely wrapped in a sweat-drenched towel, trying hard to breathe while the Latvian occupant of the sauna poured still more water onto the heat, taunting the westerner by making the air a burning hot liquid which attacked her lungs almost as fiercely as it did her skin. She had just quit the blistering steam cabin and thrown herself into the long, cool pool in the ante-room when Greg came in. He carried glasses and a bottle of white wine, water quickly condensing on the outside of the bottle.

Saz, suddenly shy of Greg seeing her scarred body, stayed under the water, "You're having a party?"

Greg shook his head, "Not exactly. I got bored listening to Siobhan give the same answers to the same old questions, so I left her to finish up. She's just got one more to deal with. We've asked if we can have the sauna to ourselves for an hour or so."

"Oh, right. Sure. I'll leave then."

"No, don't. I meant all of us. I had to pay an arm and a leg for it, but they've said we can turf out any other guests—there's another sauna next door—and have our own little band party. I think we deserve it, the gig tonight was fucking brilliant."

"A party with just the one bottle of wine?"

"No. Alex is in the bar sorting out a delivery. He has a more winning manner with the staff than I do."

Saz, who knew that Alex's manner just involved larger bribes and more shouting, forced herself out of the water. While she didn't exactly feel like exposing herself to Greg, she was even less likely to enjoy Alex's scrutiny of her scars. "Are all of them back?"

"Nah. Just Dan and Alex. It seems that Shagger Steve's scored with the local talent. He's confined to bed."

Saz picked up her towels and headed for the door, "Well,

I've been here for a while really, I might just go back to my room."

Greg looked at her, taking in the scarred backs of her legs and quickly diverting his gaze, "Sure. That's cool. But if you wanted to get dressed and come back for a few wines and the view, you'd be more than welcome." He stretched an arm past the wide, clear windows, "We might as well make the most of all this."

Smiling at his sensitivity, Saz nodded, "Ok. Thanks, I will. I'll be back in ten minutes."

Alex was struggling up the stairs with five more wine bottles as she left. He acknowledged her with a grunt and then called out after himself, "Check Siobhan out, will you? I think that journo's probably boring her to death. They're in the bar."

Showered and dressed, Saz went down to the bar to look for Siobhan, who caught one glimpse of Saz and immediately stood up and called her over, mouthing a quick "save me" over the head of her intrepid interviewer. The man Siobhan introduced as Torril was probably in his mid-forties, tall, broad, very big and very dull. After the other journalists had left, content with the usual answers on how, who, where and why, he'd stayed on to ask Siobhan exhaustive questions about her training—none; her background—traditional; and her ambitions—vast. He had just launched into his third page of notes when Saz walked in. Siobhan told Torril that she was the band's general assistant and dogsbody. Saz was only too happy to sit obediently and listen to Siobhan's answers. Anything that would give her more info on Siobhan was welcome and she knew that the businesswoman side of the pop star would keep Siobhan answering questions until even her ambitious patience was exhausted. Saz listened politely as the eager man faltered out his next question. "And you are happy then, from what you have said, to be a sex star?"

Siobhan sipped at her vodka, "A sex symbol? I suppose so. If it sells, right?"

The man nodded gravely, laboriously writing down her answer in what Saz assumed was Estonian.

"Yes. Sales. These are important to you?"

"Hell, yeah, I'm not just in this for the applause, you know."

"No. Of course not. And you do not feel the need to protect yourself?"

"From what?"

"The public. Those who would take your . . . image too far?"

"People who believe in it?" Siobhan pulled her coat closer around her shoulders, covering a little of her bare flesh, "I can't help what people believe."

"You don't think you are responsible for your image?"

"Well, naturally I am, I'm responsible for what I believe I look like. But I can't be held accountable for what other people do with that. It's obvious to me that the stage Siobhan is different from the real Siobhan. You'd have to be an idiot to think I went down the shops in my hot pants or that I really do fuck strange men for breakfast."

Torril didn't look up as he said, "You don't? That is a disappointment."

Siobhan shook her head, not quite certain if she was meant to be insulted, "I'm sorry, I don't think I understand? What's your point?"

He glared at her, "Of course you don't understand. Girls like you. You never even think about what you do. All over the rest of the world and now here."

"What?"

"You are not exactly what we hoped for from democracy."

"I'm a singer, for God's sake!"

"And, as if we didn't have enough to deal with, you bring in your cheapness and defile our country. This was not what we stood up to the tanks for, your type pollutes us by simply being here . . ."

The last comment was too much even for Siobhan's good-girl act and she pushed her chair back, "Look, I've got to go. Really. I'm tired, it's been a long night, and I certainly didn't come all this way for a lecture. If you'll excuse me . . ."

As she tried to stand, the man reached out a huge arm, grabbing her wrist. Siobhan pulled back from him, but his grip was too strong and he twisted her arm, forcing her back into her chair. With his other hand, he reached across to clumsily stroke Siobhan's hair, "You see, I had hoped that I might be able to educate you . . ."

Saz didn't give him a chance to explain just what it was he was hoping to teach. She picked up Siobhan's glass, quietly praising the choice of neat vodka and even more grateful that for once Siobhan hadn't downed the glass the moment she laid eyes on it. She threw the contents straight into Torril's face. The pure biting alcohol blinded him long enough for Siobhan to grab her bag and for Saz to pick up Torril's notepad and the two women ran from the bar, Saz stopping briefly just to explain to the burly security guard that the large man rubbing his eyes and dripping vodka from his face seemed a little more drunk than was seemly in Tallinn's premier hotel.

Having delivered Siobhan safely up to Greg in the sauna, Saz took the notepad to the desk clerk she'd befriended earlier in the day. When she asked him to translate the writing, however, she could see that she was in grave danger of mortally offending the embarrassed young man. Quickly explaining that it was a job for her boss and a matter of band security—and therefore vital that she know exactly what was detailed in the foreign language—he finally agreed to tell her, but only by writing a translated paragraph on the next blank page. Reading over his shoulder, Saz could readily see why the poor guy was so red and flustered. Every second word was "fuck", several lines detailed the finer parts of Siobhan's anatomy and after a whole sentence of blatant—and very specific—porn, Saz thanked him and took the pad away. She returned to her room and put in an urgent call to the local booking agent to confirm just who Siobhan had been supposed to talk to that night. It didn't take long for her to realize that Torril, if that was his name, should never have been there in the first place. She then went upstairs to the sauna to break up the party.

There followed an exhaustive discussion with hotel security until Saz could be assured that, having been safely ejected from the building, there was no chance Torril would get back in that night. And further, once locked in her room, Siobhan would be perfectly safe as the hotel would place a guard outside her door who would stay with them all the way to the airport the next morning. Siobhan was less convinced when she actually saw the guard, who looked more like a Russian mafia cliché than the man who had caused all the fuss in the first place. Greg was furious with himself for leaving her to talk to the press alone and before they allowed Siobhan to go to bed, he and Saz promised that any future interviews would only take place with either himself or Saz present.

When Siobhan eventually calmed down enough to sleep two hours later Saz lay in bed and counted the hours until they would have her safely home in London—where at least the stalkers wrote their nasty letters in good old-fashioned Anglo-Saxon.

EIGHTEEN

He was easy actually. He drinks too much. Drank too much. It's easy to kill a drunk. Even a bullying drunk. They are soft, pliable. They fall swiftly, crumple easily.

He was drinking alone too, that helped. I joined him at his table. He was an angry bastard at the best of times, but that night he was really bad. Furious with the world, the band, himself. But most of all, he was furious with her. She didn't appreciate him, he said. She never had really valued him. Understood his art. His talent. For a moment there I thought he was going to venture as far as his genius. But even he wasn't quite that arrogant. Not then, anyway.

He was drinking bitter. I joined him and ordered whiskys for the two of us. He was surprised that I wanted bitter. I was bitter that he still wanted her. And he did want her. Had done since the first day they met. It doesn't surprise me. Everyone wants her, I think. At least they think they do. Want to have her, hold her, own her. Everyone wants to possess her.

Everyone except me. She isn't worth having. I know.

After that I killed him. With a baseball bat. I know, it's a cliché and actually, to tell the truth, it was a softball bat—all I had to hand, I'm afraid. His skull was bloody hard. His skull was bloody.

Not immediately after, you understand. I am expeditious, not hasty.

More speed less haste, my piano teacher used to say. Then she'd smack my knuckles with her wooden ruler. Smack is a small word for that splintering caress. She'd splatter my knuckles with her wooden ruler. She left a cut in the knuckle of my left index finger once. A long thin wooden splinter, it tore my skin and bled when I pulled it out. Extradition can be a very bloody process.

I took him home first, we ate, I gave him a sandwich—a thin last supper of white bread and processed cheese—and opened another can. Lager this time. And then another. And more. It was very late, three, four in the morning. We shared six cans of Heineken, and a half pint bottle of whisky. I drank little, listened to him. He drank and talked, ate another sandwich, talked, dribbled, whined and then he cried. Actually, it's lucky that he cried. If he hadn't cried I might not have been able to do it. Merely angry, I just wanted to hit him. To smack him, in the jaw, the nose. I wanted to hear that swift crack of knuckle against his cheek. To spite him, surprise him, shut him up. But I held back my itchy fist. He was my guest, I had to be polite. And I hadn't quite decided that it really was what I wanted to do. I had a moment of wavering self-doubt, contradiction. The tears though, they made me pity him too. So after that it was easy. I was just putting him out of his misery. Putting him out of my misery.

Once he'd really got himself into a state I offered to take him out for a walk. Walk the unpleasing puppy dog. Help him to clear his head. As it were. It was dark in the hallway, dark outside too. A gentle rain was falling. One of those soft rains. My mum calls it Scotch mist. Though I don't suppose he'd have seen what I was carrying even if a five hundred watt bulb was shining on it. He only had eyes for her. We went to the park and, in a pretty little copse with the autumn leaves fast turning to life-enhancing mulch, I beat his brains out. He was leaning over to throw up and presented me with such an easy target. I don't suppose he suffered, the first blow seemed to knock him right out. Actually, he probably died fairly quickly but I needed to be sure, it's not as if I've killed a lot of people before. Or any. His skull was very hard though. It took several swings, batter-up! I heard the crack. It was a small sound, shallow. His head breaking, blood and bone and a little brain—I suppose it was brain—spilling out, splashing out. It sounded more like a splintering twig, more natural than anything I'd been expecting. Because, then, I didn't know what to expect. Of course, I do now.

When you plant a new garden you clear all the old debris first. Or, indeed, when you uncover the foundations of a garden laid long ago. That's what I'm doing now. Clearing the path.

Once it was all over I went home. The rain was much heavier now. Opaque waves of it starting to wash the blood away from me even as I walked home. Washed it all away from him too, I expect. Lucky, really. You always see on the TV, don't you, how they find the bad guy from an old bloody shoe print? But not after two inches of heavy autumn rain, I wouldn't have thought. I put my clothes in the washing machine, rinsed off the bat with soapy water and a pot scrubber. Just an old-fashioned wooden bat. With a few dents in it now. Wood is so much more natural than aluminium, yielding to touch. I washed my clothes—my upstairs neighbours were away so the machine didn't disturb them. Not that I'd care if it did. They vacuum at eight in the morning on a Saturday. Bastards. Vacuum to make their flat shiny and perfect before one of their happy-young-couple shopping trips, coming home laughing and smiling together as if all that was needed to keep them content was a good bargain on their fabric softener and yet another chrome and glass shelf on which to stack their CDs. Actually, I think it is all they need. They're fairly simple.

I sat in front of the machine and watched the mechanized water rinse his blood from my jeans and shirt. Sitting on my bathroom floor staring at the machine like the sad old git in the laundrette. I even put my socks and trainers in too. They needed a wash, stinking from too much running around, from putting too much effort into my life. I put the powder in that little dispenser thing, added the fabric conditioner— I always buy the yellow one—and turned the hot tap off at the base so they were being washed in cold, clear water. My mum always said to wash blood out in cold water. Not hot. She's good on handy hints, my mum. Knows how to get red wine out of the carpet too. You must never attack any stain with hot water. Hot water means the blood never really goes away. Always a ghost of a stain left behind. I got a lot of nose bleeds as a kid. But I didn't do my own washing then. Not like now, I'm very domesticated now. Almost tame. I watched the water rinse through the blood and bits of him, heard it all gurgling down the waste pipe. Then I ran myself a long, hot bath. I lay in the bath for ages, until the water was cold and scummy with my flaking skin. After a while I took the plastic shower attachment and hosed myself down with icy cold water. By the time I was finished, the washing was done and I hung my clothes over the shower rail, trainers upside down to let the collected drips fall out. I took my time, measured my actions. I was very precise. My German teacher at school used to say, "The Germans are very precise." I can hear his voice now. "*Fernsehen*—far-seeing— television. You see? The Germans are very precise." My German teacher was Czech, so I don't think he valued German precision especially highly. I don't think he'd have valued my night's activities either. But I was very precise. I've learnt that you have to be. I was going to eat, I thought

I might be hungry but when I went into the kitchen I saw the plate he'd left on the table. The crusts from his cheese sandwich. So I threw them out my window for the pigeons and washed the plates and cups, swept the floor. Made it all nice. It was too nice to mess up with making toast for myself so I just left it. Clean and bright and shiny and new. Like me. Then I went to bed. I slept like a baby. I didn't expect to. Didn't think sleep would come so easily. But it did. Must have used more energy than I thought.

I do have one regret. I regret I had to be quite so fast about the actual act. I should have liked to spend a little more time with him. I have questions about the lyrics, about the music. Questions about her. And I wish I hadn't been so nervous with the hitting. I should have liked to have been more exact. Less messy. But then a softball bat is hardly a precision instrument, is it? I can't be expected to kill a drummer in perfect three four time. Not without a lot of practice anyway.

NINETEEN

No one other than Saz, Siobhan and Greg had any cause to link Alex's messy murder to the letters and anonymous bouquets. The police least of all, because Siobhan refused to tell them. Or to show them the flowers that arrived the next morning, this time with no note attached but two red roses deep inside the yellow bouquet. Saz felt horribly certain that ignoring the possibility of a link meant another nasty surprise was lying just around the corner for them. She tried to explain as much to Siobhan, but to no avail. Siobhan, lying in bed—where she'd spent the twenty-four hours since Alex had been discovered, only two days after their return from Estonia—once again refused Saz's attempts to discuss the matter. She swallowed another mouthful of too warm vodka and shook her head.

"No, Saz. It's got nothing to do with them. I don't want the fucking cops getting in on this."

"But surely, just telling them you might think there's a link?"

"You think there's a link. I still don't know."

"Well, let me talk to them instead."

"I spoke to those two detectives the morning they found him, then in the afternoon I repeated everything I knew to the policewoman and then told it all over again this morning to that dim bitch from victim support. Look, as far as they're concerned, this is just another gay bashing, they don't even want to find who did it. They don't give a fuck about gay bashings."

"Right, and you'd know."

Siobhan rubbed a hand across her tired face. "Well, of course I wouldn't, but that's the impression I get. That's the impression everyone gets, or are you suddenly a member of the police-loving right?"

"They're not all fascists."

Siobhan sighed, "No, and all priests aren't child molesters either. It's irrelevant anyway, I can't just suddenly jump up and say, oh by the way, I forgot to tell you, I'm being harassed by a fan who won't leave me alone."

"I don't see why not."

"Because of the tour, Saz. Because of the band. If the cops knew about the flowers as well, we'd never get out of the bloody country without an entourage of police and hangers-on."

Saz stood up to look out at the autumn trees. She turned back to Siobhan, both worried and frustrated. "That might not be such a bad thing. Maybe you could do with some visible police presence."

Siobhan finished her vodka. "Yeah, and maybe I could do with writing 'victim' across my forehead and seeing just how well that adds to the sex-goddess image."

Saz moved away from the window and sat on the edge of the bed. She refilled Siobhan's glass and stroked a wisp of hair away from the younger woman's face. "Listen to me, Siobhan, I know you'd rather just pretend all this isn't happening, but you can't. Cowering in bed isn't going to make all this go away. If you won't tell them about the letters, you could at least mention the guy in Tallinn. Anyway, the cops already know that something isn't adding up. They know Alex isn't gay."

"Wasn't gay. But they know he was at a gay pub with Dan. Dan says he left Alex there and went home alone. What more do they need? It's just another sick bastard who thought he'd lucked out and killed a deserving queer. You know what Alex is like, he'd talk to any bastard who was buying the drinks." She started to cry again, "Or he'd fight with any bastard who was buying the drinks."

"The autopsy, Siobhan. This person was with him for longer than just a couple of drinks in the pub, whoever it was had coffee with Alex."

"Or Alex had coffee by himself. And a cheese sandwich by himself. Yes, I know all about it."

"How?"

"No mystery," Siobhan replied wearily, "You got the autopsy info from your police lady friend, right?"

Saz nodded, "After a little persuasion, yes."

"You told Greg, Greg told me. He tells me everything. I don't know why you didn't talk to me about it in the first place."

Saz pointed to the empty vodka glass in Siobhan's hand. "How about your lack of sobriety for a start? That and the fact that Greg thought we shouldn't worry you."

"Yeah, well, he stops being quite so sensitive about my worries when he's coked out of his head and panicking about his own problems at four in the morning. Shame you aren't here in the middle of the night to try and win him round the way you do with me." Siobhan screwed up her face and finished off the rest of the vodka from the bottle, "Coke's a brilliant drug for partying but probably not ideal when your best friend has just been beaten to death and you're the one who has to identify him."

Saz winced and tried one more time. She got as far as, "But couldn't I just ...?" when Siobhan's irritation flipped over into rage.

"No, you fucking can't. You can just bloody leave it alone. You can do what you're paid to do and take care of me, and if that isn't enough for you, then you can fuck off. I've worked on this for years with Greg. Our band. Eight, nine bloody years. We will go to LA. After that we will go to New

Zealand and have our far-too-fucking-brief holiday and then plan the next nine years. The next album. The next tour. I'm sorry about Alex, I'm really fucking sorry and the man I love is devastated. I've barely slept for three days. About the only thing that's keeping me going is the thought that there's more work out there. Another gig to do. And with the record company kicking up a stink about us having to get on with the business regardless and the boys falling apart all around me and the police and the tabloids sticking their noses in every bloody place, I'm damn well going to cope as best I can." She paused to catch her breath, "You know, I thought Greg and I had been through a lot, but this is worst thing that has ever happened to me, and I'm telling you, Saz, I'm fucked if I'm going to let some homophobic bastard killing Alex stop us. Not this, not that big git in Tallin and certainly not the inconsequential cunt who's trying to scare me with his pathetic little letters and nasty fucking flowers. So you can either drop this whole idea of telling the cops right now or you can just piss off too. Now, if you don't mind, I'm going to get up, get dressed and exercise away some of this self-pity and alcohol and I'd like a little privacy to do that. Thank you."

Siobhan threw herself back down into her pillows, pulling the duvet over her face and Saz, dismissed and stunned into silence, let herself out of the bedroom, walked down the stairs and out into the damp street. By the time she'd furiously wolfed down two bars of milk chocolate and one packet of smoky bacon crisps, Saz was feeling just about ready to face Kevin.

Kevin was less interested in talking to Saz. He came to his front door, opened it a crack and tried to slam it in her face. Saz got her winter booted foot through the door just in time. Kevin tried squeezing it but the steel toecap of the shoes

Molly loathed most of all Saz's apparel worked their trick and the door stayed firmly open.

"What the fuck do you want?" Kevin's eloquence was matched only by the warmth of the snarl across his face.

"I wanted to talk to you about Alex. You do know . . ."

Kevin walked away from her and back into the dark recesses of his home, "Of course I fucking know. It's in all the papers. It only fucking happened around the bloody corner."

Saz followed him, pushing the door to behind her. She didn't quite close it. In the kitchen Kevin turned to face her, "So are you a cop?"

"No. But I'm not a journalist either. I'm working for Siobhan."

Kevin slumped down in front of a nearly finished bottle of cheap whisky, "Working as what?"

Saz reached for a glass from the newly wiped draining board, "Can I help myself?"

Kevin watched her help herself to half of the remaining whisky and take an unappreciative mouthful, "You've got some nerve, haven't you?"

Saz sat down opposite him. "Sometimes. Siobhan Forrester's being stalked. Someone's been sending her nasty letters and bunches of roses and making anonymous phone calls and now someone's killed Alex. She's employed me to find out who."

"Yeah, well, you're barking up the wrong tree here, sweetheart." He looked around at the plain room, "The budget doesn't stretch to roses these days."

"Can I ask what you were doing . . ."

"The night Alex got his head caved in?"

"Yes."

"Sitting here feeling sorry for myself as usual. I went to the newsagents Friday morning. Bought the *Guardian*, thought I'd give myself a treat and choose not to check out the job section. I cracked a bottle, watched Richard and Judy, went to the shops, bought a can of tomato soup for lunch, watched the lunchtime news and then Neighbours and then whatever other crap was on the telly until Countdown. I thought about having a wank over the lovely Carol Vorderman but I just couldn't get up the energy. Then I went to the pub where I stayed until chucking out time."

"That's very specific for someone who must have been pretty pissed."

"No, darling, that's very specific because it's what I do every fucking day."

"Weekends?"

"I go to church."

Saz got up, scraping her chair against the floor as she did so. Kevin's lolling head jolted up, "Mind the fucking floor, I've just washed it!"

Looking around at the depressingly clean emptiness of the room, Saz asked, "Why bother?"

Kevin smiled and poured the last of the bottle into his glass, "My mum's coming for tea. Don't forget to slam the door after you."

Just as she was crossing the threshold, Kevin called after her. Saz looked up and saw his heavy frame taking up most of the kitchen doorway, "There is another reason I remember what I did that day."

"Which is?"

"I figure I might even have passed them in the street, at closing time. That pub's on my way home. I might have actually seen the bloke who did it. Bumped into him even. I keep replaying that night in my head, I keep thinking maybe I could have helped him . . ."

Uncertain whether to believe him or not, Saz chose to take the kindly understanding option, "I doubt it, you probably couldn't have done anything for Alex . . ."

Kevin laughed out loud, "I don't mean Alex, you stupid bitch."

Saz slammed the door behind her and ran down the street as fast as she could.

As soon as she got home, Saz put in a call to Helen at home. She was relieved to find that Helen and Judith's answerphone was on, glad not to have to explain her position any more than absolutely necessary.

"Look, I think you should let whoever is in charge of the Alex Cramer investigation know that they should check up on a Kevin Hogan. He's a real charmer. The guy used to work for Beneath The Blonde and he's not exactly happy about the treatment he received from them. Not enough severance pay apparently. And we must do dinner sometime. Bye."

Molly knew Saz well enough to know that her interest in the case would only be heightened by the latest developments and so wasn't at all surprised that Saz had decided she would accompany the band to the States and then on to New Zealand. She wasn't too pleased about it either, but she kept her displeasure to herself, feeding an unusually quiet Saz homemade pasta with fresh basil pesto and two-thirds of a bottle of oak-aged chardonnay. Dessert was Molly's own pistachio ice cream, laboriously churned and frozen all afternoon, supplemented with a third of a bottle of amaretto between them and thick, bitter coffee to wash it all down.

With Saz's appetites for food and drink sated, Molly worked a little sexual blackmail to try to make her change her mind. She took Saz to bed and made love to her in as many ways and for as long as she could manage until all the muscles in her own body were screaming in exhaustion and Saz lay in her arms half-laughing, half-crying from fatigue and uncontained satisfaction.

As Saz closed her eyes, her head curled into the crook of Molly's arm, Molly whispered, "See? How could you even contemplate going away from all that?"

Saz smiled and lifted her head just enough to allow Molly's lips to nuzzle her cheek, "Good try, babe. It'll certainly give me something to remember in my lonely hotel bed."

They drifted into sleep, slowly disentangling their limbs, Saz to dream fitfully of Kevin and Alex holding broken heads and broken roses while occasionally having a single lucid thought about what she could wear to the wake and Molly to fantasize about living with a lover who actually stayed at home.

TWENTY

Waking up the morning after the wake the night before, Saz had one moment of pure blissful calm before the reality of the day set in. When she opened her eyes four seconds later, however, two heavy truths dawned on her. The first, and most pressing, was that she had only a day and a half in London to sort out whatever she could about the flower sender before she flew to LA with the rest of the band. That she had woken in Siobhan's room and that she was also suffering from the worst hangover she'd ever experienced left her wanting to kick herself as hard as possible—something she might have done had not the mere action of opening her eyes provoked a headache more distressing than any kick might have been. Saz was suffering the after-effects of Alex's wake, an event more fierce and more partied than any she could recall. Though she wasn't at all certain just how valid her own recollections were.

Given that Peta was understandably incapacitated by grief, the wake had been personally stage-managed by Cal who flew in the morning after the news broke about Alex's murder. Cal had enlisted Saz as his assistant, working her full-out on the funeral arrangements and leaving her even less time to get on with her real job. Following two days of bargaining with the authorities and another day and a half of frantic preparations, Cal announced that, with police permission, they'd hold the funeral twenty hours later. He also announced that he fully expected it to not only be a better party than Alex could ever have envisioned, but that it would also "get the hot journo butts off this front doorstep and right into the music stores to order their copies of the new album and send you babies straight into the top ten". His only disappointment was that the record company couldn't get the album out any sooner. When Siobhan remonstrated that she didn't think that the loss of Alex should necessarily be treated as a great marketing opportunity, Cal snapped back that unless she let him have his way, Alex's euphemistically referred to "loss" would also be a death knell for the band and she had damn well better get used to the idea. As far as he was concerned, the only way to cope with a dead drummer—and even worse—a dead lyricist, was to make the dead man into a living myth. As quickly as humanly possible. Which is how Saz came to find herself poring over sheets of Beneath The Blonde lyrics and highlighting with a shiny new yellow marker any lines that might just hint at Alex's premonitions of his surprise demise. For Cal, the pathos of Karen Carpenter's singing "Goodbye To Love" was going to be as nothing compared to the fact that Alex had written a song for the new album, now rapidly promoted to single status, the last line of which was "And I never knew a friend's kiss, to beat the kiss of death, miss". The only thing that made Cal happier than underlining the words "beat" and "death" was one of the many bunches of flowers delivered on the morning of the funeral—he made sure the paparazzi got a clear shot of the card, handwritten by Courtney Love.

The funeral itself was a masterpiece of overstatement. Alex, an ex-Catholic atheist whose anti-belief was so fervent it was almost a religion in itself, would probably have been hugely impressed by Cal's purposeful rejection of all things traditional. For a start, there were the invitations— embossed silver writing on black and purple cards inviting those "close to or touched by Alex Cramer to a passionate commemoration of his brief but vital life". The celebratory service (for one hundred invited guests only) took place on the Tuesday afternoon at a tiny South London pub, the scene of the band's first ever gig, followed by a private cremation and, while the service was band and family only, the paparazzi still had easy access to great camera angles through the wire-link fence surrounding the cemetery. Those invited to the ceremony were told to wear "yellow, pink, sky-rocket blue—anything but black". Kevin Hogan made it to the service dressed in a faded brown suit and looking suitably hung over. His mother sat by his side throughout and he smirkingly introduced her to Saz as "the chick who thinks I did him in". Clucking her disapproval, Kevin's mother pursed her lips and stalked off. Kevin wandered away in Siobhan's direction to offer his condolences and the depleted contents of his hip flask. Surprisingly, even Alex's family complied with the dress code, his mother wearing an elegant suit of dusty pink, edged in black piping. It was all the more striking when Siobhan and the boys arrived, each of them dressed in a smooth black velvet suit and Siobhan with the added touch of a veiled pillbox hat, looking for all the world like Jackie Kennedy. Cal had thoughtfully provided her with Alex's besuited four-year-old nephew to hold her hand just in case anyone missed the comparison.

After a couple of hours off (to allow Siobhan to change costume and the photographers a chance to reload their cameras), the party started in earnest. A converted warehouse in Shoreditch became the inauspicious site for three hundred hand-picked members of London's glitterati to dance the night away at Alex's wake. Every now and then proceedings were interrupted to allow another primed and rehearsed friend or family member to give a speech about

Alex, about his talent and his daring, sad, wasted life, though none of the speeches were allowed to dwell too long on the fact that he was actually dead, let alone the fact that he'd been brutally murdered by an unknown killer, just in case the press might pick up any hint of desperation from the band. The desired effect was that the press and music business people should walk away from the wake in no doubt whatsoever that Beneath The Blonde had lost a serious songwriter and a great musician. That his death had left behind a legacy of amazing songs and fantastic lyrical poetry but—and this point was rammed into Saz every time Cal ordered her to pick up the phone and invite another journalist—they must also be unequivocally convinced that, despite this great tragedy, despite this "appalling waste of creative lava juice", Beneath The Blonde would go on. Beneath The Blonde would rise from the ashes in order to find themselves renewed, born again and invigorated by Alex's spirit "which would always suffuse their work and guide them to even greater heights with inspiring vibes from the other side". Cal also refused to allow anyone to acknowledge Alex's atheism just in case his inspiration might be lost to the ether and, against Alex's parents' wishes, he insisted Alex was cremated. Though he himself quite fancied a grave which would at least allow them the possibility of a Jim Morrison headstone in years to come, he also knew for certain that a phoenix rises from fire and ashes, not from a lead-lined box at the bottom of a six-foot hole. He didn't bother to tell the band, but he had already decided that the third album would continue the rebirth theme anyway, and it was important for him to get the embryo concept firmly lodged in the minds of potential reviewers and promoters.

The party was everything Cal had hoped for and Saz was utterly exhausted by the time Molly arrived. She'd spent five hours on the phone to the press since the police gave Cal the body release time, and then divided her time on the actual day of the funeral between shoring up Siobhan and vetting every phone call and bunch of flowers for any sign of the mystery caller. She would have willingly left the minute Molly pulled up had not a motorbike messenger arrived at the same moment. Saz's glance was arrested by the blaze of yellow roses he carried in his left arm and, waving Molly to wait, she collared and interrogated him immediately. Within minutes, she had his own home number, his company's number and was talking to a very pissed off radio controller on the messenger's radio.

"Look, sweetheart, I don't know what you do with your evenings, but I'm a bit too bloody busy to sit here and chat all night over a bleedin' bike radio. Some homeless kid comes in and drops off the flowers, the address and the cash right? I don't need a whole lot more than that. So if you want to come in to ask me about that, fine. Come into the office tomorrow. If not, bugger off back to your party and let my Stan get on with his work. All right?"

After a hasty apology and a request for a meeting, Saz took the roses and handed the radio back to the smirking Stan.

When Molly was ready to leave the party half an hour later, her more sober tastes quickly affronted by the excess in the warehouse, Saz took her outside and gave her a kiss and the bunch of flowers. Molly was decidedly unimpressed with Saz's decision to remain with Siobhan and spend the night with the band. She left with a goodbye as frosty as the night that was starting to settle on the parked cars around them. Saz stayed completely sober until the dregs of the revellers left and then she bundled Cal, Siobhan and the boys into two taxis and back to the house. Cal took one cab on to his hotel with an injunction that everyone make a meeting at five the next afternoon to get on with plans for a replacement drummer and the LA trip. Saz then joined Siobhan and the boys in yet another bottle of lemon vodka and a few lines of Cal's justifiably expensive coke. He'd given Siobhan three grams that afternoon as a bribe to get her to wear the flamboyant red velvet dress she'd spent the evening parading in. The bribe worked. The overwork of the previous couple of days and the unaccustomed use of illicit substances caught up with Saz very quickly and within an hour, Siobhan had taken her upstairs to the attic room and put her to bed on the gold chaise-longue. At Saz's insistence, she set the alarm for eight in the morning and kissed Saz goodnight.

And it was that kiss which prompted Saz's second worrying thought when she woke up the next morning. She was slowly and reluctantly becoming aware that, all previous indications to the contrary and against every grain of sense she possessed, if she wasn't careful she might just start falling in lust with Siobhan Forrester. If, that is, she hadn't already. With a groan resulting from the combination of her overindulgence four hours earlier, the seeming impossibility of ever finding the flower sender, the lack of any proof to link Kevin to the matter and her fear that she was stumbling into an emotional minefield, Saz dragged herself to her feet with an even further sinking heart when she remembered that this morning she had a date with a grumpy and no doubt suspicious radio bike controller.

She glared at her exhausted self in the mirror, muttering, "Jesus girl, don't do this to Molly—don't do this to yourself."

Yet, even as she started down the stairs, she caught herself hoping against hope that Siobhan might have miraculously woken early and would be making coffee in the kitchen. But the house was silent night asleep and she let

herself out into the grey morning, denied even a glimpse of
Siobhan's sleep-crumpled morning face.

TWENTY-ONE

The party was good. And in a way it was my party. After all, I was responsible. They wouldn't have had it but for me, would they?

I watched them. Standing a little back. You can get in anywhere in black and white. London parties are full to bursting with blank and anonymous waiting staff. And as such, I had no need to revel quite so much as some of the revellers. Nor reveal quite so much as some of the revellers. We couldn't all look like crossing the River Styx was a picnic. I noted the mourners and the dissemblers, each one trying to outdo the other in more and more inappropriate, unseemly costumes. Each effort to make themselves stand out, be more fascinating, creating a perpetual effect of amorphous glitter and shine. In the end, through the reflected glare of themselves, they all just looked the same. The women bare-skinned, the men pierced and shaved, the silver, the gold. Truly, it was a glittering occasion.

I wish I could have seen him one last time. Said goodbye nicely. But it was impossible. Closed casket.

My fault again.

She was very beautiful though. Really so beautiful. She'd certainly done a good job on herself. You could see she'd been crying, but even the slightly swollen eyes suited her. As if her flesh had puffed up just enough to greet the tears, but not too much, not enough to hide the lovely eyes. The red suited her too. Thin pieces of lush cloth, falling one from the other, an overall effect of joined up, disjointed seams. When she moved, I saw her flesh beneath. We all saw her flesh beneath. I suppose we were meant to. All that worked-out tone, the taut tanned skin stretched tight over bones just softened by the barest hint of rounding off flesh. She hasn't always been so gorgeous, of course. Like other man-made girlstars, like Cher or Madonna, you could look up the old photos (if you knew where to find them, if she'd allow it), you could note the progress of the achievement of her self-created body, trace carefully along the pattern lines of that cut-out-and-keep dressed up doll. I suppose that's why she wears those clothes, so we can all know how hard she's worked, how much effort has gone into making her the woman she is today. It's very impressive. Really.

They stood side by side all night. I couldn't tell who was taking care of whom. They are so very together, the two of them. The way they look at each other, I wonder sometimes what it is. Love? Lust? Or maybe it's something more. Each wanting the other's strength, the other's power. Wanting to be each other. Or maybe that's just me?

I don't know if she got the funeral flowers. I sent them for Alex, to the wake. Out of respect. But I hoped she'd see the bouquet though. The pure yellow. That single hue splash. I spent so much money on flowers that day. One hundred perfect yellow roses. And, hidden deep inside, a third tiny red rosebud. No reason. I just like the spilt red on yellow. But it was worth it. It will all be worth it in the end. Every last bloody thorn. I must get on with the clearance.

And everyone was so frivolous, so glib and nonchalant. At a wake. A time of mourning for the lost man. Yet the loss was made to seem a farewell party, not a death. The American smoothed it all over, made it bright and shiny. I surprised myself by being shocked at the drinking and drug-taking. I don't mind a little alcohol myself, a lot of alcohol myself, a joint or two, a line of speed or coke. But they took everything, all mixed in together. They have always taken everything. They have no discrimination. And she, with her constant vodka bottle. I know she used to try not to drink much, to be careful about drugs and alcohol, to be careful about her body commodity. She doesn't try so very hard these days. Something must be winding her up. Or someone. She's not quite as in control as she likes to think. She doesn't know who is in control anymore. I do.

I watched her dancing. She moves like a constructed angel. Each limb in perfect accord with the others, teetering on the edge of balance only to flick herself upright at the last impossible moment. When she dances she throws herself around the room, ignoring the walls. I've seen it before. She can't possibly know where she's going, arms and head spinning. People move out of her body trajectory or run to catch her so that, no matter what she attempts, there's never a single scratch on her. Never even the tiniest visible scar. She lives like she's always just about to fall from a cliff. After all that work she's done to make her life so perfect, all the time and effort it's taken to build them all into what they are, you'd think she'd be more careful with herself.

I mean, you would think she'd be more careful, wouldn't you?

TWENTY-TWO

Trawling through the West End of London just at the start of the morning rush hour was hardly Saz's idea of fun at the best of times, with a raging hangover and in climatic conditions that could only make an ice sculptor happy, her mood was worsening by the minute. And it wasn't exactly enhanced by her meeting with the bike messenger's controller—who also happened to be his dad. The fat father sat in an over-heated room, the air drying fan heater turned to his ankles, puffing on Gauloises, and allowed her ten minutes before his morning calls started coming in. From the filthy state of his office Saz guessed business wasn't exactly booming, the chair she sat on creaked dangerously and she'd nearly broken her ankle on the ripped carpet as she came in. The two windows were covered with a couple of years of grime and the walls had yellowed to a fine shade of dirty gold—to match the smoker's fingers.

The controller began their interview by turning off his dated radio and berating Saz's dress sense, "Wot d'you wanna come into the West End looking like that for, then?"

Saz looked down at her clothes. She thought she'd been eminently sensible when she went home to change into old jeans, Molly's gardening sweater and a plastic anorak they kept in the back of the car for emergencies, "I'm sorry?"

"You look like a right scruff."

Saz bit her tongue, hard. She reminded herself that this man was so far the closest she'd come to confirming the identity of the flower sender and she couldn't afford to antagonize him. She nodded and tried her hardest to keep the sarcasm out of her voice, answering him brightly, "Yeah, I know, and I really hate coming into town looking a mess. It's not like me at all. But, well, you know ... if I went looking for this homeless kid, all dressed up like I normally am ... well, I wouldn't get very far, would I?"

Stan's dad puffed more smoke in her direction and took in Saz's body with a leery glance over the top of his greasy bifocals, "I bet you'd look a treat in a nice outfit. We deliver loads of stuff to those posh shops down Bond Street way, you should go down there. Or I could put you in touch with the wholesalers. Nice line in office suits, girls' suits, I mean, good quality stuff too. No back of a lorry junk. Cost you, though, it would. Stan met a lovely girl in one of those shops once, least she looked nice, started out nice enough too—turned out to be a right little trollop, broke his bloody heart ..."

Saz interrupted him before he could give her any more paternal musings, "Yeah, well, those posh girls, all the same I 'spose. Anyway, I really do need to try and find this kid. The one you said brought in the flowers last night?"

"Look, luv, some pissed kid comes into the control office, stinking of alcohol and God knows what else, drops off this bunch of flowers and a fifty quid note. I check the money is real and I send Stan out with the flowers. Now, that's what we call a cash job, darling. I can't ask for bloody ID from every bastard that comes in, can I?"

Saz dropped her attempt at charm to point out that if he didn't ask for ID, he might well find he was engaged in drug deliveries for all he knew and that perhaps the police would be interested in his work methods. At this his face turned an even brighter shade of red.

"They were flowers, doll. A bunch of bloody flowers—what's more, I did check them. I checked them myself. I run a clean bloody shop here. I unwrapped the bloody flowers.

I know there's not a bloody ounce of nothing hiding in the friggin' petals so don't try that bloody mullarkey with me! Now, all I can do is tell you about the kid who brought them in last night. If you want to know?"

Saz nodded, her polite tone back in place, "Yes, please."

"Yeah, well, it was a different one to the last time though . . ."

"There's been more?"

"Three. I looked up the records last night. All delivered to the same girl. In Chalk Farm. That singer, right? Stan says she doesn't look half as good at home as when he saw her on the telly. Top of the Pops, would that be?"

"Um, I think so, I'm not really sure."

Saz looked around the room, vainly searching for anything that might resemble a computer or even a good old-fashioned filing cabinet.

"You keep records?"

"What kind of a Mickey Mouse outfit do you think we are? Course we keep bloody records. Look!"

With that, Stan's dad heaved himself out of his torn leather chair and opened the door behind him. What Saz had assumed was another part of the office turned out to be a pungently filthy toilet. On eight or nine shelves above the cistern, reaching right up to the ceiling and hiding behind the semi-naked dollybird calendar, were piles of neatly ordered slips of yellow paper. Hundreds, probably thousands of them.

"There's your filing cabinet, sweetheart. Every single day of business since I first started up six years ago. Those are the carbons of what we send the lads out with. They take the original, get it signed on receipt of delivery and then bring the signed original, that's the white copy, back here at the end of the day. We keep the yellows in this office . . ."

"And the top sheets?"

"In the ladies, down the hall. Everything's kept in

bunches—each day, each week, each month. Then, at the end of the tax year, I tie 'em all up together. All receipted, all documented, all honestly declared to the tax man. Can't say fairer than that now, can you? Shame about the stink, mind—drains." Then he wheezed out a laugh, "And Stan's arse!"

Saz was a little dazed. The combination of the care and effort gone into his records and the stench emanating from the toilet propelled her back to her seat. "Well, I'm very impressed. So you actually have records of every time a delivery was made to Siobhan Forrester?"

"If it came through us, I certainly do."

"And this information is going to cost me how much?"

Stan's dad sat back in his chair and resting his cigarette-free hands on his belly, he smirked, "Not me, love, you can have what you want from me gratis. I'm always happy to help a fellow professional in their line of duty. I'm a good bloke, after all. Like to do my bit. Nah, it's those scummy streetkids you wanna watch out for. With that lot, you don't get nothing for nothing."

She left the office with two descriptions, one for the flowers delivered a fortnight earlier, that of a young girl, maybe aged as much as eighteen, though more likely fifteen or sixteen, Geordie accent, cropped and dyed red hair. Having seen her around the streets on his way to and from work, Stan's dad thought she lived—though he admitted to using the term loosely—somewhere between Tottenham Court Road and Holborn. As he said, "It's easier for those street kids to get to Centrepoint that way. If they want to stay in for the night. It's close. Closer to the tourist trade too, if she decides to do a bit of work of an evening—you know what these little tarts are like."

The other description, for the person who'd brought the

flowers both for the wake and those delivered a month earlier, was rather more specific: "Gentle Ben."

"I'm sorry?"

"The lads call him Gentle Ben. You know, that kids' programme about the bear? Stan used to like that one. He's a great big bastard. Six three or four. Now, by 'lads' I mean my lads, you understand. I don't know what they call him on the street. Maybe the same, maybe not. Half those bloody street kids don't know what they call themselves, let alone anyone else. And off their heads most of the time, so I don't suppose they'd recognize their own mothers calling them by name. But he's always around, Ben is. Soho Square, Oxford Circus, stops around Berwick Street Market a lot. Likes bananas. You can't miss him, the bugger's vast."

"And gentle?"

Stan's dad wheezed his emphysemic laugh again.

"Nah, darling, that's comedy, you see. Irony. He's a right vicious bastard is Gentle Ben. My Stan likes nothing better than seeing the cops trying to move him on. Says it beats Giant Haystacks any day. I reckon they only send the baby cops out to do it—you know, get them used to the real city, away from their poncing bloody Hendon crap."

Then he shuffled her out of the office with copies of the white top sheets, Siobhan's childlike signature scrawled across them.

"I've got work to do now, love, business to run, official records to keep. And you've got yourself meetings, haven't you? Best be off then, don't want to keep Gentle Ben waiting!"

And he slammed the door behind her, nearly choking himself with a great wheeze of delight as he thought about Saz out in the cold and the wind.

Stan's dad had been right. Trying to get information certainly had cost her. She'd spent thirty quid in pound coins and more precious fivers trying to find someone who could direct her to the red-headed Geordie. She gave up after two hours of walking the streets when her Hansel and Gretel money trail finally led her down to the Embankment and a Glaswegian boy who, hardly more than sixteen himself, carefully pocketed her five pound note and then started screaming at her, "We don't want any bloody social workers around here, she's not going home and you can't force her to, so why don't you piss off before I make you?"

Saz muttered something about not being a social worker, just being interested in finding the girl, wanting to talk to her and he then launched into an attack on students, doctors and do-gooders, culminating in a raging invective against what must have been his pet hate—"fucking TV researchers". Reasoning that a fury like his wasn't likely to dissipate in a hurry, and suddenly only too aware that she was in a deserted and very tight alley, Saz thanked him for his time and backed off as fast as she could. Which was not quite fast enough. Just as she was turning to exit the narrow street, the ranting youth held his breath long enough to take aim with a full can of Red Stripe which smashed into the back of her head. Saz decided against discussing the matter further with him and took off down the street, the unopened can bouncing off the back of her head and rolling down her left calf. All the years of early morning running helped to jolt her jellified legs into action despite the shock of being hit and she didn't stop until she was back in the relative safety of Charing Cross Road. Shaken and more than a little pissed off that she'd allowed herself to get into a side street for a one-on-one with a kid who had no hope of being either sober or safe, she slipped into the Books Etc Aroma to placate her nerves and the cricket ball sized lump forming on the back of her head with a huge steaming mug of hot chocolate and four large chunks of gooey nougat. Half an hour and another hot chocolate later she was, if not willing, then at least ready to face the fray again.

This time she decided to tackle the big fear face on. If Gentle Ben was such a monster then at least he was a monster who was said to live in the open. She tried Soho Square first. The summer cram of bike riders and office workers who had been lounging all over the grass only a month ago had now gone for another gestation hibernation, the only residents were two gardeners raking leaves and a trio of old drunk men. The least drunk of the three accepted her fiver and sent her to St Anne's Court where, outside the Mexican restaurant, she found what she assumed to be the dozing mass of Gentle Ben. He was sprawled across three concrete steps, lying on a couple of broken-down cardboard boxes, a pair of filthy shoes and an empty milk carton on its side by his vast left thigh, that morning's *Telegraph* spread out across his knees. He opened his eyes as she came to a halt in front of him, looked her up and down and then, barely raising an eyebrow, he indicated the empty piece of step to the right of him and told her, in a faintly accented voice, "Sit down, my dear. You must be exhausted. It's taken you quite some time to find me, has it not?"

Ben Koserov was a Hungarian-German painter who'd arrived in London in the sixties and liked it enough to stay, even though it now offered him little charm and less hospitality. He was six-foot four without his shoes, immensely wide, with a mane of grey hair and beard. He was also the campest man Saz had ever met. Koserov and Gordon, Stan's dad, were old friends and sending Saz off in the wrong direction had been Gordon's idea of a joke.

"I think he thought it might do you a bit of good, sweetie, see how the other half live and all that."

"Yeah? Well, I must remember to buy Gordon a couple of cartons of Gauloises next time I'm passing duty free. For an education like I've had this morning, offering him a stronger carcinogen is the least I can do."

Koserov agreed that perhaps Gordon had been a little unchivalrous and then intimated there might be a more pleasant place to sit, especially as he knew the restaurant proprietor would be along at any moment and he didn't like to be any trouble. Koserov put on his mammoth boots, slowly lacing them with swollen fingers, bundled his newspaper and assorted effects into a neat pile and then left them behind the telephone box five yards away. When Saz asked if his things would be safe, he smiled down at her, "Sweetie, I appreciate your concern, but I am Gentle Ben. People know this is my autumn residence. And after all, I am the big hairy scary monster, am I not?"

He led her to a small greasy spoon off Broadwick Street where Saz bought them a late lunch. She had hot toast with more pure melting butter than she'd allowed herself in years and swallowed down the heart-stopping cholesterol with a mug of sweet tea in the hope of calming her still mounting fury at Stan's dad. Koserov had toast, eggs, chips, beans, three sausages, crispy bacon, mushrooms, tomatoes and fried bread—all rinsed down with a cup of boiling water into which he whisked a teaspoon of salt, a few grains of sugar and a dash of Worcester sauce—"To help with the digestion, my darling."

Koserov was very helpful. He hadn't touched a drop of alcohol since 1973, had smoked two joints since then, though he claimed they had no effect on him—"I'm too big for little puffing things like that"—and seemed to have perfect recall of everything that had ever happened to him. In fact, that was Saz's only problem. The man was a brilliant story teller and, in getting him to stick to the matter in hand, she felt like a parent denying a small child his favourite sweet and forcing him to eat badly cooked Brussels sprouts instead. Koserov didn't just love to talk, he positively relished the act of placing one word after the other. Eventually he got back to the flowers.

"Yes. Twice I have been given the task of taking the money to Gordon. But other people? Who knows how many your flower sender has tried? Or other couriers. Sometimes the people take the money and keep the flowers for themselves and then your friend the singer does not know 'that her admirer has sent the flowers today. But I am honourable. A gentleman. And really, twenty pounds to pass on the flowers and the fifty pound fee to Gordon? It is a generous gesture, no?"

"I suppose so. Gordon's fee seems a bit steep."

Koserov shrugged, "Needs must. I remember once there was a boy I loved, I was young myself, you understand . . . we both were, we were children—seventeen, eighteen . . . I sent him roses. White roses. For purity. His father found them though. Burnt the roses. Burnt my card. I do not think the boy ever knew I had sent them. Or why his father beat him that night."

Saz nodded sympathetically, trying at the same time to lure him back to the subject at hand, "That's very sad, really. But, if you don't mind, this flower sender, does he never check? I mean, how does he know if you actually take the flowers to Gordon?"

Koserov stared at her for a moment and then he burst out laughing. "You have been following many false leads today, no? He? Who is this he? We talking about the flowers for the singing lady in Chalk Farm, yes? They call her blonde one?"

Saz nodded and Koserov continued, "But, my darling, the flowers are not from a man. No no, they are from a girl. A woman. A beautiful woman. I like her—not like that, you understand, not for the fucking—but yes, I do like her. She is very fierce, very strong. She is very angry."

Saz noted his detailed physical description of the woman and then paid for their meal. She offered fifty quid to Koserov, who took ten, telling her that his wait this morning had been immensely enjoyable, as had his lunch, and he couldn't possibly charge her so much. They parted back at St Anne's Court where Koserov bowed to Saz and told her to stop by any time for tea—as long as she brought it herself. Saz then wandered slowly to the tube, walked home from the station and ran herself the longest, hottest bath she could. While she waited for the water to cool she examined the swollen lump on the back of her head, relieved to see that it had receded a little and that although it felt vast to her, it wasn't something Molly would necessarily notice, at least not without running her fingers through her hair and Saz felt sure she could at least keep Molly's hands off one part of her anatomy. As Saz lay in the bath and attempted to regain some feeling in her frozen fingertips and toes, she counted the cost of the day. The cash wasn't hers anyway, being part of the expenses Siobhan would have to pay her later. She was freezing cold and did have a runny nose, but that would pass and she knew that the sinus trouble was due more to the coke of the night before than the mellow fruitfulness of the season. She had a dreadful headache, part dregs of a hangover and larger part can of Red Stripe on the back of the head. And she'd stupidly put herself in a dangerous position without backup and without support. That was the worst bit. Her own stupidity. On the other hand, she now had a clear description of the flower sender.

Who obviously wasn't Kevin. At least not directly. Finally, having informed Koserov she'd be out of the country for the next ten days, she'd extracted a promise from him that the next time he was approached by a tall, well-built woman with perfectly cut jet black hair and a bunch of yellow roses, he'd call Carrie on her mobile and endeavour to follow the woman for as long as he could. As subtly as possible. On balance, Saz felt that the day had come out with her just about on top. Though she had an uneasy feeling that she should maybe be a little more concerned about the alley situation and then, when she heard the key turn in the lock and Molly call her name, and noted that her heart didn't quite make the leap at her voice that it was expected to make, she knew that she also needed to be concerned about the feelings-for-Siobhan situation. Those feelings, however, could wait for twenty-four hours and Los Angeles. For now she was content to hide under the lukewarm water, easing her aching muscles and ignoring her uncertain conscience.

TWENTY-THREE

With her LA flight leaving Heathrow at 3.30 that afternoon, Saz decided she might as well put the day to good use. She had been for her morning run as usual, though not for as long as before the tedious period of her recuperation. It had taken Molly hours of persuasion after the fire to convince Saz that she couldn't run quite so hard and fast as she had before the burns. Her tightened skin and the scarring, especially on her upper legs, meant that she had to try various other forms of exercise to nudge her body back to the realm of peak condition she had come to expect. Days of swimming (and then plastering her legs and stomach with industrial strength moisturizer) were followed by new classes in yoga. Saz happily took to the swimming; after forty or fifty lengths she could emerge with some of the endorphin rush she had been used to getting from her morning run. The yoga was less successful. She stuck it out for ten weeks until the end of class lecture on "Breathing For The New Millennium" meant that she decided she'd rather suffer pulled burn scars than go through one more cat stretch ever again. Two weeks later, when her specialist gave her permission to return to running, she'd done so with unadulterated elation. After three months of working up to speed, Saz eventually returned to a slower but regular four miles in the early hours of every morning, her limbs gradually becoming her own as some scars faded to nothingness and others settled into being the new body that she was beginning to acknowledge as her own.

By eight-thirty Saz had finished her run, showered, special scar-moisturized, dressed, packed and was making a phone call to Carrie. Since their messy break up four years earlier Carrie had eventually become Saz's friend, her tenant and, on occasion, a part-time, cash-hungry, freelance employee.

"I know it's early to wake you . . ."

"Damn right it is, Saz. Better be good."

"Come looking with me today?"

"Clothes, gifts or business?"

"Business. But it's in town, so you can make it all that girl-shit too if you get a move on."

"Only if you give me cash today. I'm broke."

Saz, cradling the cordless phone between her ear and left shoulder, grabbed her alarm clock and threw it in her bag, "When aren't you ever broke?"

"When I've just been visiting granny-bitch-queen-from-hell."

"I really think you ought to view your visits to granny as a time to commune with the wisdom of the elderly, not make a fast buck."

"You only think that because you don't have any slob-bering aged relatives of your own to put up with. Anyway, this is different broke. I'm taking Blair to Prague . . ."

"With no money?"

"Close. I'm taking Blair to Prague because the guy I've been life modelling for has this cousin with a travel agency . . ."

"Of course he does."

Carrie ignored Saz's sarcasm and continued, "And if I do six more free sittings for his class, that's the rest of this term, he'll get me a deal on three nights in Prague, central city hotel, flights, B&B, all for one hundred and fifty quid."

"Each?"

"Both. It's a bloody good deal. And I've already borrowed the fifty from Blair . . ."

"For her own surprise?"

"She thinks it's for the rent."

"Not such a bad idea."

"I know you're a very patient landlady, Saz. So if I come out with you today . . ."

"And I pay you a hundred quid."

"Cash. Then we'll all be happy, won't we?"

Saz wasn't altogether certain that Carrie's services were quite worth one hundred; she'd been thinking more along the lines of fifty herself, but Carrie had been very helpful to her in the past and even though the rent was always late, it did come eventually—usually with a bunch of flowers or a good book. More often than not those flowers were stolen from the park down the road or the book was shoplifted, but they were gifts all the same.

Saz and Carrie headed down Charing Cross Road, chatting up street people as they went. Carrie was much better at it than Saz. For a start, she was just a far better liar. Depending on who they were talking to, she put on a variety of accents from London posh to Midwest American and told people they were looking for the Geordie girl for a selection of reasons from being a sister, cousin, aunt, to believing she might have bought a winning lottery ticket from their shop in Tottenham Court Road and finally, in desperation, claiming that they had a reward for the girl who had fought off a bunch of muggers when Carrie was getting out of a taxi in Russell Square the night before.

Words weren't necessary, however, when Carrie and Saz entered the gardens by the Embankment. Sitting on a damp bench underneath a tree of soggy brown leaves was the boy who'd created the lump on the back of Saz's head with his well-aimed lager can and lying along the bench, her head in his lap, was a small thin girl with cropped bright red hair,

ripped jeans, extremely old trainers—very likely the object
of their search. Saz was just whispering to Carrie about the
pair when the young guy looked up. He had obviously not
grown any more trusting in the past twenty-four hours and
within seconds he was on his feet. Whatever he thought Saz
and Carrie were after, he evidently guessed it involved both
himself and his girlfriend as he tugged her up and tried to
pull her along behind him. Despite his efforts, however, the
cheap alcohol or drug combination that had probably got
her through the night before meant that her reactions were
nowhere near as fast as his and, after calling her name,
shaking her several times and slapping her once, he gave
up and she flopped back down on the bench. He took off
away from Saz and Carrie down towards Waterloo Bridge.
Carrie, who'd turned red when she saw him slap the girl,
had started to follow him, fury rising in her fists but Saz
held her back.

"Don't, Carrie. He was just looking out for her."

"By smacking her around the face?"

"Wake her up, get her away from scary old us."

"Have you forgotten how you got that bump on your
head?"

"No. But he was trying to protect her then too. He obviously thinks I'm out to hurt her."

"You're not the one punching her in the face. Or the one
who's just run away."

Saz shook her head. "Neither's he. Don't look, but he's
still there, about a hundred yards up. On the left."

"So let's try and get something out of this chick before
he comes back with a six pack ready for bowling practice."

Getting sense out of the thin girl, breath strong with
alcohol and eyes glazed with substances somewhat stronger,
took a while. Carrie managed to get her sitting up and then
despatched Saz to the McDonalds on the Strand for "a
couple of burgers—sane fish ones if possible", two apple

pies and a full sugar strength Coke, in the hope that charging up her blood sugar level might also charge up a few brain cells. The girl revived enough at the smell of food to open her eyes fully, run grubby hands down her over-large jumper by way of a wash and wolf down the burgers one after the other without a pause. She drank the whole container of Coke and then burnt her mouth on the first of the apple pies. All before she'd said thank you. Which she did, after wiping her mouth very politely on the tiny paper napkin and speaking, to Saz's surprise, with only the faintest trace of a Newcastle accent. The girl sneered when she saw Saz's puzzled look at Carrie over her head.

"Don't panic. I know you're looking for me. Some of them call me Geordie but my name's Linda, if you care to use it." She laughed at Saz, "Not every bloody Geordie talks like they do on the telly. I talk how I want when it suits me. When it'll get me a quick fiver. Or not. Pie?" She held her hand out for the second apple pie, cooler and safer to the lips now, "You want to know about that mad flower woman, right?"

"Yes. Please."

Biting into the pie, warm apple goo dripping on to her fingers, the girl nodded. "Yeah, well, let's make it quick. I've got a very busy afternoon."

Saz quickly kicked Carrie before she could annoy the girl by asking just what she might be busy doing.

Linda continued, "And it'll cost you."

Saz reached for her wallet. "How much?"

The girl shook her head, "Not money. I don't need your bloody money."

She stood up and shouted down to the end of the park, "Tim! Tim!", and the dark figure of the boy started to run towards them, head down and both fists clenched, ready to throw himself into whatever violent action was needed. Linda walked towards his flying figure, one hand out, oblivious of the scattered food cartons she was trailing in her wake. When he got to her, she grabbed his shoulders with both hands, pulled him round and whispered fiercely into his face. After a few interjections he finally nodded and then went to sit on the neighbouring bench, fifteen feet away, never taking his eyes off Linda. She came back and sat between Saz and Carrie, wiping the last crumbs from her mouth.

"Ok. I want those." She pointed to Carrie's pink platform trainers. "And Tim, wants this." She tugged on the sleeve of Saz's pillar-box red suede jacket.

Saz stood up and shook her head. "No way, kid, I'm sorry. In the first place, the most I was going to offer you would have been maybe fifty quid. Now, as my friend's shoes are probably worth about thirty—"

"Fifteen on sale, actually." Carrie interrupted.

"All right, fifteen on sale. But this jacket cost far more than that and, seeing as it was a present from my sister, would also cost me my most valuable family relationship to give it up. And even if I was prepared to make that sacrifice, I certainly wouldn't be giving it to your vicious bloody boyfriend, given the fact that I've still got a hell of a lump from when he smacked me in the head with a can of lager yesterday afternoon."

The girl looked up at Saz and shrugged. "He's my mate. He was looking out for me. But ok. Your friend can keep the shoes and I'll just take the jacket."

"Seventy quid, and we all keep our own clothes."

"Keep your fucking money, I want the bloody jacket."

The wind had picked up, bringing with it a spattering of yesterday's unseasonal sleety rain and Carrie, turning up the collar of her own fake zebra skin coat, hissed in Saz's ear, "For God's sake, Saz, give her the bloody jacket. It's fucking freezing, the poor bitch has got hardly any clothes on and it's not even winter yet. And Cassie's never going to know."

Saz looked from Carrie's angry face to the pinched, thin little thing trying not to look as if she was shivering as she sat on the bench. And then Saz reluctantly handed over her jacket. The sharp spits of rain pierced Saz's thin cotton jumper, chilling her in five seconds flat, and she demanded that Carrie sit close beside her on the bench to keep her warm.

The girl nodded in approval, running her small, scratched hands over the red-dyed animal skin. "This is bloody nice though. I'd not be happy to lose it either."

She hugged herself into the jacket and turned to face Saz. "Ok. Let's be quick about it, Tim and me have a full agenda today. Your woman, right? What do you want her for?"

"The recipient of the flowers doesn't like roses."

"Fair enough. Ok, I don't know her name but she's been coming down here, down to Soho Square and a few other places on and off most of the summer."

"What time of day?"

"Well, if she's got a job, it isn't in an office."

"Not the right sort of clothes?" Carrie asked.

Linda looked pityingly at Carrie. "When was the last time you had an office job? They wear what they like these days. No, it's the hours she keeps. Doesn't just pop into the square for forty-five minutes at lunchtime."

Saz thought she'd better move things on before Linda annoyed Carrie any more, "When did you first meet her?"

"Three months ago must have been, it was hot then. She comes up to me, big bunch of flowers and seventy quid in her hand. Offers me the twenty to take the flowers and give the fifty to the cab man. He's the one who told you to find me, yeah?"

Saz nodded and Linda continued. "Ok, so I take the flowers, give him the cash and me and Tim get to go to the pictures that afternoon. Popcorn, hotdog, the lot. Just like the tourists. Easy. Then a couple more times the same thing. Twenty quid for me, fifty for the bike and a big bunch of yellow roses. One time I didn't bother handing over the roses though. Tim and me went and stopped at this B&B in Kennington for a couple of nights. It was brilliant—we watched TV in bed for three days, had big fry-up breakfasts and then just used up all those little tea and coffee sachets in the daytime. Don't know why they complain about living in B&Bs, those families."

Saz frowned, "Yeah, well, maybe it's different when you've got four kids in the same room with you. Anything else? That's not a huge amount of info for a bloody good jacket."

"That's all I know. We don't exactly go for a drink and a chat. She offers the money, I take it."

"She didn't say anything else?"

"Listen, I wasn't doing it because I needed a new friend."

"When did you last see her?"

"Last week, maybe the week before. Not so much since it's turned cold. They go back indoors in the cold."

"They?"

"Yeah, daytime homeless. Part-timers. Nutters, Tim reckons. Got homes of their own but don't like being in them. So they stay out long as it's warm. Makes them feel they know people, you know, got friends."

"Did she ever say anything about who the flowers were for?"

"That singer, right?"

"Yes."

"I told you. Just here's your money and here's the cab money and here's the flowers. The basics. Nothing else."

"No reason?"

"What, like happy birthday or something?" Linda shook her head, "It'd be a hell of a lot of birthdays, wouldn't it? She told me about the flowers though. Gets them from all over."

"Steals them?"

"Nah. Bought they are. Like ten from one place and another ten from another place. Buys them all up separate, then gets them put into a bouquet at some other flower shop."

"You don't know where?"

Linda shook her head. "Look, she gave me the money, I took it. I didn't ask where she buys the bloody flowers from. I don't care."

"Any idea why she chose you?"

"'Cos I'm so fucking cute?"

Saz elicited as detailed a physical description as Linda could manage, pretty much tying in with Ben's. Though where Ben had assumed late twenties, early thirties, Linda just damned Saz with, "Kind of middle-aged. Like you, I reckon. Your age."

But she concurred with Ben's description of a tall slim woman, faded freckled skin contrasting with her dark hair. The description complete, Saz handed Linda twenty pounds anyway and her mobile number. The wind had turned and was driving the spitting rain into their faces along with the sour smell of train brakes from Hungerford Bridge. Linda took the money and called Tim over who came trotting up like a well-behaved puppy. They ran out of the gardens together, hand in hand like little children. Saz remarked to Carrie as they paced themselves against the wind back up to Soho, that was probably because they still were little children.

Back in Old Compton Street, Saz asked Carrie to keep an eye on Linda, maybe visit her sometime in the next week and see if she had remembered anything more about the woman, ask if she'd seen her at all in the intervening period. She handed her mobile over, telling Carrie that both Ben and Linda had the number and that it was therefore to be used for incoming calls only. Carrie agreed, kissed her goodbye as they left American Retro and had already started dialling Blair before she hit Charing Cross Road. Saz met Molly long enough to pick up her bag from her, drink two very strong espressos and share a piece of sticky chocolate and carrot cake and several long and equally sticky goodbye kisses. Then leaving Molly, she shouldered her bag to walk down to Leicester Square tube. She was just trying to get herself and the bag through the unaccommodating ticket barrier when a familiar loud laugh made her turn. It was Linda and Tim, arms around each other, jumping over the barrier, and past the two overweight and under-motivated guards. Linda looked elated but still cold and thin in her big holey jumper, Tim looked fantastic in Saz's red suede jacket.

TWENTY-FOUR

Once, when Gaelene was fourteen, she came back to the area with her parents for the May holidays. It was cold already, the wind saline sharp off the sea, slamming the car doors for them as they got out. After tea and chat Gaelene left her parents talking to the friends who had moved into their house and wandered outside in her old front garden, walked down the wide, even streets, turning corners without thinking until, just a short distance later (though it had once been a long walk for the thin legs of a six-year-old) she was standing outside Shona's house. At the back door she just managed to stop herself from walking right in, unannounced, no informing knock, just like in the old days. Shona's mother let her in with a smile and a hug. Remarried and remothered, she was playing housewife for the day, and a plate of hot fresh scones were sitting on the table waiting for Shona to come back from her Saturday job at the dairy. In fact, Shona's mum said, Shona was already half an hour late. Maybe Gaelene should just pop down to the dairy to find her?

Gaelene set off, scone in hand, dripping warm butter and raspberry jam down the front of her fourth form school jersey. The one she was supposed to keep for school. Clean for the winter term. The one she'd put on this morning, late, to leave muggy Auckland, grabbing whatever she could as her mum yelled from the front door that the weather was cooler down the line and her dad honked the car horn, anxious to get away, get their duty done. Get it over with, impatient to get home again two days later.

Gaelene took the short cut through the school to the dairy. Past the sandpit where she and Shona had played as best-friend five- and six-year-olds, past the monkey bars where Shona spun around faster and faster, one leg knee-clamped to the bar, the other straight out behind her, two short pigtails hoping the Olga Korbut image would make the physical impossibility a reality. She finished her scone and started to climb the wooden log stairs up to the play fort in the Standard's play area where as "big kids" they had made homes and wars and battleships, when she heard scuffling on the floor above and two voices in low, stifled moaning.

Gaelene was fourteen and though she had no experience to tell her so, she knew that the sound, so easily mistaken for pain or trouble, was not the sound of distress. Or at least not the sort of pain you were meant to complain about. Gaelene did not know what she was hearing, but she knew enough to move more quietly, to hold her own breath tight, to creep up to put her eye close to the knot in the wood that would allow her access to the source of the sound. Up close, the sap smell of untreated pine stabbing her nostrils, she watched John and Shona fucking. Fucking on the top floor of the play fort, open sky cold above them, shielded from the empty school grounds by a four-foot wall. She stood there for three or four minutes, fascinated and moved. And disturbed. Then she crept away as quietly as she had come. As quietly as John came noisily. As quietly as Shona, fourteen-year-old girl fucking the sixteen-year-old visiting cousin she had asked to enlighten her, did not come at all.

The day turned and Gaelene did not find Shona at the dairy and when they met the next day they had little to say to each other and Gaelene went home to the city, glad deep in her heart that she now lived in a place where she had no history and the by-product of this gladness was that she had even less reason to talk to Shona. And the following year when John came visiting his cousins, back from boarding school, he, unlike Gaelene, was revelling and blossoming in the uncovering of his own history and now he was Hone and now he did not have much to say to Shona either.

TWENTY-FIVE

Saz arrived at Heathrow via a crowded, tunnel-stopping tube journey in time to join Greg and Siobhan at the check-in. She managed to get a few minutes alone with them while they queued; Dan and Steve, who'd arrived far earlier, were having another "quick half" in the bar. It took little time to give them the basics of her latest information. Siobhan scoffed at the possibility of Kevin being involved, though Saz noticed that Greg seemed to take it more seriously and was relieved she had contacted the police about him. When she told them about meeting Linda, omitting the details of lager cans and the suede jacket, Siobhan seemed genuinely puzzled that her stalker should be a woman and insisted that Greg write down every one of the few physical details in his notebook. She fretted for a few minutes more, scanning the hall for tall, dark-haired women and then, seeing Steve and Dan round the corner from the bar, she went straight into dippy blonde mode. She picked up her bags, planted soft full kisses on both Saz's and Greg's mouths, sending Saz's stomach on a Ferris wheel turn and flounced up to the now free counter where she demanded a window seat, non-smoking, extra legroom upgrade from Business Class to First for herself and Greg. She got it too. Saz of course, would have to slum it back in company-paid Business with the boys.

A confirmed US-ophile, Saz had always loved the flight into

any American city—the descent into the vast country, alternately terrifyingly empty and then crammed full of people, the knowledge that she was about to step foot, not just on a land, but a whole continent. She adored New York; the pace and adrenalin of Manhattan fitted her rhythms almost as well as the tight-fitting black leather dress she'd bought in Greenwich Village last time they were there. Molly had taken her away for a little post-operative rest and relaxation following an extended period of surgery. The new method of grafts had left her considerably happier with the look and use of her legs but rather more depressed about the prospect of several more years of treatment until her doctors would consider her "well". Molly diagnosed basic depression in her girlfriend and suggested R&R in New York as the cure. The Rest she'd managed while sleeping on the plane there, the Relaxation she had collapsing on the way back, the three days in between had been pure acceleration. Ideal for London blues. Saz also loved San Francisco—the roaring, polluted Pacific, the dirty rainbow flags of the Castro, she even quite liked the pretentious coffee bars and the time-lapsed hippies still mooching their way around Haight. She'd visited Boston, Seattle, Chicago and Detroit and found something moving or charming in every city. For work she'd crisscrossed Northern California, Nevada and even ventured into parts of Idaho. At gatherings of friends and acquaintances in London, she was used to finding herself the only guest standing up for America, always the one to find some piece of real gold under the tackiness. Saz still believed in the Statue of Liberty, four trips out to the Island hadn't dented her enthusiasm for the sight of her stained copper green, though each time she was disappointed to be reminded again that Liberty isn't quite as big in real life as she looks spread across a cinema screen in glowing technicolour. To Saz, America was still a land of excitement and adventure. Until, that is, she went to LA.

In LA, Saz realized what people were talking about when they said they hated America. Only somehow what she felt was worse than hate. She didn't hate LA because she couldn't summon up enough feeling about LA to actually emote enough to hate it. She just didn't get it. She couldn't see the point. With Siobhan and Greg locked up in meetings all day, she had no choice but to sit by the pool alone or, on their free day, play with Dan and Steve in their over-large hire car as they tried to understand the plastic tinsel of the city. They were as perplexed as Saz. For people who had just lost one of their best friends (and in Dan's case, not long after losing his lover) the guys weren't too bad company. Every now and then one of them would point out a shop or restaurant that Alex might have liked—or have liked kicking shit out of—but in general they concentrated all their efforts in trying to enjoy what they could of this, their one day off in the angel city. Well-meaning people at the record offices had told them the things to do. They went to look at the Hollywood sign and there it was, shrouded in hazy smog. They followed directions and drove through Beverly Hills and up past the big fancy houses in the canyon, they went to Rodeo Drive, they looked at the Beverly Hills Hotel, but as Steve pointed out to Saz when they retrieved the car from yet another $5.00 a day vacant lot carpark, "If I'd wanted to reconfirm my view that rich people have no taste and shouldn't be allowed to spend all that money so badly, I could walk down Bishop's Avenue at home. I didn't have to come all the way here to find that out—and as for Rodeo Drive, it's so bloody short!"

Dan added that it may have been short, but he'd spotted at least three hair-implanted queens trotting up and down the street which was taken by Steve as a sign to turn the car around and get his own bald pate out of there as fast as he could.

After lunch by the hotel pool they walked down to Venice

Beach and Steve wondered aloud why anyone would choose to put Camden Market next to the Pacific Ocean, thereby spoiling both. Saz tried not to be grumpy, Dan tried to have a fun time and Steve tried not to mind that the bronzed, blonded barbie-doll people were obviously shocked by his looks. But both boys had been seriously thrown by Alex's murder and it hung at the back of every strained and sarcastic comment they made. Sitting on a bench looking out at the Pacific, Dan finally said, "I'm sorry, kids, this isn't going to work. I can't talk about Alex and I can't not talk about him and it just feels so fucking wrong to be here without him."

Steve nodded and laughed, "Yeah, he'd have been really good at ripping the shit out of this place. All this sunshine—he'd have fucking hated it. Fucking loved hating it!"

They both laughed and Saz, sitting a few feet away on the sand, turned to see the broad, bald, tough Steve lean his head onto Dan's shoulder where a clean white T-shirt awaited his tears.

By the time they arrived back at the record company offices they were very relieved to find an extremely bouncy Siobhan waiting for them. She insisted that she do the driving back to the hotel and all three were able to push away the silence that had grown between them in the sound of Siobhan's giggling excitement at everything around her—particularly the dozens of pet washes they passed—that, combined with their own terror that she was about to kill them as she kept forgetting to turn into the right lane when she took corners.

That night Cal took them to a tiny restaurant overlooking the ocean where Siobhan rejoiced in the vegetarian, fat-free delights of the Californian menu and Saz secretly rejoiced in Siobhan's laughter. Saz then shocked Cal by stating that she thought the best use for Santa Monica Boulevard was probably as a running track and that she'd use it as such at six the next morning to jog up to the hills—or as close as her lungs would take her. The dire warnings elicited by her suggestion almost put Saz off the peanut butter cheesecake she'd been planning for dessert, but she knew she needed something to cheer herself up and as the thought of the creamy goo had kept her going through the interminable music talk all night (that and the slight turn at the pit of her stomach every time Siobhan smiled at her) then she'd have to put the run on the breakfast menu as well. The dinner itself was something of a celebration anyway, in that the contracts were finally signed and the boys were all extremely relieved that Cal had even managed to persuade Siobhan to agree to his suggested replacement for Alex. The other guys had taken Cal's word that the substitute drummer was good enough until they had the time to look for someone perfect, but Siobhan, throwing another "I need privacy" trauma had raised every objection she could think of. Eventually Greg had taken her out into the office corridor where they exchanged a few very loud and several more very quiet words. And when Siobhan re-entered the room, she'd apologized to Cal and agreed to whatever he thought best. Cal had nodded his thanks to Greg and wisely accepted her apology immediately, knowing from past experience that dwelling on the subject would not only provoke a retraction of her regret, but would no doubt unleash an even greater fury. During dinner Cal didn't mention the replacement drummer until Saz was eating the last mouthful of her cheesecake and then he merely noted they'd be meeting him at a late breakfast the next day, before the car arrived to take them to their last meeting, followed by lunch and the airport later that afternoon. Then he hurriedly paid the bill and gave kisses all round so speedily that even Siobhan didn't have time to think of an objection.

Back at the hotel by eleven, Siobhan, a little tired and a

lot emotional, made Greg take her to bed. Saz quietly nursed her sexual tension in the bar with Dan. Steve had evidently befriended one of the other hotel residents because after a quick word with Dan he ordered a bottle of champagne in his room and said goodnight. Dan explained that his cheery handshake indicated yet another waiting shag and was not surprised to see the back of a tall, blonde woman rise from the other side of the bar and follow Steve at a not particularly discreet ten paces. Saz stayed another hour drinking lite beers and listening to Dan's stories of Alex's legendary bad temper. Dan went to bed at midnight, and Saz, before she went to sleep twenty minutes later, put in a sleepy, guilty answerphone message to Molly.

Saz woke bolt upright two hours later and lay in the semi-darkness, trying to work out what the motorized noise was that had woken her. She unlocked and opened the patio doors of her room and realized that the sound was coming from the outdoor jacuzzi just around the corner. Knowing that she would never get back to sleep with the irritation of the constant hum, she pulled on her costume and headed out for a moonlit swim herself. She dived in and swam a quick underwater length, coming up at the deep end, closest to the jacuzzi. From the small bubbling pool hidden by a variety of ferns and blossoming trees, she could hear voices, a man and a woman. Saz stood in the water quietly listening, slowly realizing that not only could she hear the sounds of a couple making love, but also that the man of the couple sounded distinctly like Steve. Embarrassed, she was about to turn and swim back to the other end of the pool when she clearly heard him call out "No" over the bubbling hum. She pulled herself out of the pool, started to head towards the jacuzzi and then stopped short. They were fucking. In the water. And Steve had just called out "No", which had to be open to some interpretation given the circumstances, and she was about to run in on them. Remembering her job and throwing caution to the warm Californian wind, she charged around the corner of thick foliage to see Steve, partly lit by the orange sky night, his arms outstretched along the sides of the jacuzzi, his face contorted in a mask of pleasure, a blonde head bobbing just underwater, a blow job clearly in action. Steve looked at Saz, Saz looked at Steve, she muttered "Whoops. Sorry" and slunk off back to her room. As she dried herself and got back into bed, Saz hoped she hadn't entirely ruined Steve's evening. Or the blonde's.

Six o'clock the next morning found Saz greeting the hotel desk clerk and heading out hopefully to discover that maybe LA wasn't only the Baywatch version she'd seen the day before. She wasn't disappointed to find, as she did in London, that the best time in any big city is first thing in the morning, when the sun is almost up and the air is about as clear as it gets. The breeze was kind and cool, the light behind the hills showed that the sun was starting to think about rising and the sky was not only a soft and unsullied shade of aquamarine, but there were even a few twinkling stars to add to the picture. Saz ran the whole distance up to Sunset, the golden sheet of the Pacific narrowing to a thin silver sliver behind her and, with the sun now fully risen, she found herself breathlessly thinking that the Pacific was a truly fantastic thing and any city so close to such a fine ocean couldn't be all bad. The thought lasted a good ten minutes, but then the no-bus ride back to the hotel changed her mood. She'd walked a good three miles before one finally appeared to carry her back to the Pacific horizon.

She eventually got to the hotel at around eight-thirty, surprised to find Siobhan up and waiting for her in the foyer.

Steve was missing, he hadn't arrived for breakfast and one of the hotel staff thought she might have seen him heading for the beach at about four that morning.

TWENTY-SIX

Drowning, they say, begins with extreme pain. The lungs hold what remains of the air as long as they can, the heart smashes itself against the chest wall, hammering at the ribs as it tries to pump oxygen through to the choking brain, the blood vessels, too, constrict, squeezing out the last remaining drops of life force. And then the will gives in. There is an involuntary rush as the mouth opens, the diaphragm swings back into place and the lungs flood with water. For a tiny moment it is all torment, choking, fighting and then the pain is gone. There is not enough oxygen for the brain to continue its chemical electric work, the mind becomes spacey, stoned. There is a whole minute, maybe even longer, of intoxicated ease and then the body slips down under the blue and the green. It sinks away.

At least, I believe that's what happens when the drowning is accidental. I don't know if Steve had any moments of peace. It didn't look like it from where I was dog paddling. It's true Steve is big, was big. Not so terribly tall, though very strong, well built. But the single most beneficial power of water, from my point of view, is that it removes the effect of gravitational pull. Water changes the dimensions of strength and weakness, repositions the impotent, making the clear arc of a single freestyle stroke a force to be reckoned with. If, like me, you are at home in water, if you can hold your breath for moments or minutes, if you couldn't care less whether the sand bar is ten inches or ten feet below your toes, then you are the master in the water. If you also savour crashing waves, feed on surf, if you are weary of passionless smooth shores, if for you the only real sea is the Pacific, well, then, you're practically Poseidon and to be caught in the surf is to see that all around you Aphrodite is rising from the sea-strewn sperm of Zeus.

A little florid I know, but this one felt so much more epic. And rather more elegant than a softball bat.

Los Angeles is a tedious city at the best of times, but in terms of killing it is deadly dull. It sits there in a blocked basin of its own heat, stirring its tepid, stagnant self only to sip the scum as it rises. Shootings and muggings, detached urban crimes, there is no passion in the murders of that city, no joy. No commitment to the killing. And yet it has a coastline full of terrors, dark crevices of hills and mountains within touching range, so why do they always resort to their antiseptic guns? Their distant murders? Los Angelenos prefer their deaths to be a drive-in McDonalds, slaughter untouched by American hands. But I don't.

Steve wasn't quite as easy as Alex. He doesn't like to drink too much, though he does it anyway. I had to bide my time, wait until the grief got him. I knew it would eventually. The grief gets us all eventually.

I'd watched him all day. An accomplished parader of man flesh himself, he fitted snugly between the over-built and the under-made on Venice Beach. Few people swim in that misnamed section of the ocean, but he did briefly. Very late at night, a sobering stroll from the hotel, with a near full moon yellow behind the smog and a quiet, almost empty beach. I knew he would. I waited for him. I knew that once alone he would be drawn to those waves. I'd seen him watching them in the daylight, watched his grief from a distance. I knew that later, no joy in the flesh, he would attempt to find comfort in the sea. I walked a safe distance behind him in the shadows, knowing that soon he would want to slip off his T-shirt, and that he'd find a better reason than mere vanity to ripple those muscles under the waves. He removed the outer layer and strode purposefully into the surf.

Once actually in the water his bravado slipped away, quietly. It is dark in the ocean. Secluded and dark and private. A unique selling point. The hotel is rightly proud of its elemental access. He swam around a little, the cold of the water no doubt educating him as to just how drunk he was. An unaccustomed drinker of spirits, he probably didn't realize what five Southern Comforts can do to a big, sad man. His fear crept up on him as the tide did. As I did. He didn't notice how worried he was until he heard the tiny rippling splash. He'd been able to hold on to his myth of strength until I passed him with my slicing strokes and fast kick, my head as happy underwater as above. My breathing regulated and attuned to the swell of each new-built wave. The deep holds no fear for me. When I caught his legs and pulled him out and down he was disoriented immediately. By the time he came back up coughing and spluttering I was three feet away, turned in concern and went to him fast, held him in the life saver's position, the one they taught us at school, my arm crooked around his neck. I told him not to worry, he'd be safe. I soothed him. Whispering soft in his ear and the mother water close against his skin, he relaxed in my grip, closed his eyes and I began choking him with my elbow. Then the surf was there to do it for me, water that I floated over and through while he turned and twisted in it. Like a single sock in a violent washing machine. His colours weren't fast and his screams came quiet, muted from under water and blown away on a warm night wind. I looked and the moon gave me light but I didn't see any moment of peace on his face. He sank.

I waited for five, ten minutes. Long enough to be certain, then I swam a long way up the beach, far past the Santa Monica pier, where the signs warn of pollution and dirt.

As if there were single locations in the city that could be pinpointed, circled and declared, just this piece here, this is the unsavoury part. You must beware of this particular area. As if everywhere else was clean.

I didn't need to wash myself this time. This was a much cleaner death. I retrieved my towel from where I had left my things, neatly bundled into a dark corner. I suppose I should have been scared—muggers, thieves. Murderers. The night was too gentle for fear though. I dried myself and slipped into cool, clean clothes. I walked out on to the road and in an easy distance I slipped into an all-night cafe, smiled at the waitress. She was about to finish her shift. I asked her if she wanted to join me in a drink, to celebrate the fact that the sun would be with us again in an hour or so. She had other plans though, a bath and bed. I sat alone, relaxed against the cane of a bar chair and toasted myself— Two down, two to go."

Pretty soon it would just be her and me.

I finished my beer and walked back to my little room; I was humming "Hotel California". I hadn't thought of the Eagles in a very long time.

TWENTY-SEVEN

And then it was police and coast guards and police interviews and more interviews and fielding requests from offices they didn't even know the record company had, from the hotel, from the airline. Saz told the police what she could about the blonde. Nothing other than that she was blonde. And even that information was dismissed as the hotel receptionist remembered the tall woman leaving the hotel foyer just after three in the morning, her hair still wet. There was Cal raging and simultaneously hugely efficient and Dan crushed and crying and Greg placating and the record company solicitously teetering on the edge of throwing the whole thing in and then police again and the coast guard again and calls to and from England, to and from Peta, and the poor replacement drummer left waiting alone in the foyer for hours before anyone remembered him, remembered to politely tell him he wouldn't be needed just now and, in the middle of the tempest, Siobhan sat still. She was quiet and sincere. She was makeup free and perfectly tear-stained. She spoke in a small gentle voice, answering the hundreds of repeated questions politely and patiently in measured tones. She behaved impeccably and dealt with each moment as it came, pre-empting no one and keeping up with the pace of everything and everyone around her. Surrounded by a choking sea of chaos, she was one tiny piece of perfect calm. And her hands were so tightly clenched in her smooth linen lap that her French manicured nails dug a row of bloody stigmata into her palms.

At seven o'clock that evening, their New Zealand flight having left hours earlier, Steve's body was spotted ten miles down the coast, pulled from the weed and frothy sewage that lined the shallows. At midnight Cal made a formal identification. At ten the next morning the police examiner got through four gunshot deaths, two recreational drug overdoses and one barbiturate suicide, had a quick look at the fluid in Steve's lungs and scribbled drowning as the cause of death. She'd had a long night. Two days later the body was released and the record company flew Steve's parents and brother out for a tiny, very private funeral. He was cremated in West Hollywood and flown back to London, a puny ash pile, perfectly reduced to hand luggage proportions. Everything was quietly and efficiently and expensively taken care of, almost before the press had a chance to point out that someone was missing.

Two hours after Steve's ashes left LA International Airport, Cal issued a brief press statement stating that Steve had drowned in the Pacific Ocean. He took great care to emphasize that, while Steve had been very upset about Alex's death two weeks earlier, as indeed were all members of the band, there was absolutely no suggestion of suicide. The drowning was a terribly unfortunate accident—an accident confirmed by both the LAPD and the Coast Guard. Confirmed only in that they didn't bother to propose any other suggestion; there was no way for the officials to know for certain whether or not Steve had meant to drown. It was just another wet death for them. The authorities didn't much care whether Steve had floated away accidentally or intentionally but it hurt no one for them to write "accidental" on the form and certainly made the paperwork a damn sight easier. Cal added to his press release that Steve had been in good spirits—all things considered—and very much looking forward to the band's short holiday in New Zealand. His death was a tragic and devastating accident. There was a coda to the statement which asserted in no uncertain terms that any mention, covert or otherwise, of suicide in press coverage would result in immediate and very expensive legal action. If "accidental" was good enough for the weight of the American judiciary, then it was certainly good enough for Beneath The Blonde—and therefore for the tabloid-buying British public. By and large, the press accepted Cal's statement, Steve had been found to have a high blood alcohol level and he had chosen to go swimming in the middle of the night. The right-wing press took it as yet another opportunity to lecture on the loose morals and life-wasting antics of a new generation of "foolish and arrogant youth" and the left-wing papers found another way to blame the long years of Tory government for the dissolute deaths of the young. There was no reporting of funeral and wake as with Alex's murder, there was no big celebrity party to photograph. This time Cal presented the band with a funereal image of quiet composure and restrained suffering. What press coverage there was centred on Siobhan's elegant grief and, after a day or so of dignified silence, Cal's hopes for the future of the band.

Only *Loaded* chose to point out that to lose one band member could be considered an accident, but to lose two looked like carelessness. Saz, feeling particularly negligent, couldn't help but agree.

TWENTY-EIGHT

The girls had remained friends until they were just thirteen. Best friends, through Shona's first period started early and painfully at eleven. Proud of her new status as woman, she explained all that needed explaining to Gaelene, who knew little enough about her own body to be terrified and disgusted by what was to happen to it and had her innate horror confirmed when Shona scratched a picture of a sanitary napkin and belt into the top of her desk with Gaelene's compass. They stayed best friends even though John deserted their threesome somewhere around eight or nine, acting as if he hardly knew them when they went to Ruby's in the holidays and could barely wait to get home when it was his turn to spend a week at Shona's house. John's desertion hurt Gaelene more than it hurt his blood cousin. In a way, though she resented the change, Shona was now glad of the chance to have her best friend all to herself, but for Gaelene the growing separation between boys and girls was a gulf she didn't want to acknowledge and one which John made sure to rub in every morning when they were at the beach and he set off early to go fishing with his uncles, leaving the girls behind to peel and chop potatoes for the chips that would go with the fresh snapper Ruby would cook them all for breakfast.

Back at school after the holidays, the year before they went reluctantly into double figures, Gaelene took the only route she could find around the enforced separation of the sexes. She became a leader of the girls, as tough as any of the boys, heading the little groups of girls who would meet at morning break to play four square or marbles. And when one of the boys would steal their four square ball, the other girls would not fight him themselves but come running for Gaelene. She would chase the boy, catch him and, often as not, give him a good hiding before taking the ball back. The second time she gave a boy a black eye, Mr Stephens the headmaster came into the playground himself and, in front of the whole school of almost two hundred children, Gaelene was given the strap. If Mr Stephens had thought that the punishment—and what he assumed would be humiliation—would deter Gaelene from her violent activities, then he had reckoned without the heroine factor. To see Gaelene given a punishment reserved for boys, to see her hold out her hand and not flinch as the strap came down, its leather twice as thick as that of her dusty red roman sandals, was to watch a little girl become a star. The girls thought she was brave beyond belief and even the boys had to admire her courage. That night, walking home from school, Gaelene was surrounded by other little girls all offering her glow hearts and pineapple chunks and bites of their peanut slabs. Not pretty like other little girls, not startlingly clever like her best friend Shona, Gaelene was, for the first time, basking in her own glory—and loving every minute of it. In fact, the only person who didn't like it so much was Shona. Other people wanted to play with Gaelene now, and Shona wanted her all to herself.

Their friendship continued through Intermediate, through Spelling Levels one to seven, it continued through Gaelene's father's promotion and their subsequent acquisition of a colour TV, it even survived Shona's new dad and the sickness of the new baby and Shona having to stay with Gaelene's family for two months, sleeping on the floor of Gaelene's bedroom. It went from Janet and John books to a shared library of Trixie Beldens. But, like so many other friendships—adult or child—it couldn't withstand geographical relocation. And when Gaelene's father's promotion meant a move to Auckland, Shona waved goodbye to her best friend, not knowing that they could never be best friends again.

Shona visited Gaelene in Auckland, they went out to Devonport on the ferry, admired the reaching span of the harbour bridge, went to the zoo and walked down Queen Street, Gaelene proudly showing off her new home. But the city was too big for Shona, the cars too fast and shiny, the people too many and the next time Gaelene invited her up, Shona said she was too busy to come. She had a place in the marching team now and needed to practice.

Gaelene went to Ruby's for the next two summers, told all the kids about how they'd finally got that big house she'd wanted. Everyone was enthralled by her stories about the Farmers' Christmas parade and her new big school, everyone except Shona, who told her she was skiting and should just shut up about boring bloody Auckland. After that Gaelene didn't really bother any more, she wrote to Shona a couple of times but Shona didn't reply and before the next summer came round, Gaelene had found a new best friend and her unanswered letters to Shona became unwritten.

Gaelene eventually forgot about Shona, or if she did remember her, it was only in passing. As an adult, Gaelene preferred not to think much about her childhood at all; as far as she was concerned, she had been a completely different person then. But Shona never forgot Gaelene. She always remembered Gaelene's birthday, just two days after her own. And she always remembered how hurt she felt when Gaelene had left to go to Auckland. How she felt

deserted. Gaelene had been her only real playmate, the only
one she could really talk to. Even when there were other
kids around, it had always really been just the two of them,
ever since Gaelene had first started kindy. Just the two.
Shona blamed Gaelene for leaving her. Blamed her for
wanting to move away, for being excited about Auckland,
pleased about the new house, happy to be living a new life.
Shona blamed her and eventually, damned her.

Gaelene had no idea she'd left such pain behind her. No
idea at all.

TWENTY-NINE

The late eighties' coffee wave trickled down the West Coast of America from Seattle to San Francisco where it gathered a Pacific momentum, rolling in a great percolating swell across the ocean to New Zealand, smashing against the harbour bridge in Auckland and splattering itself in small cappuccino-coloured pools the length of the two narrow islands, leaving sticky puddles and stains all the way down to Queenstown and beyond. Saz had sampled the pleasurably pretentious delights of groovy "speciality" coffee shops in several cities in the States and in the few places that were starting to infiltrate the filter coffee hell of central London, but she had hardly expected to spend her first morning in Auckland accosted by menu after menu detailing in a variety of coloured chalk fonts, the allure of thin latte and double latte and moccachino and triple mach and double espresso freeze and pale black regular with choc sprinkle. Her second postcard of the morning to Molly catalogued the charms of excess caffeine intake and how very much their London sanctuaries could do with such improvements. She also sent a guilt-laden double dose of her love.

The afternoon before in LA, Saz had tentatively suggested to Siobhan that perhaps it would be more sensible if they all just went back to London, maybe they should even give the police at home the description of the flower sender and see what connections they could come up with, but Siobhan would have none of it. Tired of restraining herself for the press and the cameras, terrified to believe that Steve's drowning was more than it seemed (while simultaneously incapable of accepting it as just an accident), she was still not willing to give up any of her travel arrangements. Saz turned to Greg for some support, to try to get him to convince Siobhan of a more sensible course of action, but Greg had retreated into a safe musical world with Dan, churning out new songs and rehashing old ones, anything to keep their minds off what was really going on. With her lover hiding in the safety of his music (to Cal's delighted relief), this long-planned trip was all Siobhan had and she was determined to hold on to it. To the trip and, as her access to sanity, to Saz. Nine years of becoming The Blonde, concentrating on her work, locked in the silk worm cocoon of her four men and all the attendant band paraphernalia, meant that Siobhan had pretty much rid herself of any of the female friends she'd ever had. As far as Siobhan was concerned, if everything else was falling apart and if her demands on Saz's time meant that Saz wasn't able to get on with her first unofficial function, she was at least very well placed to contribute to the second—being Siobhan's girl-friend. Girl friend.

A few hours after the funeral, they were back at the LA airport, bags repacked, tickets reissued just ten minutes before check-in closed. Siobhan then presented Saz and the remaining members of Beneath The Blonde with their itinerary. Arrive in Auckland Wednesday midday, stay there until Friday morning, catch the early flight to Queenstown for one night so Siobhan, Dan and Saz could see the mountains Greg kept bragging about. Fly back to Rotorua late on Saturday afternoon, pick up a hire car, drive to Greg's aunt and uncle where they would spend three whole days in one place before returning to Auckland and their direct flight back to London exactly a week after they had arrived. Greg looked aghast at the hand-scribbled sheet of paper, "You can't possibly be serious. This is stupid, babe, we're exhausted. There's no way we can do all this. Even if any of us had slept at all in the past two days, this would be mad—we can't possibly hope to cover all this ground, you don't know what the roads are like in New Zealand."

Siobhan ignored him, "Darling, they're roads, aren't they? You're the one who's always telling me the old homeland is so very modern."

"New Zealand is, the geography's not. It's all mountains and lakes and winding roads two lanes wide—it's hardly the same as a straight bloody motorway run from London up to Birmingham."

Siobhan ignored him and handed the sheets of paper out to the others. "Fine. At least if you're concentrating on the bumps and curves, you won't get bored driving. Anyway, you haven't lived in New Zealand for years, they must have made some improvement in all that time?"

"That's not the point. You just don't realize what you're suggesting we do. This whole thing is ludicrous."

"Maybe, but we've done plenty of ludicrous things in the past and I don't intend to stop now."

She countered Greg's other claims by pointing out that if he and Dan were going to continue shutting the world out and being "creative", then at least she and Saz should be allowed to do some fun things. And when Greg said he didn't feel much like having fun, nor did he really care whether or not they went to his aunt and uncle's place, Siobhan finally rounded on him. "No. But I do. I want to meet your family, Greg. You know I do. I want to know where you come from. That's the whole point of going all that way. For you and me. Remember?"

Siobhan was gripping Greg's hand, pinching his knuckles with her manicured fingers and spitting her love into his face. Saz, listening to the half-whispered, half-shouted interchange and watching the minutes tick away while the airline's ground staff tried to hurry them on, could see the determination in Siobhan, hear it in her voice. As could half the airport terminal. She didn't quite know exactly what Siobhan was after but she did understand that at least part of it was to help her recreate her relationship with Greg. The two of them were completely tied up in Beneath The Blonde; their relationship was at the centre of it. Siobhan obviously felt that not only had the events of the past month taken the strength of the band from her, but they were also starting to take Greg away too. And Siobhan would lose everything before she lost him. Greg glared back at her for a moment and then cracked his angry face into a smile. He pulled her away from the group that surrounded them and their pile of bags and reached his arms tight around her body, squashing her breasts to his chest and his groin into hers. And then the two of them kissed for longer than most LA airport attendees had seen since the last time the dingy building was portrayed as a place of glamour in a 1970s jetset movie. Saz allowed herself to feel the full vent of jealousy twisting her stomach. She promised to beat herself up later and, sitting back down in the red plastic airport chair, forced herself to swallow the gritty dregs of her watery coffee, muttering quietly into her empty cup, "Serves you right, you silly bitch, we don't fall in lust with straight girls, remember?"

So Saz had come to New Zealand with no idea of what she was going to—*The Piano* and an Australian-centred view of what the Antipodes might hold had not prepared her for streets of cafés, groovy clothes shops and beautiful ceramics. To be fair, it was only four or five streets, but it was four or five more than she'd expected. What's more, it was lit with stark white southern hemisphere sunlight and dotted about with the Victorian villas of central Auckland, all packaged up in balmy late spring weather. Delightful for the day and a half of jetlag recuperation Siobhan had allowed them. And that only under duress.

Saz did what she could in the four spare hours allotted her. With seven phone cards, a copy of the Yellow Pages and a flimsy city map in hand, she called twenty-six florists, just in case. Telling them she was a researcher from the BBC, looking into flower-buying habits across the world, she asked each bemused shopkeeper to please make a note if anyone should possibly come in asking for yellow roses at any point in the next week. She gave them the number of the hotel in Queenstown and Greg's aunt's phone number on the coast. By the time she'd called the eleventh in the centre of town and worked her way around four others in the North Shore suburbs, she had her speech so well worked out that no one got a chance to tell her what the first six mentioned straight away: "Did you know that yellow roses stand for hopeless love, dear? Not a very good choice, really."

She quickly slipped in that the programme was about the lack of true love in modern Britain. The New Zealanders didn't seem to have any problem believing her.

Before dinner that night she called Carrie to check for any news from London.

"Well, on the Kevin front, Helen called to say I should tell you that they've got nothing on him."

"Are they going to keep trying?"

"Unlikely. They don't think it's him, doll. The guy can barely afford plastic flowers, let alone bunches of roses."

"Yeah. I suppose so. What else? Any developments on the flower woman?"

"Nope. But Linda sends her love."

"She does?"

"She called yesterday. Said your jacket got drenched in the downpour after we left them. Mentioned that the dye seemed to run rather a lot too."

"I hope it ruined his jeans. What about Ben?"

"Nothing, sorry. But if they're supposed to be calling me on this phone, won't the batteries on it be dying soon?"

"No, Carrie. Not if you're only using it for incoming calls like I told you."

"Oh dear."

Saz sighed, "Jesus, kid, you can't ever do what you're told, can you? Give Moll a call and ask her to drop the battery recharger off to you. Tell her I lent it to you because your phone's been cut off. She shouldn't have any problem believing that."

"Why can't I just tell her the truth?"

"Because she already thinks you take far too much advantage of me and my innate generosity as it is."

"And there was me thinking it was just ex-lover sexual jealousy that made her that little bit off with me."

"It is, but it's the other too. She can't help it, she loves me. So is that all?"

"I think so. Oh yeah, there is one other thing, Linda mentioned the flower woman has an accent."

Saz froze, "What sort of an accent?"

"Australian she thinks. Isn't that a coincidence? I told her that's where you are now."

"Carrie, I'm in New Zealand."

"Yeah, sure, same difference. So I suppose if this woman's an Australian, then maybe . . ."

Saz interrupted her, "Which is it?"

Carrie paused, not at all sure what she was being asked, "I realize the time difference is a big one, but you did wake me. Which is what? What are you on about?"

"This might surprise you, but there is a difference between New Zealand and Australia; they aren't the same country at all . . ."

"Darling, we can't all be brilliant globe-trotters like you."

Saz tried unsuccessfully to hide her frustration, "Listen

to me, will you? If the woman's a New Zealander then maybe she's here. Maybe she knows Greg. So what exactly did Linda say about her accent?"

"Just that it was kind of Australian. So . . . I don't know, maybe you're right. I imagine 'kind of Australian' might also mean New Zealand."

"But you didn't ask her."

"It didn't occur to me."

Saz screamed down the telephone, "Brilliant, Carrie. That's just fucking brilliant. Perhaps you might go and check today? If it's not too much trouble? I mean, why didn't she tell us sooner? Why didn't you tell me sooner? What the hell's wrong with you people?"

Saz yelled a little more, then slammed down the phone and stalked off to the hotel gym to work off some of her fury. Two hours later Carrie called back to say she'd gone straight into town and Linda had confirmed that, as far as she was concerned, Australian and New Zealand accents were exactly the same, so it might well be that the woman was a New Zealander. A little calmer from her workout and long hot shower, Saz grudgingly apologized to Carrie and then hurried off to meet the others for dinner, rehearsing in the lift mirror the best way of breaking her new concerns to her employers.

Saz wasn't able to get a moment with Greg and Siobhan where she could tell them the news without involving Dan in the conversation and had to force herself to wait throughout the meal during which Siobhan, whose scant regard for the etiquette of traditional table manners had her eating sautéed potatoes and courgette strips with her fingers, animatedly told them all about the great dream she'd had while taking an afternoon nap. It had been a sense-and-sex dream featuring the steward from the plane, Brad Pitt, a tiger cub and an empty yellow and blue painted building.

Even as she enjoyed the bright and brittle entertainment,

Saz quickly saw that Siobhan would no doubt flip from charm straight into fury if she told her the news tonight, so she jostled her off to bed as soon as she could. Siobhan readily went to her room and, once Dan had also done so, Saz managed a quick exchange in the hallway with Greg to tell him about the woman.

"She's a New Zealander?"

"Or Australian."

"Your friend couldn't tell?"

"No."

"Typical. British cultural racism at its best."

"Sorry. But at least we now know the woman sending the flowers in London is Antipodean."

"But we don't know if she's from New Zealand or Australia. Nor do we know that the woman you saw with Steve in LA was the same person as the flower woman in England."

"No, we don't. Unfortunately we don't know anything for definite. But I just wanted to fill you in."

"To let me know what you don't know?"

"Yeah. Well . . ."

Greg shrugged, "I guess knowing what we don't know is something more than we've had so far."

Saz agreed and added, "I really do think we all need to be a whole lot more careful from now on. If she is a New Zealander, she's going to be a lot less obvious than we are. And we ought to let Dan know what's been going on. I don't think it's fair to keep all this from him any longer."

Having reached agreement from Greg on that front, with a promise that he would tell Dan all in the morning, she then tackled him on the next issue, "And maybe you could do something to persuade Siobhan to talk to the police here?"

Saz noticed that Greg physically inched away from her, his face clouding over, "Well, I don't know . . ."

"But this woman could be here. Now."

"Yes, but as you said, we don't know anything for certain."

"Fine. Then tell them that. At least we'd have more people looking out for Siobhan. I mean, it's ludicrous after everything that's happened, with Alex and Steve, that she still won't let the police know about the threats."

Greg frowned and bit his thumbnail, "Look, Saz, you and I need to talk a bit about this. I think . . ."

Siobhan then appeared at her bedroom door wearing only a pair of Greg's boxer shorts. She put an arm around Greg's shoulders and pulled him away, slurring her speech in Saz's direction. "Whatever it is, sweetheart, he can tell you all about it in the morning. I want him all to myself right now. G'night!"

She blew Saz a giggling giddy kiss and Saz went to bed alone and frustrated. In more ways than one.

THIRTY

To Saz, brought up in the rolling suburbs of urban Kent and transplanted for the past fifteen years to London where Hampstead High Street was thought steep enough to be a luge run, Queenstown was dauntingly beautiful. Siobhan looked at the view of the lake, the sun splashing itself across the water and whispered in awe to Greg, "You're right. This place is amazing. It's a bloody good thing Alex is dead—he'd have hated it."

Peta had booked them into a B&B for the night—the luxuriousness of "Queenstown House" rather negated the title "B&B" in Siobhan's eyes. Though they were now almost inured to posh hotels, the term B&B still recalled the unchanging imprint of five years stopping at orange and brown carpeted versions of cigarette-stale rooms the length and breadth of band-touring Britain. They weren't exactly used to a landlady who offered them cocktail hour glasses of sauvignon blanc. Nor were they used to sleeping in rooms lit by lake view windows with fat feather pillows. Had they not been reeling from the messy deaths of Steve and the more cynical Alex, who would indeed have loathed spending two days in anywhere quite so perfectly the personification of Antipodean tourism, the three remaining members of Beneath The Blonde would have had a blissful time. Dan, however, was still in shock from the information Greg had given him on their flight south that morning. He was, quite naturally, worried for himself, feeling as he said "like some ignorant guest at an Agatha Christie hotel, just waiting to be bumped off". But while worry was one of the emotions he was feeling, his overriding response was fury at Greg and Siobhan for having kept him in the dark about what had been going on. As he said to Saz, "I'd never have agreed to come all the bloody way out here if I thought any of this was going on. This was supposed to be a holiday, a rest before we get into the really big stuff. Prancing about at the bottom of the world while some maniac makes up their mind about when's the best time to do me in isn't exactly my idea of a rest-cure. I feel safer at home than I do in this tourist trap."

While Saz tried to reassure Dan that she didn't think it was quite that bad, she could hear the uncertainty in her own voice and knew she hadn't done much to calm his fears when he announced he intended to spend the rest of the afternoon locked in his hotel room and that he thought he'd just like to fly home the next day if possible.

Saz found herself wishing she too could just throw a tantrum and retire to daytime TV and the view, but Siobhan was having none of it. She had convinced herself that even if the stalker were a New Zealand woman—and she forcefully pointed out that neither Greg nor Saz knew this for certain—they'd only been in the country for forty-eight hours and without prior knowledge of their schedule no one could catch up with them quite so quickly. Saz's comment that, as Peta had confirmed all their flights and arrangements on the Internet, their plans were open to anyone who knew how to look, was brushed aside as Siobhan flounced upstairs to demand that Dan accompany them on a quick sightseeing trip before dinner. The four of them then went out for a wander around the small town, an incongruous group to be tour bus partying. Dan was strained and silent, Greg alert and holding tightly on to Siobhan and Saz still angry with Siobhan for yet again refusing point blank either to speak to the police or even discuss the matter. Only Siobhan was having a good time, her incessant chatter and bright manner belying any worries at all. Saz thought she was behaving like a small child on Christmas Eve, rushing headlong through one day to get to the big event the next. What she wasn't clear on was what on earth Siobhan had found to be so happy about.

After early evening drinks at the hotel, Siobhan insisted they spend the evening at the Tex-Mex restaurant they'd passed in their afternoon walk. Though Greg had been hanging out for Chinese food, they were all pleasantly surprised by the vast portions and the speed and sexy charm of their waiter who took it into his head to flirt outrageously with first Saz, then Siobhan. And then, much to Greg's chagrin at being missed out, he spent the rest of the night proffering larger and larger portions to Dan—which at least cheered Dan up a little and brought a semblance of a smile to his face. Saz stayed sober throughout the meal. Unable to relax at all, she'd positioned her chair flat against the wall from where she could easily view both the main entrance and the kitchen door and she spent the whole meal scanning the room for tall women with very dark or dyed black hair. Half way through the first course she remembered Steve's woman in LA and her own experiences with peroxide and extended her gaze to include any woman in the room over five-foot six. There were only three, sitting at a large and raucous table together with a selection of lads. All of them were American, all drunk and all very loud. Saz kept an eye on them anyway.

Dinner finished and three jugs of margaritas down, Siobhan lurched from her seat to join the regular Wednesday night band. After a quiet, slurred word with the lead singer she took the mic. Despite three moderately successful singles in New Zealand, Beneath The Blonde weren't exactly megastars in his home country, Greg having refused point blank all the record company's attempts to make any publicity mileage out of his being born there, but Siobhan's voice was known. Known and noted. And while nobody really cared or noticed as the tall, lean woman slightly stumbled her way up to the raised corner where the musicians were standing, they immediately sat up and took notice when, after three introductory bars, Siobhan's voice rang out loud and untamed, clear over the now silent heads of the stunned diners.

Even without the wig and the clothes and the makeup and despite the hollow dark rings under her eyes from combined nerves and jet lag, Siobhan could make the whole room shut up and pay attention with just a single held note, breath catching and voice cracking as she let each moment fall from her mouth. Which is what she did for four more Beneath The Blonde songs. Then, after a heart rending version of "Diamonds and Rust", she left the band to return to their set and came clattering back to their table to fall into Greg's arms, hiding her face in his neck as the applause of sixty knives and forks on plates rang out into the street.

Dan finished his drink and whispered pointedly to Saz, "Please note, our little songbird's physicality isn't quite the classic pose of the reluctant star." And he indicated the clenched fist Siobhan was punching into Greg's upper chest as being just the start of a pay back, since Greg had earlier bet Siobhan she wouldn't have the nerve to sing tonight, the bet taking place just at the moment the plane took off from Auckland airport.

When Siobhan looked up and mouthed a sweaty and grinning "Yes!" across the table to Dan, Saz noted with disgust the stirring in her own stomach. She hoped it might have something to do with the char-grilled tuna steak and extra hot chilli sauce, but was rather more certain that the cause was now sitting opposite her, face flushed and beaming, chest panting and voice hoarse from doing what she did best. And who was now doing what she did second best. Kissing the man she loved.

Saz managed to ignore her own inopportune lusts and listened to Dan while she waded her way through the small mountain of chocolate and coffee cream that was pudding. Relaxed from the alcohol and food, he shifted his attention from his immediate worries to those waiting for him back home. He told her about his break-up with Jeremy—and proved just how very much still in love he was with a bloke Saz could have told him to write off in about ten seconds. Jeremy was not out, not planning ever to come out and wanting Dan to pretend to be flatmates to his parents. All that and an inability to cope with Dan's success in the band and complaining whenever they went away on tour—though not when Jeremy could come too. Funnily enough, Jeremy didn't have a job of his own either. Or a flat, or a car. Though he was making good use of Dan's while Dan was away.

Half hearing the story, Siobhan, two more margaritas down and even less tactful than usual, turned from her whispered conversation with Greg to butt in with, "Dan, you're being so damn stupid. You're too bloody nice for your own good. What are you doing letting that little creep stay at your place? He's obviously a user and a liar and a coward."

Dan had to agree, but when Siobhan had turned her attention back to biting the loose skin around Greg's little fingernail, Dan leaned his head to Saz and whispered, "She can talk. We all know what's best doesn't mean we're going to do it. I know Jeremy's a bastard. A beautiful, charming, blue-eyed bastard. But I still love him. What does she expect me to do?" Saz shrugged, listening to him, but her eyes still travelled around the rest of the room.

Dan continued, "It's like all the crap with this stalker. Everyone knows Siobhan's wrong, we all want to tell the police, but, as usual, she's the one with the power and she's the one who's vetoed the sensible solution. It's all very well to say do the right thing, when you have no intention of doing it yourself."

Saz had no answer for him, nor did she much want to answer his questions about her own relationship with Molly. Dividing her attention between observing the room and watching Siobhan laugh with Greg, she would far rather torment herself with a perversely enjoyable guilty tension for Siobhan than answer questions about how she and Molly met. But she played with her dessert and gave Dan all the right answers. She professed her passion and love for Molly, all the while trying to ignore the little voice in the back of her head asking, three years on and routine setting in, if any of all that wonderfulness would prove to be enough to get her past this teenage infatuation with Siobhan. At the end of the evening, Dan managed a prolonged and probing goodbye with the waiter, then the four of them stumbled into a cab and up the steep hill to their beds. Saz was adamant that Siobhan should not walk the short and badly-lit distance. She was teetering on the verge of picking up the phone and calling Molly to tell her everything and was therefore surprisingly grateful to see that while they were at dinner a huge bunch of yellow roses had been delivered for Siobhan. At least it sobered her up enough to realize there was no point in disturbing Molly just to tell her every-thing about nothing.

When Siobhan walked into her room five minutes later Saz was just wondering what to do with the flowers. In too much of a hurry to get the roses into her room and away from Siobhan, she hadn't yet got around to barring her door. Siobhan stood, staring at her, mouth a little open, in surprise or inebriation, Saz wasn't sure which.

"How lovely. For me?"

"Ah—yeah. They were outside your room when I came upstairs. I grabbed them while you and Greg were making coffee. I was going to throw them out."

"Without telling me?"

"Maybe. I'm not sure, I hadn't really thought about it yet, I just didn't think you'd want to see them tonight, after having such a good time at the restaurant and everything."

Siobhan's head dropped and her hands started shaking, "Fuck it. Fuck it. We're not even ok here."

Saz shrugged, "Yeah, look, it seems churlish to say I told you so . . ."

"But?"

"Well . . . I did."

Saz put the flowers down and put her arm around Siobhan, sitting her down on the bed. Knowing that the last thing they needed at one in the morning was another tantrum, she decided that lying was likely to do the least harm and chose to reassure Siobhan, all the while desperate to run out and shake their landlady awake, demanding she reveal the identity of today's floral deliverer and how she could get her hands on her. She smiled, hoping that what felt like a tight-drawn grimace and sharp baring of the teeth would inspire comfort and ease, "Look Siobhan, we're all right tonight. You stay here for a few minutes. You can lock the door after me and I'll go and get Greg for you, ok? Then I'll have a word with the landlady, ask about the delivery. I'll get her to check that all the doors and windows downstairs are locked and we can all get to bed. In the morning I'll find out who left these." And here she added a relieved chuckle to her theatrical repertoire, "I mean, really, there really can't be that many bloody florists in this little town."

Siobhan looked properly at the flowers for the first time. "There's a card."

She took the small envelope from the cellophane encasing the roses and ripped it open. Saz saw her hand start to shake as she read it. Siobhan held the card out to Saz who read: "Welcome to New Zealand! Now it's just all us girls together. How nice! PS—tell Greg that Gaelene misses him."

Saz turned the card and envelope over; neither had a florist's address on them. "I don't get it. Who's Gaelene?"

Siobhan shook her head, "Nothing. I don't know."

"Well what about the 'all girls together' bit? What's that?"

Siobhan's whole body was shaking and she started to cry, "I don't know, ok? I don't know what any of this is about. I just want it all to go away. Make it go away."

Saz's right arm was around Siobhan's shoulders, her left hand holding both of Siobhan's shaking hands in hers. She really wasn't thinking of anything other than making Siobhan feel better, feel safe, of looking after Siobhan—simply thinking about the best way to do her job.

Sitting on the edge of the bed, their height difference was marginal, their eyes level, Siobhan's extra long legs reaching out across the thick carpeted floor. Saz poured all the reassurance and calm she could cram into one fabricated stare. Their eyes held and then Siobhan's lips were on hers and Siobhan's left leg had swung up and around, was smooth and low across her hips and they lay long on the bed together, Siobhan leaning over her, breathing hot, tired margarita breath into Saz's eyes, ears, mouth, breasts. Siobhan and Saz pulling each other's clothes off, light clothes, thin clothes, the easily removed clothes of an almost summer evening. Siobhan locking the door. Saz and Siobhan kissing and touching, Siobhan's fingers prying, trying the new scars, unseen by anyone other than Molly, anyone other than the many, many doctors. New skin untouched, unloved by any other than Molly. Saz's hands running fast over Siobhan's long limbs, straight waist, full breasts. Saz's mind choosing not to look at the difference, not to register a difference. Not to register that there was anyone to be different from. Saz's cowardly mind retreating, shutting off and letting her subversive physical self take over. Only Saz's hands noting the difference between this new body and Molly's, noting and revelling in each fresh sensation, fingertips and lips with minds of their own craving virgin sensations and untouched body to satisfy impatient, easily bored lusts.

When Saz and Siobhan fucked it was not as if Siobhan had not done it before. She did not wait, a lesbian virgin to be taken and saved by Saz's knowledge. She held Saz tight as she fucked her, Saz's body deliriously surrendering to wide-awake dreams of fantasy finally made flesh, her mouth open to kiss Siobhan, her body wide open to take her in.

Saz woke the next morning to a bed littered with broken roses, petal yellow smeared against the sheets, ripped green leaves staining white linen pillow cases and her back rose-thorn scratched. She ached the bruised ache of the hour's incessant unexpected passion until Siobhan had left her, half sleeping and returned to her own bed where Greg dreamt quietly, so many pints down that even his dreams poured slow as Dublin Guiness.

Saz had fucked Siobhan with all her body, most of her heart and some of her soul. Unfortunately, with sharp day-light, her tardy conscience had finally decided to join the party.

THIRTY-ONE

I haven't been here before. Not as a grown-up anyway. Once we came here, very early in the morning, a long way from home, driving south, even further south than this. I was a small child. I sent you a postcard and Mummy had to write the big words, put the stamp on, lift me up to put it in the box. I did the licking part myself. I never liked it here though. Never even liked the idea of it. The mountains are too big, they ring the sky and don't let you see behind. There is not enough sky here, too much earth, too much rock. I like the edge of the sea, the depth of sky. I want to see far out into the distance. The straight and curving line that defines the horizon parameters of our future.

I've been so far to find you, been to all those places you've visited. And now we're here. So very far. Little criss-cross lines scarring the world map, gouging lines out of the globe. Noughts and crosses all over Europe. Backwards and forwards from town to city. Some you went to more often. Some places you really laid claim to. I followed the scent, sniffed you out though you tried to cover your tracks. And now I've followed you all the way back.

Home again home again jiggety jog. To buy a fat hog. Or pig. Maybe it's pig. But do they eat meat? Well, who doesn't these days? Even the cows eat meat now. How much meat can this cow eat?

I watched them. Kissing and fondling. Both so public and unashamed. I hated her then. Weaving herself around that table, that room. She thinks she's Pygmalion, looks at what

she's made, plays with herself, with them, with her creation.
Plays with me. I should never have let you take it this far. I
should have told the truth from the beginning. You've got
away with far too much.

But she is beautiful. They are beautiful. You are beautiful.
A conjugation of loveliness.

Beauty is in the eye of the beholder. Does she have any
idea just how beholden she is to me? Don't worry, I won't
forget the debt.

This place used to be much nicer, I'm sure. Smaller. More
real. Now it's full of Americans and Japanese and the tourists
with their bloody tourist dollars and their bloodier tourist
minds. I would expect that in London, in New York.
Somehow I'd hoped for better from here. I'd hoped that this
little piece of the world wouldn't change. I believe in the
sanctity of stasis. But you can see it has started already. The
small towns are all decaying—those that aren't dead already.
Shutting off shops and whole streets in an attempt to beat
the gangrene of poverty, to stem the flow of dollars that
props up the economies of the fat greedy cities. I lived years
in a small town, they are the same the world over. I loved
it. But its life blood has been siphoned by Auckland and
Wellington and Sydney and LA and Tokyo and Paris and
London. Spirit killed off to feed the names on a plastic
carrier bag, a T-shirt. You'll see them as you drive north
from here, follow the spine up the islands where the mountains turn into white-crossed roads, all those little towns
slaughtered, sacrificial cows to feed the rampant drive, the
empassioned "we can be as big as the rest of the world".
Yes, we can be that big. We can be big and bad and beautiful
and deny the little people too. We can forget our pasts.
Pretend it never happened. We can turn our land inside out
and change it all. We can be brand new. And no doubt she
thinks it's worth it. After all, she did the same to herself.

Can you imagine how hard it is to find yellow roses in

Queenstown at this time of year? It was the devil's own job to get enough to make a bouquet. But, as always, it was well worth the effort. "Must try harder" they used to say on my school report. Term after term. Not these days. These days I can't try hard enough. I really am a great success. In my own way. Just like her.

THIRTY-TWO

It was a sober and embarrassed Saz that greeted Greg and Siobhan at breakfast the next morning. Saz felt sick and confused, Siobhan was bright and strangely excited, given her unhappiness of the night before. Saz assumed it was to cover up what had happened between them and arranged her breakfast with little appetite, avoiding Siobhan's eyes as much as she could. Greg was subdued, fielding questions with "Don't no's" and "maybes". Dan hadn't made it down to breakfast, nursing his hangover and the late-sleeping waiter in his bedroom with a tray of dry toast and two vast glasses of orange juice retrieved an hour earlier from the breakfast table.

Saz waited until Siobhan had eaten her third piece of toast before she told Greg about the flowers, acting as if Siobhan didn't know about them either. He looked concerned enough until she told him about the card when he jumped up from the table, spilling lightly poached egg all over the polished wood.

"Right, that's it, I've had enough of this shit. We're leaving. Now. Siobhan, you can get your bags, I'm transferring the flights, we're going straight to Auckland and then getting out of here."

Surprisingly, Siobhan didn't argue with him. She merely ignored him.

Greg continued, "Siobhan? Did you hear me?"

Siobhan smiled at him, her mouth full of toast and boysenberry jam, "Yep. But we can't go just yet. The flight's not till four this afternoon."

"I know that. We'll go on to Auckland instead of changing at Rotorua. I'll call Aunty Pat and tell her we're not coming. We'll just go to a hotel in Auckland, book in under someone else's name—Saz, you'll do. We'll just be the Martin party, then get the first flight out. There must be one tomorrow. I don't care what airline it is, we'll just go. Ok, Saz?"

Saz nodded, unnerved by Siobhan's disinterest, "Yeah, sure. Whatever you want. I mean, I think there's probably more I can do to find this person while we're still here though. I plan to go downtown and check later, as soon as the shops open. They'll know if the flowers were ordered here or by phone. At least then we'll know a bit more. Um, and about this Gaelene . . .?"

He ignored her question, watching as Siobhan stood up and crossed to the dresser, picked up a thin china bowl and spooned homemade muesli into it, topping it with slices of peach and apricot and a dollop of plain yoghurt.

Greg stood with his fists clenched, glaring at her, "Siobhan, what are you doing? This is hardly the time to develop an appetite."

"No, I don't suppose it is." She slowly returned to her seat at the table. Greg and Saz both watched each deliberate move, neither convinced that she wasn't about to pick up the bowl and throw it at them, Saz terrified of what it could be that Siobhan was gearing herself up to say. When Siobhan finally picked up her spoon and pointed it at Greg, Saz could have sworn she saw him flinch.

Siobhan's voice came out, just above a low whisper, "Greg, my darling, I'd love to do just as you say. In fact, in three hours' time I won't have any choice. But just for now, until I make that rash promise to obey, you'll have to excuse me for not doing what you want. We're not going direct to Auckland tonight because Aunty Pat will have spent all day making ham sandwiches and tiny sausage rolls and we don't want to upset her. Uncle Dennis is probably polishing the family silver as we talk. Anyway, you don't really have time to spend the morning on the phone to Auckland, you probably ought to pop into town and do a little shopping."

"What are you talking about?"

Saz had no idea either and while she was wondering whether she should get a cloth to wipe up the congealing egg yoke or just run away then and there, Siobhan spooned up another mouthful of muesli and fruit and held it out to Greg, "Marry me?"

Greg, confused by the contrary action and words, looked at the cereal and at the woman offering it, "I don't like mue . . . I mean . . . what . . . I can't, you know . . . I'd love to, we've both said that . . . what?"

Saz stood up, desperately wanting to get out of the room, away from the bizarre scene, away from the vomit she felt rising through her stomach, away from the eyes fixed on her, but Siobhan had already put down her spoon and grabbed Saz's hand, "See, my darling, we'll have Saz and Dan for our witnesses. Won't we, Saz?"

Siobhan looked at Saz and her eyes were both hard and pleading, "I've checked it all out. I took our passports in yesterday when you were looking in the ski shop, it took no time at all. I filled out the forms . . ."

Greg shook his head, "I must have to sign something?"

"Forged it. Told the nice lady you were taking a photo, went outside and forged your signature. Been doing it for years, you know that. What a wonderful country this is! Normally you have to wait at least a couple of days but when I explained who we were to the woman on the desk—you see, darling, we are a little bit famous here after all—she said she'd see what she could do. I told her we wanted to avoid the English press. Seemed perfectly plausible."

Greg seemed to come to his senses for a moment but

Siobhan didn't give him a chance to jump in, "So then the nice lady came back and said we were in luck, her boss had agreed that they'd process the forms fast for us. All we had to do was bring ourselves and a couple of witnesses. Isn't this just so cool? We're fitted in right between a couple of Americans who only decided to get married on Friday and this Japanese couple who've come to New Zealand just for the ceremony. Apparently they do it all the time. The Japanese, that is."

Saz managed to extricate herself from Siobhan's hand, rubbing her fingers where her rings had been squashed together, her skin pinched from the strength of Siobhan's grip. She forced herself to sit calmly beside Dan who had arrived at the table during Siobhan's speech and was immediately wishing he hadn't.

Saz stuttered, "But Siobhan, it's so soon."

Siobhan shook her head, "No. Greg and I have been talking about getting married for years. We just didn't know we could do it, that's all."

Greg came and sat beside her, "Sweetheart, we still can't. This is crazy."

Saz interrupted Greg, "Don't they have to read the bans or anything?"

Siobhan kissed Greg lightly on the mouth and leant her forehead against his. "Haven't you always told me what a groovy country this is? Apparently our passports would have been enough. I brought our birth certificates with me just in case."

Greg questioned her again, "She saw the birth certificates?"

"Don't you trust me? I did everything right. It's all real, babe. I checked."

"Everything?"

"Yep. Right down to the last teeny tiny little detail."

"You're sure?"

"Yes! It's all done, all legal, all above board. It really is possible." She looked at Saz, "They don't do the bans thing here."

Turning back to Greg, she continued, "I called last week and checked everything. Then the nice lady went and checked everything. Again. We can do it, we can have the lot, you and me, Mr and Mrs Siobhan Forrester-Marsden and Greg Marsden-Forrester just like all those silly dream plans we've ever had. All those three-in-the-morning talks. The world is actually going to let us do it. All you have to do is say yes."

Greg was crying when he said yes and Siobhan was crying when she whooped with joy and Saz was crying when she went upstairs to find something to wear for the immediate ceremony. Saz knew her tears were jealousy and betrayal and anger, but she wasn't certain if she was jealous because she wanted Siobhan or angry because Siobhan and Greg were about to do what the world wouldn't let her and Molly do or just furious with herself for having let things get so out of hand. Taking her clothes out of the wardrobe to pack, she was hoping the local shops held more variety than her suitcase.

Siobhan was right. Everything was in order. They went to the local courthouse where their forms were checked again, Siobhan and Greg signing a couple more declarations. The ceremony was conducted in a small ante-chamber by a Justice of the Peace who made a lovely speech about joy and love and spontaneity turning into permanence and reality, Siobhan and Greg read the simple vows from a card she gave them and improvised a couple of their own. Siobhan didn't promise to obey, but Greg did. Siobhan wore a full-length green satin skirt and a very fitted red Chinese silk top, with maximum cleavage exposure. Removing the clothes from her bag, she'd confessed to Saz that the wedding was her main reason for coming to Queenstown all along. Greg had told her ages ago that couples on holiday there were able to marry with a minimum of formalities and with maximum speed and ever since she had thought how exciting it would be to get married that way. In response to Saz's hurried question, she told her that Alex and Steve's deaths had simply prompted her to turn the whimsical thought into a reality. In Siobhan, the finality of death provoked not despair but an overkill on life.

Answering the other question, Siobhan merely told Saz she'd been interested—"Wanted to find out the difference, babe. Between a boy and a girl. I mean, you have a girlfriend right? It was just sex, yeah? I wouldn't want to come between you and her, that's not what I meant. I know you love your girlfriend and I know I drive you crazy, but I do really like you, so I figured, well, I assumed you felt the same as me." She stopped her ironing long enough to look up and ask, "Did I fuck up?"

Saz shook her head. "No, Siobhan, you didn't fuck up, you probably didn't even do anything wrong. I did." And then she went shopping, hating herself all the way.

Greg wore an old red shirt and a pair of jeans, the shirt ironed by Dan while Saz dashed out and took half an hour to shop. Five minutes in the florist to confirm that, yes, a woman had come in early the day before asking for a huge bunch of yellow roses, they'd even had to send to several other shops in the area to make the number up—she did hope the flowers were ok? Saz assured her they were lovely, the scratches on her back beginning to itch and took another five minutes to get a full description of exactly the same woman Ben Kaserov had described to her. Except this one had bleached blonde hair. Saz remembered the blonde head in the jacuzzi in LA and felt sick. She looked forward to getting through the ceremony and on to Greg's aunt's house where she had decided she would force Siobhan and Greg to go to the police. And if they wouldn't, then she'd just go by herself. She then took just twenty minutes to buy a long summer dress in pale pink silk for herself and a pink linen shirt for Dan. As he said when he handed over his cash, "I don't care what you buy, but I do think the two witnessing queers ought to make some sort of a statement."

So the witnesses were gay and pink and Greg was tearful and casual and Siobhan was, of course, stunning, beautiful, charming and completely over the top. She also—just in case a certain someone was looking—carried the biggest bouquet she could buy. Forty, long stemmed, velvety dark red roses. With a single yellow rose set in the middle.

THIRTY-THREE

She really thinks she can get away with it. That no one will find out, that her little secret won't be uncovered. She thinks she can smother it in white lace and satin and I won't see.

Of course they don't do that though. White lace and satin would be too traditional. No, they take the fashionable route. The path that will give them maximum exposure and minimum truth.

I know who is to blame. With their passive attitudes and glib natures, they have created this. A world in which that woman can swan around in red and green on her wedding day. A world in which an occasion of such dignity and solemnity can be reduced to this farce of hurried decisions and cobbled together vows and crude sexual innuendo. My darling is worth more than this, but she has forgotten. Has spent too much time with them. Has changed too much.

That's ok. She will be alone eventually. Alone and herself again. And anyway, we are going home. Going back to the beginning. A very good place to start. And finish.

THIRTY-FOUR

When Shona and Gaelene were nine years old their favourite game was weddings. Planning their own. Shona would draw up detailed lists of all the possible variations on dress, attendants, churches, reception venues. The groom would be added at the last moment, an afterthought, primarily there to stand smiling in a suit and take her hand from her first dad and place the shining golden ring on her perfectly manicured outstretched finger. Blissfully unaware of the laws of God and man, she usually nominated her cousin as groom because she didn't yet like any other boys or, if she was planning her favourite combination—the double wedding for herself and Gaelene, then Gaelene was allowed to marry John and Shona would have whoever they minded least that week at school—Craig or Paul or Shaun or Mike— a seventies' boy with a seventies' one syllable name.

The ceremony always started with both girls getting ready at Shona's mum's house. The two of them would be grown-up ladies now, as old as twenty-two or twenty-three, getting dressed in Shona's bedroom. This being a really special occasion, they would be allowed, once they were fluffed and flounced, to stand on Shona's mum's bed and look at themselves in the longer mirror above her dressing table, the added height of the bed allowing them a magical full-length view of the total princess picture. Then, fairy-tale perfect, they would go outside to the waiting car—driven by Shona's first dad, her real dad, come back home to her mother for the occasion and happy to be there, smiling at

Shona's mum, kissing her like all the fights and the shouting and the holes punched in the thin particle board walls had never even happened. Shona and Gaelene would get in the polished car, a Jag or a Rolls covered in ribbons and flowers, watched by all the girls they were at school with. Watched by the prettier girls, the clever girls, the girls with posh houses with separate loos and the girls with Raleigh Twenty bicycles and mums who didn't work and dads who didn't go away, girls with big sisters who were at nursing school in Rotorua or training college in Hamilton and wore mini skirts and maxi coats, girls who had big brothers in the First Fifteen. And these perfect little girls, who hung around in all the wealthy Pakeha groups, who didn't have Maori friends, Maori family, who went to their cousins in Auckland for the holidays, not just down the coast to their rellies, these Debras and Andreas and Yvonnes with perfect blonde hair and perfect straight teeth would stand there in seething, thwarted jealousy as they stared at Shona and Gaelene, paragons of bridal superiority. And at the church, Gaelene and Shona would walk in, hand in hand, their fathers tall on either side of them, their mothers crying at the front. They would walk up the aisle, all the heads turning to look at beautiful Shona and beautiful Gaelene. At the altar they would say their vows to whoever was waiting, capture the rings and then waltz down the aisle together in a rush of satin and lace, married ladies, irrelevant things like husbands and parents and friends trailing after them. The reception at the rugby club would be the biggest the town had ever seen, the partying would go on all night and the next morning the two couples would leave for their honeymoon—a week in Auckland or Christchurch or, if Shona was really getting carried away, four nights in Sydney. The girls would of course share one room and the boys another. These were the plans of a nine year old.

It was all Shona's dream. Gaelene didn't care so much.

Knew her family might be moving to Auckland anyway, didn't know if she wanted to get married, didn't know if she cared, didn't know if it mattered all that much. But it made Shona happy, making the plans, all the details, the dress styles, the shoes, her and Gaelene getting married together. Always the two of them together. And naturally, everywhere they went would be flowers, roses at the church and roses at the rugby club and roses for their first flight in a plane and roses for their first night in a hotel. Beautiful roses, red, white, pink and, of course, yellow. Shining yellow roses for Shona's favourite colour.

Gaelene had forgotten lots of things about Shona. She'd completely forgotten Shona loved yellow. In fact, she'd pretty much forgotten all about Shona. But that was all right. Shona would help her remember.

THIRTY-FIVE

Given the days' notice Siobhan had allowed them, Greg's Aunty Pat and Uncle Dennis had done wonders. The dining table at the far end of the large blue-painted kitchen looked as if it was about to topple with the weight of chicken, cucumber, egg cress sandwiches, what seemed like several carcasses worth of sausage rolls and a flotilla of butterfly cakes. After the nuptial fuss and hurried photos in Queenstown they'd caught the plane as planned, picked up their hire van at Rotorua and driven the two hours it took to get to Pat and Dennis's "batch". On hearing the word Saz had assumed a small cottage by the sea, perhaps a New Zealand version of Derek Jarman's Dungeness cottage, if a little less horticulturally stimulated. She couldn't have been more wrong.

The Marsden's home had been created from the shell of their forty-year-old weatherboard house and added to at weekends and holidays over a three year period until what Pat and Dennis had fashioned was a five bedroom, newly finished, extremely desirable retirement residence. Greg's aunt and uncle had lived by the coast for the first fifteen of their married years and when Dennis's work had taken him to Auckland they had chosen to let rather than sell the small house where they had started their marriage. When Dennis retired they had sold the big house in Auckland and returned to the coast, remaking their environment with the extravagant proceeds from the Auckland house sale. Using their old home to create the core of the new house, they had transformed a small wooden bungalow into a show home. Inside it was all huge windows and wood-panelled flooring. A lifetime of pouring over copies of *New Zealand House and Garden* had left Pat with a wealth of ideas and finally she had the real wealth with which to achieve them. Greg was astounded. Though he had seen photos of the work in progress, he had not expected his aunt and uncle to have achieved so much. Or that they would have done it in quite so much style.

They arrived at eight in the evening, with the sun just setting behind the distant Kaimai range. At first Greg was convinced they had come to the wrong house, shaking his head at the size of the building in front of them, but the number on the letterbox was the same and Siobhan assured him that the woman wiping her hands on her apron and waving at them from the balcony was definitely her—"It is your Aunty Pat, babe"—she whispered to him just before she jumped out of the passenger seat and bounded up the steps and into Aunty Pat's outstretched arms, shouting and waving her wedding ring hand the whole way.

The whole day had been bitter for Saz. She was unable to run away, stuck in New Zealand with the happy newly-weds, stuck in the plane with the newlyweds, stuck in the car with the newlyweds. She couldn't talk to anyone about what had happened, Molly, her usual sounding board, being the last person she wanted to confide in and, because Siobhan insisted on celebrating her wedding with her "new family", her day was given over to doing nothing but dance attendance on Siobhan's whims. None of which involved coming clean with the police about what had been going on.

Late that night, after poring over the Polaroid wedding photos and listening to the new album, after the praising of the wedding ring, after all the sandwiches and sausage rolls had been finished—carefully made to a special vegetarian recipe just for Siobhan—after the pavlova had been brought in and crowed over, the endless cups of strong tea finally turned to wine for the ladies and bottles of beer for the men, and just as everyone was starting to settle down, Saz made the mistake of asking Pat about the pretty little blonde girl in the variously aged photos on the wall.

She realized she'd made a huge error as Pat stuttered, "That's our . . . daughter . . . she's, um . . ."

Dennis tried a little harder with, "She was . . . something happened to her . . . she was . . ." then he too turned white and his speech ground to a halt.

Greg jumped in to save his aunt and uncle further distress, "That's my cousin Gaelene. She's dead. She died years ago. When she was sixteen."

Saz muttered a quiet "Sorry" and Dan shuffled to the window, overcome by a sudden intense interest in the full yellow moon.

Looking around at the embarrassed faces in the room Greg continued, "See, we're no better at talking about this kind of shit than the English . . . oh fuck . . ."

He ground to a halt, looking at Siobhan for help but she was too interested in the light glancing off her wedding ring to notice. He tried again, "Um . . . how about . . . must be a while since we measured my height, eh, Aunty Pat?"

His aunt, glad of a chance to change the subject and well into her fourth dry sherry, jumped up a little unsteadily and the others followed her out to the kitchen. Maintaining an edgy distance from Siobhan, Saz stood with Dan as they watched Dennis measure Greg against the side of the walk-in pantry—the only piece of wall in the whole house Pat hadn't repainted—and made a new mark beside all the other little ones that indicated Greg's growth over the years.

Saz, relieved that the subject had been so abruptly changed, was impressed by the display of extended family closeness, but nevertheless she wondered why they had no marks for their own daughter and more urgently, if this Gaelene was the same one mentioned on the flower card.

She asked Dan as they piled the plates into the dishwasher and finished the cooking pans together, "Don't you think it's a bit funny that there weren't any wall marks for their own daughter?"

Dan shook his head, "I don't know. Maybe. People do funny things when someone dies."

"Like what?"

"Well, my mum's sister died when she was in her early thirties and my gran just went nuts. Made this huge bonfire in the back garden and burnt all of my aunt's stuff. Some people make a shrine to their dead people and some just wipe them out like they were never there. Maybe they had a wall for her and painted it over. It must have been a long time ago."

"Maybe. Greg's really lucky he gets on with them so well. He must have spent a lot of time with them as a child?"

"I think so. Certainly he's always talked more about his aunt and uncle than his mum and dad."

"What happened to his own parents? Do you know how they died?"

Dan shrugged and passed her back the cake tin, "There's a bit of gunge still on this. Nah, I don't know that much about Greg's stuff, only the basics. They seem very fond of Greg anyway, the aunt and uncle."

"What about Gaelene? Do you know anything about her?"

Dan pulled the plug to drain the sink, "Saz, look, I really don't know any more about Greg than I've told you. He and I have never talked that intimately. He was closer to Alex than to me. I was closer to Alex too."

"I wouldn't have thought Alex was that easy to be close to."

"He wasn't. Which goes to show how not close Greg and I are. You know, we're colleagues and we're friends. But not close friends. I think the only person Greg ever really talks to is Siobhan. That's just how it is. If you want to know all Greg's sordid details, you're going to have to ask him yourself."

Saz nodded, "Yeah, I think I will."

When they had finally put everything away, it was already one-thirty in the morning and Dan excused himself to go to bed, "I've had it, Saz. I'm off, early start tomorrow."

Saz turned from where she was wiping down the kitchen sink, "Oh? I thought we were all just supposed to lie around in the sunshine all day—wasn't that the scenario in Siobhan's itinerary?"

Dan shrugged his shoulders, his long pony-tail lifting and waving against the weight of muscle, "Maybe, but I've had enough of playing unhappy families with the band. We've got two more days in this country and I'm not prepared to spend them doing as I'm told just to keep Siobhan calm. We've done their happy little het wedding and quite frankly, I'd just as soon get out of here right now. I'm a pretty superstitious kind of guy and the thought of just sitting here, getting a tan and waiting for the third bad thing to happen doesn't exactly fill me with delight. Particularly not if the third bad thing is me."

"What are you going to do?"

"Nice though Pat and Dennis are, I noticed signs of a thriving if small gay community in Auckland, I'm going to spend my last two days there and join you lot back at the airport." He smiled at Saz, "You're welcome to join me— where there's gay boys there's usually gay girls somewhere close."

Saz shook her head, she'd had more than enough of girls for the time being, "No. I don't really think that's in the job description. But thanks anyway. Leave me the details of where you're staying though, will you?"

"Checking up on me?"

Saz nodded, "Yeah. Why not? I'm superstitious too. Have you told Greg and Siobhan?"

Dan laughed, "I'm not that brave. I had a quick word with Greg this afternoon. He said he'd do the dirty work for me. Pat's taking me in to catch the early flight tomorrow so I'll be well out of the way before her ladyship wakes up. I mean, this is lovely," he said, gesturing at the wide expanse of night ocean through the windows, "but it's a bit too bloody much of the outdoors for me, I'm a city boy at heart and I rather like the sound of Queen Street. Goodnight, chica. See you in duty free!" Dan threw her his tea towel and turned on his heel, whistling a slightly sharp version of "Downtown" as he went out the back door and downstairs to his basement room.

Hanging up the sodden tea towel, Saz realized how frightening the whole thing must have been for Dan. Unlike Greg and Siobhan, he'd not been allowed to know the full story, fobbed off with excuses and half truths until yesterday, but like them, he'd seen two of his best friends killed within a week of each other. While he didn't have to suffer the anxiety of wondering where the next bunch of flowers was going to come from, he also hadn't, until recently, been allowed the dubious comfort of knowing that there was at least one person out there who knew a little of the truth.

Her thoughts were interrupted just a moment later when, returning from a long beach walk, Greg and Dennis clumped up the back stairs and into the kitchen. Saz was about to offer to make them both a quick nightcap when she saw that Greg's face was flushed red and Dennis's eyes were bright with unshed tears. Dennis grabbed Greg in a fierce hug, holding him tight until Saz thought the younger man just had to break. Eventually Dennis broke away and with a long look at Greg, wished them both goodnight.

Saz waited a beat and then turned to Greg, "Do you want to tell me what's going on? Tell me about Gaelene? There's obviously some link with all the stuff with Siobhan," she shrugged and held her hands out for emphasis. "But, really, I have no idea what it is."

Greg closed the door after Dennis, speaking quietly, "Yeah, I'm sorry. I should have told you ages ago."

Saz sat down at the kitchen table and waited for him to join her, "So what happened to Gaelene?"

Greg heaved a massive sigh and turned to look out at the moon, now high in the bright starred sky. He nodded in confirmation of his own words, "I killed her."

THIRTY-SIX

When Gaelene left New Zealand aged sixteen, she left with not one blessing to speed her on her way. Not from her mother who couldn't bear the thought of losing her baby and not from her father who said if she really meant to go away and follow her plan then she need never come home again. And certainly not from Shona, practically just a pen friend now, their friendship reduced to two letters a year, maybe an occasional phone call or quick coffee if they happened to find themselves in the same town, by sixteen their interests so diverse there was no basis for conversation. At least that was what Gaelene thought.

For Shona it was different. As far as Shona was concerned, she was happy just to be near Gaelene, vibrant conversation or not. Shona still made contact with Gaelene's parents whenever she was in Auckland or when they were visiting friends on the coast. She held on to her childhood for as long as she could, intended to hold on to Gaelene for as long as she could. Not that Gaelene thought to ask for Shona's blessing when she left, or cared that she didn't have her parents behind her either. Gaelene was going to follow her star. She knew they didn't understand, probably would never understand. And she also knew that as far as her own heart was concerned, she had no choice but to leave.

Her first stop was the Netherlands. She'd done the reading, visited every library she could gain access to, spoken to her own local doctor, then to the referred hospital psychologist, to the first psychiatrist, the second and third psychiatrists, to expert after expert, each one claiming to know what was best for her, each one certain she should wait, take time, take still more time, think again. Each one convinced that the reasons the medical system gave for waiting until eighteen, twenty, twenty-one, were sound, valid reasons. Each one demanding that Gaelene put off her future, delay her life, for just another year.

After a tortuous route of stopovers and delays, rescheduled flights and a long six-hour wait at Heathrow, Gaelene finally left her last plane at Schippol, caught the first train into Amsterdam, ate welcoming *pofferjes* with a cup of sweet coffee, bought a few essential items of clothing, made a phone call home to tell her mother she was safe and then took the next train out of the central station to Utrecht. She booked into a tatty hotel for one night and, locked into the shared bathroom, removed her clothes. She stood naked in front of the mirror and stared at herself, at her height, at her long legs, her narrow hips, her barely indented waist, her wide shoulders. She ran her hands over her body, lifting her fingers so they escaped touching her breasts, the small, just rounded breasts of a sixteen-year-old girl. The breasts she wanted rid of. She reached into her toilet bag and in the stark fluorescent light took out a pair of scissors. She laid the scissors on the bench in front of her and, after a deep breath, picked them up in her left hand, holding her hank of shoulder-length hair back with the right. In one fast movement she freed herself of the female indicator of long blonde hair. With a smaller pair of nail scissors she neatened the edges, leaving herself with a ragged urchin cut. She took out the wide crêpe bandage and, pulling it tight enough to constrict her breath, she bound her breasts into a masculine chest. Already her shoulders and upper arms were muscled from a daily swimming routine, hours in the gym and nightly push-ups. She threw her bra and knickers into the rubbish bin where she had earlier discarded her jeans and T-shirt. She didn't need to throw the clothes away, they were as male as they were female. It was a gesture, the deliberate disposal of her past. She opened the bag of new clothes by her feet and pulled out a pair of boxer shorts, a new black T-shirt and a new pair of jeans. She added socks and heavy black boots. Gaelene bent down and collected her belongings, joyfully dumping the old in the rubbish bin, carefully folding the new into her canvas bag. She was ready.

Greg stood up and looked at himself in the mirror. He was a tall, fairly thin, just beyond pubescent boy. He was a sweet-looking young man. He was male. And when Greg let himself out of the toilet and the old Dutch lady wagged her finger at him in annoyance and let out a stream of furious foreign babble, pointing several times to the picture of a woman on the door, he could have kissed her in gratitude.

THIRTY-SEVEN

At almost seventeen Greg started injecting himself daily with a chemical version of the hormone testosterone. Within three months the irreversible effects had started, his periods stopped, his voice had begun to break, he was developing what started to look like an Adam's apple, he began to grow the faintest fluff of down on his chin and upper lip. He also suffered mood swings, several outbreaks of particularly virulent acne and, until his doctor had sorted out exactly the right levels of testosterone, a slight degree of jaundice resulting in a yellowing of his pimpled skin. For Greg, this was a minor burden to bear. He continued to live and dress as a man. As a boy, for that is what he was.

He moved to England and continued the treatment started in Utrecht, working sixteen-hour days at two jobs to support himself and his treatment. He continued to badger his local GP for a referral to an NHS treatment centre. He was continually refused.

At eighteen he travelled to San Francisco, visited a transgender clinic and then was referred to a private plastic surgeon. He had a full mastectomy, completely removing both of his small girl breasts and repositioning the nipples. He spent only the minimum time in hospital, completing his recuperation on the sofa of two other patients at the clinic who had befriended the young man when they were receiving treatment in the Netherlands. He returned home broke, weak and very happy. He continued to work out, replacing girl tissue and sweet soft fat with solid boy muscle, his pectoral wall a rippling product of committed self-development.

At nineteen he increased his hormone intake, and drank sweet woodruff tea by the bucketload for the care of his liver. It was another year before he discovered fennel, juniper, rosemary and rose oils had the same effect. Two years later he had incorporated the herbs and the oils into a daily regimen, having also added selenium, thiamin and Vitamin E to the equation.

At nineteen and a half he increased his daily workouts and doubled his vitamin doses to prepare for the hysterectomy which left him with a thin scar line just above his increasing patch of pubic hair, in pain but tired and elated.

After the hysterectomy he took two years away from the operations and began even more intensive therapy to prepare himself for the final operation, meeting his psychotherapist twice a week and his group once a week. He was throwing money at his body and the shape changing was absorbing cash at an alarming rate. The beginning of the last stage started at twenty-one and the long and painful process finally finished close to his twenty-sixth birthday. Leaving him with a long, deep scar from tissue removal on his left arm and, through the miracles of modern prosthetics, he had a working penis. He could piss standing up and he could fuck lying down, just like any other boy.

Inside and outside Gaelene was now Greg, the person she'd always known she was, the person she'd always wanted to be, the person who had endured painful operations, worked like a dog to afford them—and when work wasn't enough, had begged, borrowed and sometimes stolen to make up the shortfall. The man who had hitched seven or eight times a year across the Channel to the Netherlands or as far as the States because he could not receive the treatment he needed in Britain—not fast enough, not sure enough and not willingly enough. Greg had pleaded and cried and suffered and laughed and eventually been so very relieved to be allowed to become the man he knew himself to be.

At twenty-one he had also met Siobhan Forrester, the flatmate who was to become his singer, his lover and his muse—Siobhan, who never for a moment doubted that Greg was a man and that she was in love with a man. Siobhan, who would do anything for Greg, who was prepared to allow the other members of the band believe she was the difficult one and cancel arrangements and even miss their first ever real gig if it meant Greg could get to his next appointment, his next round of drugs, his next surgery in New York or Rio or Utrecht. Siobhan who, once the band had achieved some success and there was more money to spare, bundled him off the plane and into waiting taxis to get him to their naturopath who would help him to stabilize his system against the foreign chemicals and drugs that he needed to maintain his new status, his real self. Siobhan, who screamed at him if ever he woke too sleepy to remember to take any of the many pills he took daily disguised as "too much good life" combating vitamins. Siobhan, who injected him with testosterone. Siobhan, who had known and aided and been prepared to take any amount of shit, throw any number of tantrums to protect Greg.

By the time he was twenty-six, Greg Marsden was "all man" and drop-dead gorgeous.

And though they were best friends, Alex never knew and Steve never knew and while Dan had a few suspicions, he'd never quite worked out what it was he was suspicious about. Siobhan knew and Greg knew and Pat and Dennis knew and eventually, with time and distance and the conditioning of unconditional love, they also accepted. Accepted that their daughter was now their son who, for the sake of his sanity and his career and the band, was now their nephew.

And now Saz knew. And, of course, Shona knew too.

THIRTY-EIGHT

Shona and Gaelene were sitting in the shed at Shona's mum's place. The shed had once been a coalshed, back when Shona's mum's house still had an open fire, but the advent of the seventies had seen the allure of glowing coals and sparkling embers replaced with the sober cleanliness and efficiency of three storage heater units. They dried out the air and gave Shona's mum headaches, but at least they weren't the same sort of headaches as the ones that came when she was trying to get herself off to work. Hurrying her own routine and at the same time clearing out the fireplace on a damp winter morning so she could dry Shona's grey school socks before the little girl left for school, Vegemite sandwiches and little packet of Sunmaid raisins crammed into the yellow plastic lunchbox beside a drink bottle and two gingernut biscuits that were guaranteed to be soft and stale by morning break. The shed, then, had become "The Clubhouse" for Shona and Gaelene. They both had bedrooms they could have played in, but the shed was much more exciting. The shed meant they actually had a Club. They had covered the dirt floor with the old lino from when Gaelene's mum had got cork tiles for her kitchen floor and they'd hung up an old candlewick bedspread in front of the open space where once there'd been a door but now there were two rusting hinges—the bedspread didn't stop much wind but it kept the rain out in winter and stopped Shona's mum being able to see in from the kitchen window when she was doing the dishes. There were three old packing chests turned upside down. One was a table covered in a lace tablecloth that had been too tired even to give to the school gala and the other two were stools, draped in Shona's old knitted cardigans to stop the jagged edges of the chests catching too often on their bare little girl legs. On the shelf on the back wall where a home-dwelling father would have kept his tools were the toys Shona was slowly outgrowing. Her first baby doll, perversely named Johnny, wearing a dirty yellow top and her father's handkerchief for a nappy, his eyelashes cut short in a game of hairdressers; a dusty silver and red velvet musical box from her aunty in Wellington and a walking-talking doll called Elizabeth who had long since refused to do either.

The girls were practising kissing, each one taking it in turns to hold the other in her arms, pressing their lips against each other in the way they'd seen the older kids do on Friday nights when they waited, hands in back pockets cool, outside the pictures. Their lips firmly shut, eyes screwed tight closed, they twisted their faces against each other, trying to work out where to put their noses and how to breathe with their mouths shut and their nostrils half blocked by the flesh of the others' cheek.

When they kissed, Gaelene felt nothing. Other than Shona's lips, she felt nothing. It was just practice, a rehearsal for being grown up. Practice for when she had a girlfriend of her own. Gaelene was only seven. She still thought she was going to grow up and become a man, the horrible truth hadn't yet dawned on her that the process of becoming un-woman was one she would have to push and force and fight for all alone.

When Shona kissed Gaelene she knew she'd found The One. Even at seven she knew she'd found The One. Sitting on her packing case, she sat back and asked Gaelene to wait for her, "Will you marry me when we're bigger?"

Gaelene looked at her, half a finger stuck in the mock

cream doughnut she had just picked up, trying to pick up the lump of oozing jam and get it into her mouth without spilling any on her yellow daisy Bermuda shorts. "Why?"

Shona's reasoning was simple. "Because you're my best friend. That way you'll always be my best friend."

She knew her mum and dad hadn't been best friends, she knew her mum said that was the only way to keep a marriage—with a seven-year-old's logic she figured the reverse must be true, if you keep a marriage going by marrying your best friend, then the way to keep a friendship was to make your best friend marry you.

She tried again, "Marry me?"

Gaelene gave it little thought, it was Monday afternoon, she wanted to eat her doughnut and she wanted to wait until Shona's mum came home from work and gave them five cents each to go and buy lollies and then she wanted to go home and watch the Partridge Family. She didn't want to talk about what might happen when she grew up. She also knew that if she didn't just agree, Shona would go on and on about it. Keep going until she got what she wanted anyway. She swallowed the cream and jam, swirling the two textures on her tongue before letting them slide down her throat, "Yeah, ok. If you want. Is John coming to stay in the holidays?"

Shona smiled, she had her answer. "Nah, my aunty's coming to get me and we're all going down to Ruby's place. You can come too if you want."

"Grouse!"

Gaelene loved Ruby, loved the relaxed atmosphere at Ruby's place, loved the way the kids ran and played and the grown-ups sang late into the night and no one shouted at the kids to shut up all the time.

Shona knew she had Gaelene interested and added her coda, "But only if you promise."

"What?"

"Promise you'll marry me."

"I just said I would."

"Swear?"

Gaelene sighed, "Cross my heart and hope to die." She crossed her heart, taking care not to touch her pale pink seersucker blouse with her sticky fingers. This careful promise was still not enough for Shona.

"Make a pact?"

"I just swore!"

"Make a pact anyway."

"What sort of a pact?"

Shona's eyes lit up, "A blood pact. Like John and Mani Pomare did last year."

"Nah, we'll get in trouble. John got a really big hiding when Ruby told his mum he'd cut himself."

"They were dumb. They shouldn't have done it with a big knife."

"Or where everybody could see."

"Yeah. So we'll do it somewhere else. We can do it on our arms, up here, not our hands. Then they won't see. Go on, or are you chicken?"

Gaelene wasn't chicken, she just didn't really care, but she followed Shona back into the house and held the chair as Shona stood on it to get at the top shelf in the bathroom cabinet where her Dad had left his shaving things behind when he left in such a hurry all those rainy nights ago. She carefully unscrewed the razor, her little fingers turning the bottom of it until the top opened and revealed the vicious two-sided blade, a few of her father's whiskers still clinging to the dirty edge. They stood in the bathroom and Shona held the blade and made a tiny nick in both of their upper arms, just above the bend of the elbow, squeezing the surrounding skin up to force a drop of blood from each of them, then they rubbed their bloodied spots together while Shona made Gaelene repeat after her, "I promise—"

"I promise—"

"To be true—"

"To be true—"

"To wait forever—"

"To wait forever . . . Shona, I have to go to the loo . . ."

"Hold on! I'm nearly finished! To wait forever, until I marry you."

"To wait forever until I marry you. Now can I pee?"

Shona shook her head, "In a minute. You lick my blood and I'll lick yours and then we kiss and then it's a real real pact."

Gaelene, bladder close to bursting from two bottles of Fanta on the way home, spare hand clamped between her legs, quickly licked the small smeared drop of congealing blood off Shona's arm and held hers out to be licked, she then kissed Shona on the lips and pushed her out of the bathroom, pulling her shorts and pants down as she did so.

Ten minutes later Shona's mum got home and they went down to the dairy with their five cents and bought mixed lollies, glow hearts and aniseed balls for Gaelene, red and black gumdrops for Shona.

The girls didn't think they were doing anything wrong. Didn't know that the world thought it was strange for two little girls to be so close. Didn't know that Shona's mum talked to her friend Pam about it, was secretly relieved when Gaelene moved away, hoped that now Shona would make more friends, get to know other children her own age, broaden her horizons.

But Shona didn't, of course. She was saving herself for Gaelene. Shona is not gay. Shona has no sexuality. She has never been interested in women. Or in men. She loves Gaelene. Only Gaelene. Always did. Always will.

But Shona didn't like it when Gaelene broke her promise.

THIRTY-NINE

Saz's head was reeling. Greg's story had left her in a state of shock. He grinned at her, slow and rueful, "You think it's weird, right?"

Confusing concepts around the shock of reality and fiction, political correctness, prurient curiosity and gender dilemmas hit her smack in the face. Saz, schooled in years of left-wing politics, knew she wasn't supposed to think it was weird. Knew in the core of her aware soul she wasn't supposed to think it was weird. "No. Of course not. No, I don't. I just . . . it's just . . . I . . ."

Greg was a man. But he wasn't. Greg had been born a girl and, until he was sixteen, had lived as a girl. But he was a man. Now.

Greg nodded at Saz and stirred himself from the deck-chair on the balcony where he'd been sitting as he told his story. "Sure you do. It's ok, Saz. It is a bit of a shock. You're allowed to be surprised. Siobhan was surprised and she still loves me."

Siobhan loved him. And she had slept with Siobhan. Had sex with Siobhan. Just a night ago. Twenty-four hours ago. Siobhan was a heterosexual woman who loved a man who had been a woman. Was brought up as a woman, conditioned as a woman. Must somewhere in there, somewhere inside, still think like a woman. Or not. Saz tuned back into the room and realized Greg was still explaining. "I mean, when I told Siobhan I thought I'd lose her. We hadn't quite got around to the sex part and obviously, she had to know.

Actually, she says it was something of a relief. Because I hadn't shagged her senseless within the first week we met, she reckons she was worried that maybe I didn't fancy her and she knew she really fancied me. So she was almost relieved when she found out that really I did. Fancy her. A fuck of a lot." Greg laughed. "Which eventually lead to a lot of fucking. Once it was all done. The operations, I mean. And quite a lot before it was done, I suppose. Well, you're gay, I guess you'd know, right?"

Saz smiled noncommittally. "Yeah, right."

What did she know? Siobhan had sex with a man who'd been a woman. But Siobhan was straight. More or less. Less probably. Greg had been a woman but now he was a man and he was living with a woman. Had just got married to a woman. Greg was a straight man married to a straight woman. So were they both really dykes? Saz's lust leapt at the passing thought and then a combined dose of guilt and political correctness crashed down on the fanciful notion. Of course they weren't, couldn't be, Greg was a man. And Saz knew that Siobhan loved Greg as a straight woman loves a straight man. And shouldn't Saz just accept that? She knew some male to female transsexuals, two distantly, one as a friend. She'd done the reading, watched the documentaries, seen the movies. And, as a woman, it made sense to her. Boys who wanted to be girls made perfect sense to her. Saz loved being a girl. Had never wanted to be anything else. She'd never understood the concept of penis envy. Thought it showed just how really weird Freud was. But Greg had wanted it. Wanted it all, the whole man thing. Greg had willingly undergone painful and—Saz winced as she thought about this, her own scars itching in sympathy—permanently scarring surgery to physically become the embodiment of the man he believed he really was. Greg had been through a voluntary mastectomy. A voluntary hysterectomy. Had paid thousands of pounds to make himself. Had worked himself into the ground to earn that money and then spent it all on creating himself.

Greg got up from his chair and rubbed his red, tired eyes, stretched his arms above his head. Saz looked up at him. Noticed the scar on his arm, the one she'd been told and believed was from a motorbike accident. Understood that he had taken part of his body to make it new. Her questions were swimming. She wanted to ask about his body, how it worked, how it felt. Instead she quieted her prurient curiosity and asked about the legalities. "I don't understand. How do you get to be married? I mean legally?"

Greg smiled. "The New Zealand judiciary is a fine and glorious thing. I present as a man, therefore I am a man. It's fairly new, but I'm legal. I got a new birth certificate and then a new passport a few years ago, after the last operation. Like all the rest of them, I'm just a good Kiwi bloke."

Saz looked at him. Greg was a tall, good-looking man in his early thirties. Just like any other. A nice man. Nice to be around, easy to talk to—really, a good bloke. She noted his broad, heavily worked-out shoulders, the well defined pecs outlined across his chest under a thin cotton T-shirt, the man's waist—straight up and down, narrow hips, no bum, his long legs and his big bare feet beside her own, a smaller girl's version. Boy's feet, girl's feet. She looked at Greg and saw a man.

Greg let out a long sigh, dragged his fingers through his tangled dark blonde curls. He laughed quietly and with little humour, "Well, I'm off to brave the real beast now. I'll have to tell Siobhan I've told you. She won't be happy but I think it's best that we all know the truth. Hopefully it'll help clear all this mess up, eh?"

Saz nodded, uncertain. "Yeah, sure. I mean, you're right. I'm glad you told me. I just . . ." She faltered, "Look Greg, I'm sorry. I really don't know what to say."

Greg nodded. "No one ever does. You'll get it eventually,

Saz, it's a shock. I understand. Sleep on it. That usually helps. I'm going to anyway."

Greg bent down, kissed her goodnight and then walked quietly through to the kitchen to make Siobhan a placatory cup of tea before waking her and telling her his news. He left behind a kiss on Saz's forehead and she felt it was a man's kiss on the forehead.

Greg was really Gaelene who was really Greg and Pat and Dennis were really Greg's mum and dad and Siobhan was really in love with a man who'd been a woman, though of course she had slept with Saz last night, slept with her really as a woman, not a lesbian myth and Saz was really confused.

Confused and tired and sick of staring at the relentless Pacific pounding on the pale submissive sand and getting no answers at all. Saz took herself off to her own single bed. The sun, setting on a peacefully sleeping Molly, was on its way up again in the Southern Hemisphere and Saz was a long way from peaceful sleep. She knew it was pointless to beat herself up about not being politically correct enough to take Greg's transsexuality on board as just another fact like Siobhan's hair really being a dull mousey brown or Greg being the only real blonde in the band. She recognized the fact and was pissed off with herself anyway. And, as she started to get undressed, she remembered the small list of men she'd slept with years ago, some of whom she'd liked very much and one of whom she'd loved. As she pulled on her T-shirt and heard Greg pad past her door and down the hallway to the bedroom where Siobhan slept, waiting for him, she acknowledged that things might have been restrictive and unyielding and exclusive in the bad old days, but they'd also seemed a damn sight clearer. It had been easier to know who and what when queer just meant gay and wasn't likely to also include women who loved men who were once women and men who loved women who were going to become men and women who loved women but quite liked men too sometimes and men who didn't care who they loved as long as they were loved back and every other trans-gender permutation that now gathered under the fluttering and expanding rainbow flag.

Saz slept and her brain was grateful for the chance to relax. Whatever dreams she may have had, she did not remember them when she awoke.

FORTY

Saz woke the next morning to hot sun falling on her face. She'd fallen asleep exhausted and strained, leaving the curtains open and by seven-thirty stark white light had cornered the house to her room and was slamming itself against her tightly shut eyes. Roaming the quiet house, she found Pat had already left with Dan and Dennis was out in the garden, raking over the runner beans before the ruthless sun drove him inside. So far she'd seen no sign of either Greg or Siobhan. She showered and slathered her`body with the vitamin E and lavender creams she used for her scars and, dressed for the spring sunshine, was just sitting down to a thick piece of toasted wholemeal bread and loganberry jam when the phone rang. It was the local florist she'd called briefly the day before. Just in case.

Saz quickly swallowed her half-chewed mouthful of food and spluttered out a reply, "Yes, this is Saz Martin, can I help you?"

"Look, I know it's probably a bit early to be calling, but this really weird thing just happened so I thought I'd better let you know about it. You know you asked me to call if anyone came in for yellow roses?"

Saz knew exactly what she'd asked and hardly needed the florist to tell her, but she kept her voice level and answered politely, "Yes?"

"Well, it happened! Now isn't that just the funniest thing?"

Being only too pleased to finally have a concrete lead, Saz would have agreed it was absolutely fucking hilarious had she not correctly guessed that Mrs Dolman of Kath's Plants and Flowers probably wouldn't extend her bad language to anything much stronger than "pissed off". Within ten minutes she had the address of the shop, had changed into her running gear and, following the directions she'd hurriedly got from Dennis, was on the empty road and heading into the town centre.

She arrived at the shop twenty minutes later, boiling hot and almost breathless. While she ran several miles most days, she didn't usually do so at quite such a fast pace or on hot mornings in a country with great sun and little ozone. As it was Sunday morning, the single main road which constituted the shopping centre was quiet. Not yet summer enough to encourage much Sunday opening, most of the shop doors were locked under the sheltering corrugated iron awnings that leant out into the street, giving an air of a small town waiting for high noon to happen.

Having admired the cut flowers on display, accepted a cup of tea, twice turned down the offer of gingernuts only to have a packet of fig rolls opened for her instead, Saz tried to encourage her informant to get on with the story, "So, Mrs Dolman—"

"Call me Kath, dear."

"Ok, Kath, do you want to tell me about it?" Saz smiled encouragingly as Kath frowned, her glance taking in Saz's tired, three-year-old trainers. She knew she might have made a better impression had she turned up looking a little more like Helen Mirren and a little less like someone who thought the concept of burn time was for sissies, but Pat hadn't been back with the car when she left and not insured to drive the van, running had been her only option. Her scrutiny of Saz's attire over, Kath swallowed the end of her third fig roll and began, "Right you are. I got in at, let me see ... seven forty-ish, unlocked the front door as I always do, locked it again after me, of course. If I didn't, I'd have all sorts in

bothering me when I'm trying to set up for the day, pen-
sioners mostly, the old dears love a bit of a gossip and a
chat when they're passing, not that they ever buy anything
most of them. Still, can't complain, won't be long till we're
all there, will it?"

Saz, thinking it would be sooner than she thought at this
rate, swallowed a mouthful of the weak tea and muttered
encouraging comments.

Kath continued, "Well, anyway, there I am, just taking out
the curly kale seedling—it's good to get the veges out on a
Sunday, the weekend gardeners just can't resist. Do you
have a garden?"

Saz gave up on smiling, "Yes. Shared. It's very small. The
woman?"

"Well, there I am with the seedlings and in she comes,
large as life and asks about the roses."

"I thought you'd locked the front door?"

"Yes, dear." Kath smiled, her greying permed bob nodding
for her.

"So how did she get in?"

"Back door."

"Right. So you hadn't locked the back door?"

"No, love, got to get the seedlings through from the yard,
don't I? Anyway, I'm on my knees with the boxes and in she
walks and says, 'So, Kath, how about a bunch of yellow
roses?' Well, you could have knocked me down there and
then. I mean, I haven't seen the little minx for two years
and in she walks large as life and twice as cheery!"

Saz stared at Kath, wondering if she was hearing right,
"You know this woman?"

"It's a very small town, dear. We're not exactly Auckland
or Wellington, now, are we? Not London either, I suppose.
You might miss out on your theatre and dinners and all that
in the city, but it's nicer for the people in a small town. You
get to know them, their families, you watch children grow

up and become parents themselves. You'd never get me living in a city." Kath brightly finished her discourse on essential metropolitan differences, "I like to think you get to know your customers better in a small town."

Saz repeated, "You know her?"

"Yes. So do Pat and Dennis actually. She used to be their girl's best friend. Inseparable they were before the Marsdens moved to Auckland. Shona Henderson. Lovely girl, but quieter than she used to be. I think she took it very hard when we lost Gaelene. They were really very close. She doesn't live here now, of course. Went to London for a while—I thought she was still there, that's why it was such a surprise this morning."

Saz was up and out of her chair before Kath finished speaking, "Can I use your phone, please?"

"Yes of course, dear."

Kath led her to the telephone in the back room where she assembled the bouquets. "I do hope nothing's wrong. That's why I was happy to call, you see. I mean, Shona— you must have got mixed up, musn't you? Whatever it is you're investigating, she couldn't have done anything wrong. She's just an ordinary girl. Right?"

The phone was engaged, Saz tried twice more and then gave up. "Is there a taxi rank near here?"

Kath pointed down the street. "That way." She hesitated and then asked, "I haven't got her into trouble, have I? I mean, I wouldn't want to . . ."

Saz shook her head, "No. You've been great. Thanks. Look, how long ago did she leave?"

"Right before I rang you. I called straightaway. Must be almost an hour since then." Kath frowned again, her hands nervously playing with the hem of her overall, "I did do the right thing?"

"Yes. Really. You've been brilliant, thanks. Look, I have

to get back to Pat and Dennis's place, I'll call you later, ok? There's probably some more questions I need to ask you."

Saz edged her way out of the shop and away from Kath Dolman's worried look. She ran down to the taxi rank, dragged a reluctant driver away from his breakfast conversation with three other drivers and forced him to take her to Pat and Dennis's house as fast as he could. He drove a little over the speed limit and then double charged her, thinking the pushy English bitch could probably afford it.

By the time Saz got back Pat and Dennis had already called the police. Greg pulled her into the car. He left Dennis holding Shona's note. The one that told him where he could find Siobhan.

FORTY-ONE

I wouldn't have been this fast if I'd had a choice. This speed has a recklessness to it which I would not normally approve. I had a plan, a strategy. One after the other. No madness, only method. Like pruning. Remove the dead wood and find underneath the shoot of new growth. And it's true, it does seem harsh to cut them back with such ferocity, to removed the rosehips, dead-head the blown bloom. Still, the bare branches are always worth the pain when spring comes. Cold winter has its reason in spring. But he left this morning, the beautiful one. He left early before I could remove him. And so the gears are moved up a knotch, graunching against their wheel cogs to be travelling so fast so soon. They'll catch up.

It was easy to get Siobhan here. Easier than I expected, although admittedly, I had not foreseen much trouble. Siobhan has always thought she was charmed. And then again, she thought this was all about her. Wrong on two counts.

Gaelene was walking along the beach with her father, the two of them, hands in pockets, faces out to the sea, looking for all the world like a pair of Kiwi blokes. Pat had taken Dan to the airport, and the English girl was in town, no doubt chatting to Kath Dolman, getting my name, my age, my telephone number. I expect she will. Eventually. It's hard to uncover the truth when you're told the story in half lies. The thief was drinking tea, sitting in the kitchen. She had not seen Gaelene on the beach, they were further up, past the headland, I passed them when I came down the road. You could not have seen them from the kitchen. Though anyway, Siobhan was looking at the paper in front of her, ignoring the real world outside. I had parked in front of the house, walked up to the door. I held a single yellow rose in my hand.

"Siobhan?"

She started, was not expecting my voice, a woman's voice. She looked around her to the back door before realizing it was me who was calling. When she stood I saw the flesh of her thighs before she pulled the thin dressing-gown around her. I think she knew who I was, saw me hold the rose out to her.

"Hi, Siobhan, I've come to explain. I met Gaelene on the beach. She's at my place. Come down to the car. I need to talk to both of you. I want to tell you why."

I didn't know if she would. I thought maybe she'd call out, and the Gaelene masquerade would come running up from the beach, running to protect the innocent girl. Maybe all of them would be there. I'd thought I might have to tell them what I'd done, why. Or not. I know it seems silly now, having made all the preparations, all the work to clear the ground, but by the time the end was nigh I was starting to feel a bit confused. Not so certain of the plan. Dan's leaving had thrown my routine. I thought I'd just go along. Improvise. See what happened. And it was far easier than I expected. She just came walking down the steps to me. Because she loves Gaelene. Cares for her. But not properly, not as much as I care for the real Gaelene. She came with me, simply because she believed me. Believed I had Gaelene. Which is true in a way, I'd always had her more than Siobhan ever had. The real her.

I held out the rose as an invitation and she took it. She followed me because she thought I had Gaelene. She believed me. She wasn't wearing any clothes under the dressing-gown, she held it to her as she walked down the steps, the thin material smooth over her breasts, the hollow of her stomach, the slight bulge of her cunt, red silk flowing open to her legs with each step.

I left a note for Gaelene, put it in the letterbox, the one piece of that old house not made new and we just drove away. Drove here.

Ruby hasn't lived here for years. She died in '81. I cried for her then, silent karanga in my small room. I cry for her still, I tangi alone and whisper a silent karakia. I hope she will accept my prayers. Ruby died the weekend the game was stopped at Hamilton. But John had moved her out of that old house a couple of years earlier. Starting to do well for himself in Auckland, he bought her a house much closer to town. She said it was what she wanted. But I knew it was too far from the sea. Closer to her daughters and their babies but too far from the sea. Too far to hear the wave lullaby at night. Too far from me. They just boarded up the house once she was gone. And it wasn't tiredness that killed her, or all those years of caring for others, or giving and giving until she was too tired to give more, but cancer. A long, slow stomach cancer that killed her from the inside, poisoning her slowly until she couldn't eat anything, couldn't swallow, until the kai that had been her mainstay became something to taunt her with.

Ruby had fed us all, holiday after holiday, fed armies of kids on God knows what, God knows where from. A dish of kumara and fresh sweet watercress usually or if we were really lucky maybe a wild pig one of her brothers would bring back from hunting. For years Ruby waded sideways through doors, creaked herself down into unwilling arm- chairs and her hand was a soft fist of fat flesh and kisses, even when it whipped the back of your legs for running across the road without looking, for talking back to the grown-ups. But the day they finally came to carry her out she weighed in at five stone. John could have carried her himself. She had been such a big woman my whole life and all there really was to her was this tiny skeleton underneath.

I planted a tree for Ruby that weekend. A kowhai. Yellow flowers to hold the sun from her laughter. I planted it in a quiet place in the bush, one of those bits of bush near the sea that the tourists and inlanders don't know about. Just me and Gaelene. We used to go there when we were little. It was our rest area. I hope Ruby is resting.

My whole life Ruby had been there, huge and warm, holding it all together, the house, her family, her own kids and everyone else's kids too. I was strange there, down at her place. Little bright white kid, a skinny, long legged Pakeha runt, I stood out long before I wanted to be noticed. Every holiday, every long weekend, my mum would ship me off down to Ruby's and then it would just be all us kids, free in the sunshine, laughing and swimming until we fell into bed, five kids to a room and no talking after ten and waking up at six because there was so much to do and so far to run. I loved those holidays, and I never felt bad about it, never felt like my mum didn't want me. It never occurred to me until I was about fifteen that she sent me to Ruby to get a break herself—I thought it was a present to me. Ruby was a koha for me, this big mountain of a woman. Just touching her dress felt like coming home.

At Christmas, in those too few years until my mum got married again, we'd go down the week before the big day and the men would go out fishing and maybe hunting, the ones without jobs or the ones on holiday, and the women would be in the kitchen. The big kitchen with the window you could lift out to make it easier to pass the plates of food through. Sometimes Gaelene would come down too, but even when we were tiny Gaelene always wanted to be out there where the men were going, wanted the fishing and the hunting, wanted to be digging in the garden. At night when we sang in the garage she wanted to be the one playing that "ringadicky-ringadicky" strum on the ten guitars, not sitting at the back, not doing the cooking, the cleaning, the harmonizing, the caring. Gaelene never could remember to sit at the back on the marae, she always thought she belonged up front. It was hard for her, I know. But not for me, I loved it. All of it. When Gaelene was there I didn't stand out so much, she had that shock of white blonde hair and it took the attention away from me. And at Christmas time anyway my aunty would come up from Wellington and she had Pakeha kids too. Well, she had one Pakeha kid and one Maori kid. Ruby used to say all she needed was a Samoan kid and she'd be all of Auckland. And she had him too, eventually.

I loved it then. There was a row of years, maybe '69 to '74 when it was exactly the same, year after year. When nothing changed and no one got older, taller maybe, but nothing really changed, at least not that you noticed. We did the same things and sang the same songs and even the first couple of years that my mum was married, it still didn't change, even after the baby came. But by the time the baby went to school it was all different, my new dad didn't like it so much down at Ruby's, he didn't really feel part of our family and my aunty met her next man and she stopped coming up from Wellington and then sometimes I'd just go down to Ruby by myself but it wasn't the same. Ruby was always there, always the same, but the people had changed. They wanted me to change too. I don't know why. John had gone away to school, to Hatu Petera, and when he came home after third form he wasn't John anymore, he was Hone and then Ruby was so proud of him. Not because of doing well in his exams or because of the rugby—though he had done well and he was going to be the Captain of the First Fifteen one day, everyone said so—but because he was Hone now. She was so proud that he was Hone. And they started to sing songs I didn't know the tunes to and Ruby said I was always welcome, I was her whanau too. I know she meant it, but I don't know if the others thought so. It wasn't that I couldn't understand the words. I knew all the words, I'd always been able to understand the words. I just couldn't follow the tune any more. The tune grew away from me.

Then Gaelene moved to Auckland and she was so different and they had a big house and our new baby came and my mum was so much nicer and happier with the new baby and my new dad and I did get a bike and everything should have been good—it looked good, all new and shiny. It wasn't good though, because I wanted what had been. I wanted it to be like when I was the little one. When I used to climb on Ruby's lap at night and get into her dressing-gown, she'd button it up around me and I would sit there while she laughed with Wai and they shared tea or a couple of bottles of beer. I was warm there between her body and the pink nylon, scarred by cigarette burns along the hem, and I felt the same as her and while her brown skin was different to mine, it was not so different. She promised me that one day the freckles would all join up and we would be the same. But they didn't. We never could be the same.

And then there just wasn't anywhere for me to be. No home. No safety. The places and the people kept changing. They changed their names and their identities and their faces and their bodies. And on the day they carried Ruby out for the tangi I tried to call Gaelene. Tell her what had happened. How our childhood was dead, my one place of safety had shrivelled and shrunk and was a thin, dried out old lady, too weak to lift her head from the pillow, too tired to want to try. Too dead to have the will. I tried to call Gaelene. But Gaelene wasn't there either. Gaelene was dead too.

FORTY-TWO

We sit in the boarded-up kitchen, Siobhan and I, sun slatting though what used to be garden centred windows. We drink tea from the flask I have with me, there are no biscuits, but anyway she is nicer than I expected, more real. I had not talked to the others, not really. The drunken conversation with Alex didn't count, the water thrown syllables of Steve not the same as words. She is quite pleasant, this woman. She asks me to explain and so I do. In the very beginning— me and Gaelene at school, me and Gaelene at my house, at hers. Here, playing in Ruby's house, Ruby's garden, the long hot summer holidays. She is smiling. "It sounds like a nice childhood, Shona, fun, warm." I agree with her, "Yes. It was. Even in winter we held a dream of warmth. I've lived in London for a while now, even though I've never liked the city, the size. It's easy to be anonymous there, plenty of work if you don't care what you do. I'm not there for me, I'm there to follow Gaelene's progress. You are easy to follow, you know. Your tour dates, the places you stay, all that information. The world is so small when you know where to look."

I remember I am telling her about the weather, the cold. "After I'd been in London a couple of years I was surprised when I came home to visit last winter, home to New Zealand. I was surprised by the frost and the cold and the rain that falls here for three days at a time. I must have rewritten my childhood. It must have been cold sometimes."

"Greg says it felt like it was always hot. His New Zealand stories are all about summer."

I frown. I don't like how she keeps calling Gaelene by the pretend name. I want her to admit the truth. "Her name is Gaelene."

She smiles at me. I do not want her to smile at me. I should be the one smiling. I am in control. This is my story.

It is on the edge of my mouth to tell her to stop smiling when I am distracted by the mess around me. Under the faded lino of dulled gold and red squares the floor is wooden, old boards laid down when rimu was everywhere and all the houses were built of the strong red wood and the pine tree was still just an idea for making money, bringing jobs to flat, thirsty volcanic land. This lino has been torn up in patches, a fire laid months or years ago against the wall where the oven stood, a cumbersome early electric model that baked cakes lighter and sweeter than any since. Children must have played here in the past few years, there are comics and empty cigarette packets. They did not know Ruby, did not know the woman to whom they have shown such disrespect. I think she would forgive them. I hope she will forgive me.

In the far corner there are possum droppings. I remember sleeping here at night, hearing the morepork on the telephone wire and the night we kids heard the possum in the loft. Tui, John's uncle, had to climb up and get it down, he went up wearing the thickest gloves and still came back, his arms scratched and bloodied, baby possum wild in his hands. I thought they would let it go, us kids standing around in our pyjamas staring into its frightened eyes, tiny young/ old face, but Tui took it outside and held it face down in a bucket of rain water. Drowned it. John and the other boys had wanted to do it themselves, talked about how they would kill the possum, John wanted to break its skull with the softball bat, but Tui said he couldn't do that. It would be too hard. Possums have the hardest skulls, he said. So he drowned it instead. Water is soft, but stronger than a softball bat. And he told us it was kinder, better for the possum, better for the land. The possums kill the native birds and trees, they are a pest, brought here by the English like the rabbits and the deer, all pests. John said that if Bambi and Thumper were pests, why were there no possums in Fantasyland? But it was too late for those questions and we had to go to bed. I dreamt about drowning the possum that night. I wondered if it just closed its eyes underwater like the kittens did when my mum had to drown Squeaky's babies. Squeaky was our big black cat and once a year his girlfriend Mama Cat would come back, leave a litter of kittens and then go again. She was wild as the possum, she had the kittens in the corner of the shed, fed them for a week or two and then left. Squeaky stayed behind, licking the kittens, crying for Mama Cat. We kept one of the babies and Tracey Myers had one and Kimberley Dickens had two but my mum drowned all the rest. I said she was mean but she said that's just what you did. When I was an adult I'd understand. You have to do the right thing. And she's right. I do understand. You have to do the right thing.

Then I am explaining about Gaelene and me, how we will be once this is all over. Why I had to make a clearing to find Gaelene. She doesn't understand. She keeps stopping me and asking for explanations. I am happy to tell the reasons, I want her to know.

"I had to make the boys go away. They were taking up too much space. Getting in the way. You are all in the way. You are all too much a part of it, you make it easy for Gaelene to live the lie. I had to stop you aiding her corruption. I want to help Gaelene find her way home."

I am telling her the truth but she doesn't know how to

listen to it. She interrupts again, "But don't you see that how he lives his life is Greg's choice?"

I stare at her, don't know what she means, why she won't let me talk.

She carries on, "Greg couldn't keep living as Gaelene. He was never Gaelene. It wasn't him. He was never really Gaelene. He had to become his real self."

I shake my head, "You've influenced her badly."

She holds up her hands in frustration, her movement too big in this quiet house. The plastic lid of the flask holding her tea shakes at the action, the table is not steady, the chairs are not level on the floor that has been vandalized by marauding ten-year-olds.

She tries to persuade me, "No, Shona. It wasn't me. Greg was already Greg when I met him. I never knew Gaelene."

I don't believe her. Gaelene is still there. Somewhere in that façade there is my best friend. My blood sister. I will find her again. Siobhan stands up, her eyes dart to the back door where we entered. I had pulled the boards away from the door to let us in. We are not ten-year-olds, we are grown women, there is no thrill for us in climbing through a broken and dirty back window. I wonder if maybe she has heard something that I have not. I stay silent for a moment. I can hear my heart and think maybe I can hear hers. Her heart beats faster than mine, less steady. But then she does not know the house, is not comfortable here. I ask her to sit down, she refuses. I move towards her. I do not know when the knife came to be in my hand. Was it before or after she stood up? Have I been holding it all along? Did I hold it at the house? I look at the knife and am not even sure when I picked it up. Maybe the knife belongs to Pat. Perhaps with this she has carved roasts and cut chops. It is a sharp knife. I know I have a plan to follow. I have to make Siobhan stop using the name Greg. I have stopped the others. Gaelene will be able to acknowledge the truth if people stop going along with the lies, colluding in her fantasy. It has been too easy for her, too many people have made it easy for her. She needs me to help her back to Gaelene.

Then Siobhan is moaning, there is blood on her face and on her silk dressing-gown. The dressing-gown is red and her blood must be red too, but it splashes darker, blacker than the dyed silk. Siobhan is holding her cheek, redness seeps between her fingers. There is another gash below her collar-bone. The knife is bloody. I am skipping time.

Siobhan is flailing in this semi-dark room, this house. She has forgotten that we came in through the back door, or maybe she does not know where it is, she is a moth throwing herself against the windows in the lounge, she can see the sunlight as it filters in, still lazy and hot, warm sunlight, dust motes held like the single note of a lawnmower on a Sunday afternoon. She smashes the one window unsmashed but cannot push against the wood nailed from outside. Now she has cut her arms on the glass, there are splinters in her hands, her eyes are wide, pupils extended to their farthest diameter to allow in the light, to let her see what there is to be seen. She is quite bloody. It is hard to know where the cuts start and the flesh ends. The dressing-gown sticks to her now, dark stained patches where the real red is stronger than the silk. I tell her again to calm down, we can sort this out, talk about it, she does not need to keep trying to run away from me, from this house, she is safe here. I tell her she should stop screaming, stop screaming that name, I cannot stand to hear that name.

She is making a mess of Ruby's home. I wish she wouldn't. I wish she would stay still. Talk to me. I try to make her stay still, to pin her down. But when I move towards her she is screaming for Greg. Greg cannot help her. There is no Greg. I go right up to her, tell her to hush, to be quiet. I am close to her eyes, see the bright in them. Then she stops screaming. She lies at my feet. She moves her mouth but there are no words. I think she is still breathing, there is a gurgling sound, I hear her heart pummelling in her chest. Maybe I can see her heart pummelling in her chest. She stops. There is no sound now. There is a small hole at her throat, just above the cavity where the collarbones almost meet. The cavity where a diamond droplet might sit. Her mouth twitches but she is not screaming now.

Perhaps she should have been calling for Gaelene. Perhaps I would have heard that.

FORTY-THREE

Greg pulled Saz into Pat's old station wagon, toppling his mother out of the front seat as he tried to force them faster to Ruby's house. To the bearer of the message left for him: "Dear Gaelene, Siobhan and I are at Ruby's place. See you there. Shona."

Greg drove as fast as he could, faster than the old car wanted to go. He'd been to Ruby's new house many times the year he left New Zealand. When the old lady already knew she was about to start the process of dying. It was her new house Greg drove them to, the one much closer to town. The new house Hone had bought for her when he had just started to earn money. At university and putting all his spare money into making some comfort for the woman who had been so much a part of his childhood, who he now wanted to hold soft in his adult life. Greg had visited Ruby before he left New Zealand, told her what he was going to do. Then Ruby in turn told Hone, shared the story with her own boy. But no one else knew. Greg had visited Hone quietly the one time he came home. Just the two of them to talk about Ruby's passing and have a quiet beer. None of the sisters, none of the grandkids, none of the cousins. It was cool. Ordinary. Like two men having a drink together. Normal. But this wasn't, not normal, not cool and not right. Greg screeched the car to a learner-driver stop and threw himself out, up the driveway, pounding on the front door. Hone opened it. Tall, dark, broad body pushing against the constraints of his suit and tie, he looked confused and then surprised when he realized Greg was standing in front of him, "Greg?"

Greg didn't bother greeting his childhood friend, "Where is she? Where the fuck is she?"

"Who? There's just me here. What are you talking about?" He looked out to Saz in the car. "Calm down, bring your lady inside. It's only a couple of hours till lunch, I'm working in town tomorrow, that's why I'm down from Auckland, but we could have lunch, right? Or dinner?"

Greg shook his head. "No. It's Siobhan. My girlfriend." Greg corrected himself, "My wife. Shona's got her. Got Siobhan. She said they were here."

Hone's smile vanished. "Shona? That mad bitch? Jesus, mate, she went crazy. Used to come round here all the time wanting to talk to Ruby. And that was years after she died. Nah, she's not here. We haven't seen Shona for ages."

"But she left this note, said she'd gone to Ruby's house."

"Sure. But no one calls this place Ruby's house. It's the old house she means. She'll be at the old house."

Hone came with them this time, Saz in the back seat. She introduced herself as Greg drove them off again, screaming tires out to the coast road and then south. Five minutes later they rounded the corner to the derelict houses down by the estuary, out where the little town had first been settled, from where most people had long since migrated to the suburban comfort of more easily manicured lawns, less exposed to the salt air elements. Greg parked the car as close as he could, still several hundred yards run from where Hone pointed out Ruby's house. In a row of boarded-up houses, it was the green and white painted place at the end, paint peeling and facing out, away from the others, one side bordered by the estuary, the other by what was now an overgrown path through the high dunes down to the sea.

Saz sprinted down to the house, leaving the unfit lawyer and the panicking Greg in her wake. She almost ran right past before she realized that while everything else was boarded up, the back door was open. She ran through the house, six small connecting rooms, the nearly mid-heaven sun now meaning that there was no angled light to slant though the boarded windows, she fumbled through the semi-darkness, waiting for her eyes to accustom themselves to the dim, heavy light.

She stumbled over Siobhan before she saw her, stumbled and then fell headlong into a naked mess of bared flesh and blood. Saz knew she should apply pressure to the wound, hold in the blood, but the wounds were so many and the light so dim, she couldn't hold it in, didn't know where to start. She tried to roll Siobhan over, listen to her heart, feel for a pulse, check her eyes, but the body kept slipping from her shaking hands. Then Greg was there with Hone, standing before them both and screaming, pushing Saz away. Greg picked Siobhan up in one move, holding her to him and screaming. The sound that came from him was not words but a deep moan, a lowing that started as a fierce rip inside his chest and came out in a choking eruption of meaningless sound. For a minute they stood, Saz and Greg, holding Siobhan up between them, standing her between their two bodies and holding her in an embrace that squeezed the limpness out and tried to force life back into her. Hone took one look at Siobhan and the dark room and, leaving Saz hanging on to Greg, ran out to call the police from the payphone back on the main road.

Saz heard the movement from the corner before she saw what it was.

Greg's face buried in Siobhan's neck, Saz with her arms holding them both, twisted as she heard the sudden beat from the corner, saw Shona come at them with the knife. She let go of Greg and he fell backwards with Siobhan just as Shona lunged at the two of them. Saz doubled down as the knife whizzed past her face, its already sticky wet blade catching her on the shoulder. She heard the thin material of her shirt rip, felt a hot shock of pain and then stopped thinking about herself completely. She saw herself touching Siobhan. Remembered the first time Siobhan had opened the door to her. Felt Siobhan warm lying beside her, heart rhythms matched by their on-the-breath kisses.

Then Shona was coming for her again, screaming at her, "Leave us alone. I need to talk to her. Me and Gaelene, leave us alone."

Saz dodged the knife, knocking Shona back against the wall as she turned to avoid the blade, kicking out at the taller woman. Scrabbling to her feet and out of Shona's reach, Saz slipped on a slick of Siobhan's blood, took two uncertain steps and then fell heavily against the window, smashing her already cut shoulder into the broken glass, a thick splintered shard edging its way through her shirt and into the earlier wound. She slid down the wall in the shock of the pain and winced again as she bashed her knee on the edge of a board of wood. Groping in the semi-darkness, the board came away easily in her hand. The searing pain in her shoulder stopped her getting a very good grip on it, but when Shona flew at her again she held the board in her right hand and smacked it clean across Shona's face. She heard the crunch of wood against Shona's nose, saw the blood begin to flow and, in a detached and surprised way, noted the exhilaration she felt when Shona cried out in pain.

The fourth time, Saz was ready for her. Greg was still moaning, Shona screaming to be allowed to talk to Gaelene, the sirens wailing outside keeping time with the blood throbbing in her temples. Shona flew at Saz with the knife and Saz knocked it out of her hand, smashing at Shona's knuckles with the lump of wood. In a single curved movement Saz dived for the knife and then turned back to stand in front of Shona. She grabbed Shona's hair with her left hand, her shoulder wrenching in pain and screamed into her face, "Did you kill her?"

Shona looked at Saz in surprise, "Kill her? Gaelene's here! She came in with you. I saw her, she ran in with you!"

"Did you kill Siobhan?"

"Who?"

"Siobhan! The woman! Did you fucking kill her?"

For a moment Shona almost knew what she meant, why it mattered. Shona looked right at Saz, spoke quietly, calmly. "Yes. I expect so."

Saz heard Hone calling from outside, heard the door slams of the police cars, heard their shouts, looked first at Shona and then at Greg and Siobhan. For a second she held Shona and the knife really very close. And then she let go of them both.

When Shona died, she fell on her own knife.

FORTY-FOUR

Siobhan wasn't dead. She was badly scarred, her vocal chords severed and unlikely ever to heal properly, but she wasn't dead.

It took one long statement from Saz and little police work to acknowledge that Shona had done the damage. The knife she had picked up from Pat's kitchen bench, the knife she had used to persuade Siobhan to go with her, had a blade which perfectly matched the cuts gouged into Siobhan's body.

Saz explained her version of events to the helpful policewoman. Then the same version of events to a less helpful more senior policeman and then the whole lot again to another man who would be able to pass the information on to those working on Alex's murder and Steve's drowning. "And Ms Martin, it didn't occur to you that these two deaths were in any way linked?"

"Of course it did."

"But you said nothing?"

"I had nothing to say. My client didn't want me to make a fuss and it could hardly have escaped anyone's attention that Steve and Alex died within weeks of each other. I didn't exactly have to point that out."

"The letters, the flowers?"

Saz's answer was always the same. "I couldn't. My client didn't want me to make a fuss."

When he finally left her to get back to the matter in hand with the nice helpful policewoman, the older man shook his head as he said goodbye to Saz, "I'd choose more amenable clients in future if I were you, Ms Martin. 'Bye now. You take care."

Saz didn't like him much but she could certainly see his point.

Shona's funeral was very quiet. Just Shona's mother—not her new father or her stepbrother—Pat and Dennis, and Greg, with Saz and Dan to sit beside him. After the funeral Greg went to talk to Shona's mother, told her his story and put in his request. She didn't take much convincing. Didn't want much to do with Shona now. Two days later they went to collect Shona's ashes and Saz and Dan sat silently on the beach when Greg and Hone walked into the bush to take the ashes to Gaelene and Shona's rest area. When they came back Greg was crying and white, Hone crying too, holding Greg close.

Hone told Saz, "There's a new tree there, in the bush. Shona must have planted it. We planted her ashes with that tree."

Saz visited Siobhan in the hospital the morning before she flew back to England with Dan. Greg was staying behind for a while to give the British tabloids a chance to calm down after all the revelations—including the story of how Gaelene had become Greg—even Cal had finally accepted Greg's reasoning that it was better for him to come out himself than for someone else to do it for him. Speculation was rife as to what career each of the remaining band members could continue with now, but as neither Dan nor Greg really cared and Siobhan hadn't had a chance to think about it, speculation was about as far as it would get.

Saz sat quietly waiting for Siobhan to wake up. Eventually

the long black eyelashes fluttered against cheeks that were now bruised and swollen, lined with purple scars and bloody tissue. Siobhan smiled a tight, strained greeting, wincing at the pain and then closed her eyes when even the wincing brought pain of its own.

Saz began her speech, the semi-rehearsed words faltering as she forced them out. "I'm so sorry. I should have been with you, stopped this happening."

Siobhan shook her head and mouthed, "You did."

"No. I wasn't there. My job was to take care of you. And she still did this to you. Fuck, Siobhan, I'm so sorry."

Greg had come into the hospital room behind Saz, stood by the door and watched her as she leant forward to kiss Siobhan.

"Don't, Saz," he said sharply, coming round to the other side of the bed. "You can't kiss her."

Realizing what he'd said, he stepped back a little, "I didn't mean it like that . . . I mean, you can't kiss her. One can't. Anyone. It hurts her. Doesn't it, babe?"

Siobhan nodded at Greg and looked back to Saz.

Greg stroked her free hand. "I know, hon."

He turned his attention from his wife to Saz, "Siobhan isn't pissed off with you. Neither of us are. At least, I'm certainly not. You did get there in time. You got there before me. You found out who it was. Perhaps if I hadn't been so bloody caught up in all the secrecy I might have figured it out sooner. We're both to blame too—we should have told you what was really going on."

Siobhan shook her head and removed her hand from Greg's grasp, pointing at herself.

Greg laughed, "Yeah, ok, babe, you're to blame. You should have let me tell the truth sooner."

He smiled bitterly at Saz, "See? It's all Siobhan's fault. Lucky you and me, eh?"

When Greg saw Saz off that afternoon, he held her tight before she left. "I know what you did, Saz."

Saz caught her breath, stepped back and looked up at him, "When?"

"Both times."

"Oh."

"Siobhan told me about the first thing and I saw the second."

Saz shifted her weight, her bag suddenly wrenching against the unhealed rip in her shoulder, "And?"

"And I don't care about the sex. I could tell she fancied you right from the start. I know Siobhan, I thought it was inevitable. It's not the first time and I don't suppose it'll be the last."

Saz flinched as he wrote off her idea of herself and Siobhan as a special entity. "Thanks a lot."

Greg grinned. "You're welcome. Once anyway."

Saz looked back at him, "And the other?"

Greg shrugged. "Nothing really. I just wanted you to know. I saw it."

"Do you think I did the right thing?"

"Probably. Who knows? If Shona had realized Siobhan wasn't quite dead she'd have gone for her again."

"I didn't know Siobhan wasn't quite dead."

"No. Neither did I. And you know, if Shona'd had the chance she would have gone for you again too."

"So I probably did the right thing?"

Greg shrugged. "I reckon probably's as close as you're going to get."

The last call for boarding came from the pilot as he walked past them and out to the ten-seater plane, swinging his briefcase and smiling at Saz as if she and Greg were lovers, "I'm off now, sweetheart, you wanna kiss the boyfriend and hop on?"

Two nights later, weary, dirty and jet-lagged, Saz fell off the plane and into Molly's arms. Home again to wash, to have her dressing changed, to sit by the fire and drink hot soup with fresh bread and be scolded and loved and warmed and held gently while she cried away the telling of everything that had happened in that house. Almost everything that had happened.

Much later, after they had made love hesitantly and carefully and then not carefully and furiously, after Molly had changed the dressing again on her shoulder, after Molly had fed her sweet honey cake dipped in hot chocolate and after they had kissed and touched and soothed and held each other long enough for it to feel almost normal again, Molly fell asleep on Saz's good shoulder, a last question whispered into the dark room, "Saz, is there anything else you should tell me?"

Saz thought about what Greg knew, what she knew, the two things that only she and Greg knew and then she kissed Molly's forehead, stroking the stream of her long black hair.

"No, my darling, that's the whole sorry story. There's nothing else to tell."

Saz lay beside Molly and lied. Then she fell asleep.

Also by Stella Duffy and published by Serpent's Tail

Wavewalker

"Very near the top of the new generation of crime writers" *The Times*

"The clever money should be on Duffy when the crime-writing Oscars are dished out" *Telegraph*

"A feisty little page-turner guaranteed to keep you up all night" *Big Issue*

Calendar Girl

"There's a lot of lesbian lore and sex in it, but it is also a fast, witty and clever crime story, with cracking dialogue and exuberant characters" *The Times*

"Steamy erotic moments, some smart one-liners and a few digs at lesbian stereotypes . . . Stella Duffy is definitely a name to watch" *Forum*

"Lends a new dimension to trips to the supermarket" *Literary Review*

"A highly atmospheric, rhythmic narrative . . . a stylish book which also warns of the destructive power of lies and half-truths" *Gay Times*